ALL THE
MISSING PIECES

Julianna Keyes

Visit our website at www.juliannakeyes.com.

Cover design by Khoi Le
Formatting by Polgarus Studio

ISBN 978-1-7772697-1-5

First Edition September 2020

ALL THE MISSING PIECES

Reese Carlisle hates her life.

Three years after her father's arrest for one of the largest embezzlement schemes in history, twenty million dollars is still missing, and the world believes she knows where it is.

Two years after her brother's death, they still think she killed him.

One year later, she's still hiding.

When the loneliness is too much, she seeks out strangers for one dark night, no questions asked. She makes up a name, puts on a disguise, and tries to forget.

One night she meets a new man. She tells him her name is Denise, she's a dental assistant, and she loves dogs. He tells her she's smart, she's pretty, she's funny. Things she hasn't heard in too long.

Things that are too good to be true...

WHEN

1

Tonight my name is Denise. I'm a dental assistant, I'm divorced, and I love dogs. My dark hair is covered by a muted red wig that hangs past my shoulders and makes my neck itch. The designer clothes I once obsessed over have been replaced with basic, bland pieces meant to be forgotten once the night is over, the same way I'll forget it.

Don't judge me. Everybody who hooks up online lies and everybody expects it. It's just something to break up this wretched monotony, to keep me breathing until the day my father's appeal is heard or I find the courage to jump off a building and put an end to my misery. Whichever comes first.

Until then, there's this.

And tonight, there's Doug.

Doug's not so bad. Over the past two years—as Angela the accountant or Beth the barista or Carmen the cartographer—I've met some good guys and some questionable ones, but no one dangerous, not that I care. The only real rule is that they buy into the evening's persona. The slightest indication that they recognize me and the deal's off.

Doug has no clue. Doug's a decent guy who's newly divorced and looking to get back in the game. He's got all the requisite first-date stories lined up, as though he's read the same hundred internet articles every other single person has read.

We're eating at Verre Plein, a small restaurant with leather-bound menus and a wine cellar so extensive it has its own round-the-clock guard. Not even at the height of my fame—or infamy—did I have a bodyguard.

The white cloth-covered tables are arranged close together, but instead of feeling suffocated, the proximity enhances the sense of privacy. Like everyone is making an effort to show just how much they're not listening to your conversation. How much they can't see you. How much they don't care.

Originally conceived as a Wall Street off-shoot, Holden City, just an hour's train ride from Manhattan, has taken on a life of its own. In two decades it's transformed from a smattering of buildings housing Wall Street rejects to a glittering city of towering offices, imported cars, people too rich to care about their money, and the people they pay to care about it.

Like ninety percent of the population here, Doug is an investment banker. He has a little office in a little building and manages money for people with bigger offices in bigger buildings. I know the world well. Daughter of the one-time richest man on the eastern seaboard, I was born into money. As was expected of me, I grew up and got my Masters in Economic Policy and, for a time, had a corner office at Carlisle Gale Investors with a pristine view of the city.

Of course, everyone hated me. I was born into that, too. They didn't even whisper *nepotism*; they shouted it. I could hear them through the walls. Math came to me almost as easily as the job, though I'd never been nearly as interested in managing other people's money as I'd been in spending my own. My hobbies were going to clubs and posing for pictures and monitoring my growing internet celebrity. It wasn't until they called me a thief and a murderer and a whore that people credited me with much of anything at all. The first two names I get, but I'm not sure where the "whore" came from; maybe they just needed three to round it out. Or maybe that infamous crotch shot did it. Anyway.

Doug is in the middle of a story about a box he found in the attic of the house he's renovating—because renovating is one of his hobbies, along with cycling and listening to jazz—when the maître d' seats a man at the table beside us. I try to appear interested in the contents of Doug's box, but I'm distracted by the man. My dad used to play a game with my brother and me: Who belongs? Who doesn't?

The man doesn't.

He orders a beer. In a bottle, not a glass. He's wearing a brown sports jacket with patches on the elbows like a professor in a movie, and the Rolex that peeks out at his wrist is a knock-off. Until they were taken away, my father had a world-famous collection.

Unlike everybody else, who is actively ignoring everybody else, the stranger is watching me when I lift my gaze. I'm wearing brown contacts, but the extended eye contact makes me feel exposed. I used to be bold, but years of self-imposed solitude and fake dates have made me awkward and ungraceful, and I look away.

The stranger is handsome, but he doesn't belong in this restaurant. I know he doesn't understand the French terms on the menu because when the server comes to recite the specials, he requests the first dish he hears and doesn't try to repeat the name.

His shoulders are too broad for the jacket, which means he borrowed or bought it last minute, probably to adhere to the restaurant dress code. It's been at least a day since he shaved, and his wavy brown hair is thick and unruly, like it's never seen product or a high-end haircut. If he cares about any of this, it doesn't show, and I wonder briefly why he would choose to come here if he had to go to the effort.

He pulls a battered old paperback Western out of his pocket and begins to read, and I do my very best to focus on Doug, who's now telling a story about a recent humanitarian trip. I missed learning whatever was in the box and I'm annoyed. I swear I can feel the stranger watching me, but every time I risk a glance his way his eyes are dutifully trained on the book. He turns a page, sips his beer, and ignores me.

I vow to pay attention to Doug, but not before noting that the stranger's fingernails are clean but not buffed, and his knuckles are cracked, like he works outdoors. I doubt even the chef here has cracked knuckles.

"...walking across this field," Doug is saying, the faintest traces of his North Carolina accent coming through, "and I see we're approaching a dry streambed with a log laying across so people can get to the other side. It's not so deep you'd die if you fell, but it's deep enough that you'd have trouble getting out. Anyway, we're about fifteen feet away when suddenly the villagers in my group start to run. I check over my shoulder to see if there's a lion or something, but there's nothing there. When I turn back around, they've all crossed the log and are waiting to watch me attempt it. They wanted front row seats."

I sip my wine, the second of the two drinks I allow myself on these dates. "Did you fall?"

He's quiet for a second. "Yeah."

A laugh slips out.

I know it's mean, but I can't stifle it. Maybe it's nervous energy. Maybe it's five weeks of limited human contact, tension searching for a natural outlet. I don't know the last time I laughed. I'm not very funny.

Doug blushes, then offers a sheepish grin as he pushes a piece of fish around his plate.

"I'm sorry," I manage, trying to shut up. "Did you... Were you hurt?"

"I sprained my ankle."

My shoulders shudder as I fail to suppress one last guilty laugh. "I'm sorry."

"It's fine. You're pretty when you smile, Denise."

I'd heard that a lot growing up. My father spent a small fortune on dental care, beating my snaggle tooth into submission and closing the gap between my front teeth. Back then, I had a lot to smile about. Or so I'd thought.

"Thanks."

I know he meant it as a compliment, an effort to get this date on track, and I vow again to try harder. I need this. I need a couple of hours every once in a while, just to keep going. To feel something. Before my father's arrest, I'd been the life of the party; after the arrest, a pariah. Now, a hermit. Doug is the second person I've spoken to in three weeks, and it will be at least that long before I speak to someone else.

The stranger's food comes and Doug talks and I listen and occasionally the stranger glances up, turns a page, and meets my eye. The connection is palpable and terrifying. I can't have it but I want it. I want it but I don't need it. Those are distinctions I'd never had to make before my world fell apart.

I tell myself I'm only feeling this way because it's been so long since I felt anything at all. That the stranger only interests me because I didn't already read his too-long biography on the Fantasy Friends website and scroll through his profile and study his photos. He's only appealing because he's unknown, and he finds me appealing for the same reason.

If only he knew.

Doug asks if I'd like coffee or dessert, and I decline. We didn't come here for coffee or dessert. Dinner is just protocol. I know he's got a condo ten minutes from the restaurant; we'd discussed it in our emails. I told him what I tell everyone: Denise rents a studio apartment in one of the artist buildings at the edge of the city. It's cluttered and the dogs bark and we'll have to go to his place, if things progress that far. Doug agreed. They all do.

He folds his napkin on the table and excuses himself to go to the restroom. I know it's my imagination, but it feels like the air in the restaurant grows ten degrees hotter. The stranger finishes his meal and closes the paperback and returns it to his pocket. Our eyes meet. When the server places my bill on the table, the stranger asks for his at the same time. He pays cash and stands, and I can't look away. I want to. I need to. Brown contacts, red wig, fake name. He doesn't know me. He can't.

His jaw flexes like he's considering speaking but decides against it. Eventually, he reaches into his pocket and pulls out a card. It's flat, shiny and black. He puts the card on the table, the edge of his thumb grazing the side of my hand. Then he walks out.

I don't turn around to watch him leave. I couldn't if I wanted to. Instead I stare at the card, the fancy silver script. *Holden City Grand Hotel.* Room 804.

I know what this means. It's why I'm here. My legs are shaved, my skin is soft, my underwear is new. But until this moment, I hadn't truly wanted it, not this way. Not really.

Now I do.

I pick up the card and turn it in my fingers.

I put it in my purse.

Then I pay the bill and leave before Doug returns.

2

I don't go to the stranger's hotel room. I want to, but I'm not ready to be murdered, my body hacked up and tossed into the Holden River, as many would agree I deserve. I won't give them the satisfaction.

Architects and city planners perfected the design of Holden years before they ever broke ground, and while the city has won awards for its beauty and sustainability, it's the network that runs underneath it that makes Holden truly remarkable. Considered naively optimistic at the time, the designers believed Holden would one day explode into a financial superpower and carefully arranged the space so every square inch would be useful. Accordingly, there are very few above-ground parking lots, and 99% of the city is accessible through an intricate network of underground parkades and pathways. Perfect for those who want to move around unseen.

Verre Plein is just a few blocks from my apartment, and I chose the restaurant for precisely that reason. If I don't drive to meet my date, no one can offer to walk me to my car, make note of my license plate, and, if they're so inclined, do some research into the stranger they've picked up for the night. Despite the screaming headlines, I'm not a criminal mastermind, and I haven't figured out how to register my car to a fake name.

The underground pathways are heated but the parking garages are not, and with the frigid winter weather, I'm the only person braving the dark and cold. It takes ten solitary minutes to reach my building's parkade, and I swipe my key card at the elevator, both relieved and miserable to be home. It's a five-degree February night, but I'm burning up. Sweat gathers beneath my arms and at the nape of my neck where the ridiculous wig twitches.

I live on the fourteenth floor but take the elevator to the top, climbing the stairs to the roof and using my shoulder to shove open the door. The roof is a gritty combination of gravel and tar, sticky beneath my feet, rolling my ankles. The air up here is cold and clean as it rushes past.

The building doesn't have a rooftop patio, and I like it for exactly that reason. If it's uninviting, no one else will come. If no one else comes, no one can see me pacing the perimeter, measuring the distance from side to side, counting how many feet it would take until I ran out of roof and there was nothing but air.

I pause at the front edge, overlooking the busy street below, the passersby unaware. There's no railing up here, no safety net. I let the tips of my shoes poke over the side and feel the icy wind whip over my fake hair. A violent shiver rolls through me, like a ghost passing from one world to the next. I close my eyes and wait for courage I know won't come. For most of my life, I had the world at my fingertips, everything I could have wanted and everything everyone else wanted. Now I have this. Up or down.

If my dad's conviction is overturned, we'll take a plane to parts unknown and start fresh. If it's not, I'll take that final step and give the world one last, dramatic display.

Until then, life, unfortunately, goes on.

I head back inside and take the elevator down to fourteen. I rarely see my neighbors, but tonight Mr. Pedersen, the frisky septuagenarian across the hall, is coming home from a date of his own, a perky redhead in a sparkly dress laughing at something he said. Mr. Pedersen winks at me and I grimace. He's not paying *me* to pretend to like him for a night.

I unlock the door to my unit. Home sweet home. "Home" used to be penthouses and beach houses and Paris pied-à-terres. Now it's a modest two-bedroom in a one-of-a-kind boutique building that resembles all the one-of-a-kind buildings around it.

Over the course of his career, my father amassed an enormous collection of real estate, sometimes full developments, sometimes a swath of units in a popular building he would rent out for "spare change." As a result, we had master keys to approximately eighty percent of the buildings in Holden, giving me and my brother quite literal keys to the city. After my father's arrest, the units were repossessed along with pretty much everything else we owned, including all of our homes.

When it came time for me to start apartment hunting, I knew I couldn't show my face. Despite my father's arrest, the angry mob continued to demand justice, tar and feathers in hand, and I needed to remain anonymous. Even without the death threats making it difficult, I knew no one would sell to the infamous Reese Carlisle, and if they did, it would be humiliating to ask to buy a place we had once owned. So I took matters into my own hands: I checked the real estate listings online, used my master keys to investigate properties until I found one I liked, then emailed the realtor and completed the entire transaction online. I had to use my real name, but a privacy clause and extra commission point bought his silence.

Now I enter the dark apartment, a wall of windows providing enough ambient light to see my uninspired, decidedly minimal decor. I drop my purse and press my back to the door, sliding down to the floor. My black skirt rides up my thighs and my legs flop apart, knees rubbery, ankles weak.

I'd like to think I had too much wine, but that's not true.

Not even after a night of halfway decent sex am I this shaky.

I know what the issue is.

My gaze flickers to my purse the way it would to a ticking time bomb. I fumble with the clasp before retrieving the shiny black room key and turning it over and over in my hand like a magician with no trick.

My phone beeps, the sound muted by the contents of the bag, and for a fleeting, foolish second I think it's him. The stranger. It's not, of course. It's Doug, being normal. Wondering where I am. What went wrong.

I close my eyes, guilty. Then I type. *Sorry. Family emergency.*

He asks if we can reschedule.

I turn off the phone. I was going to throw it away tomorrow, anyway. Just like I'll throw away Denise.

I yank off the cheap wig. I have a closet full of them, thanks to my brother's short-lived career in theater management. They're one of the few items that were returned to us after the raid. At least they came in handy. They help me become Harriet and Isabel and Jess. People nothing like the person I was. And most definitely nothing like the woman I am.

The stranger wouldn't want this woman. He likes redheads with brown eyes who laugh when they're not supposed to. My once-bleached hair is back to its natural black, my fingernails haven't been painted in three years, and I only bother to shave my legs when I have a date. I don't think the stranger would know what to do with this girl. He could read a million newspaper stories exposing my father's crimes and hypothesizing about mine and never find the truth.

Liar. Thief. Murderer. Whore.

It's in there somewhere.

I get to my feet and cross the spacious, sterile room. In the kitchen I find a pair of scissors and deftly cut the room key into twenty tiny pieces, watching them slip through my fingers into the trash.

Denise was not a success.

Maybe Elle will have more luck. She's an economist who likes Elton John and extreme sports.

》》 》》

On Saturdays I volunteer at the Holden City Food Bank. I applied here at the same time I started my alphabet dating system and thought I'd last a week. Now I'm on my second pass through the alphabet and my eighteenth month volunteering.

I park in the pothole-riddled lot alongside half a dozen cars boasting more rust than metal. I drive a black Mercedes. Before the scandal I drove the pink Maserati my father had given me for my sixteenth birthday, but that was repossessed and sold at auction to someone who professed to be in my fan club.

At that point I'd been earning my own income for years and had a sizable inheritance from my mother, so the scandal didn't leave me personally bankrupt. I considered buying something less expensive, but a cheap car would attract attention in downtown Holden, where I need to blend. It makes me stand out at the Food Bank, but I told them I inherited it and they're willing to believe me. Or at least Lyla, the manager, is willing to pretend she does, since they're always desperate for people. "I've got no time for your drama," she'd warned when I showed up in sunglasses for my interview and provided only my initials on the application. She didn't recognize me, and I'm convinced she would not have cared if she had. But someone would have. Someone would have asked why I was volunteering at the Food Bank instead of donating. Why I wasn't rotting in prison with my father. Why I was driving a fucking Mercedes instead of taking the train.

The answers are: paperwork, lack of evidence, and because I don't want to.

Lyla was as surprised as I was when I kept showing up for shifts, but we soon found a rhythm. I arrive, scribble my initials on the time sheet, and go to work in my quiet, lonely aisle, where I organize non-perishable donations by myself for six hours. Thirty minute break for lunch, then back to work. With the exception of Lyla, no one talks to me, and I don't want them to.

Voices carry in the warehouse, and I can hear their conversations. There are two groups of people who work here: Older white ladies who have retired and want to give back, and young black men whose mothers know Lyla and wrangled them jobs. I know this because when you talk as little as I do, you get good at listening. One of the white ladies thinks one of the black guys would be perfect for her daughter, but her friends think that's asking for trouble. He was, after all, once arrested for drug possession. It was pot, but still.

I awkwardly and unwillingly straddle both groups. I'm white, which puts me with the women. I'm twenty-eight, which puts me with the guys. I'm not paid to work here, which puts me back with the women. I think Janet stole Suzanne's roast beef sandwich and just put the balled up plastic wrap back in the fridge—I'm with everybody on that one. And yet despite all our shared interests, I'm an outcast. I prefer it that way.

Growing up, my father insisted we volunteer. I'd done the requisite rounds of reading to seniors and helping to build a couple of homes, not because community service was important to me, but because it would look good on college applications. At my interviews, I'd smiled and nodded and enthusiastically ruminated on all the wonderful things I'd learned while helping those less fortunate, and because I'm not a dimwit—and my father was a billionaire—I was accepted to every Ivy League school in the country. I got my degree from Yale.

"R.C.," Lyla says.

"Uh huh?" I don't turn around, too busy squinting at expiration dates on canned corn. You can hear Lyla coming from the other side of the warehouse. She's a big lady with bright red braids twisted up on the sides and spilling halfway down her back. She wears wire-rimmed glasses, at least one item of animal-print clothing, and kitten heels every day. You can track her progress around the entire space by the click of those heels. When she's angry, you know it. When she's trying to sneak up on you, you know it. It's usually some combination of both.

"You closed up last week, right?"

"Yeah." Two months ago, I'd been given the special privilege of being trusted with the warehouse keys so I could lock up when Lyla leaves early to take her daughter to swimming lessons. None of the white ladies would stay late in this part of town, and she didn't trust the guys not to lose the key. I was the least bad option and I didn't care enough to say no.

I hear her sigh and glance over my shoulder. A zebra-print blouse does its very best to accommodate her ample bosom and generous stomach. I don't want to ask, but I do. "What's wrong?"

"You see anything strange when you left? Anyone hanging around?"

"No. But I wasn't looking."

"Anyone here when you locked up?"

I nod toward the cereal corner. "Rodney." There's a two-man system in place for closing time; no one can be alone to do it, just in case. There are video cameras located on each side of the building and one at the only entrance to the parking lot, but we all know there's no money to keep them turned on. That's why I know Lyla doesn't know Rodney left with everybody else that day instead of waiting with me like he was supposed to.

She shakes her head. "Two of the cameras were broken," she says. "I just noticed yesterday. The one in the parking lot, and the one by the back door. I don't know if it's just kids throwing rocks, or worse. I can't afford too much more of this."

Unfortunately, the Food Bank is a popular target for vandals. Their favorite activity is ruining the food—leaving the freezers open over night so everything melts and meats spoil, but occasionally they'll steal anything worth taking, which isn't much. Lyla's lost two laptops and a pair of shoes. The last time was four months ago, just before Thanksgiving. I'd left an anonymous cash donation to cover the cost of some new turkey. Lyla cried.

"All right," she says, glancing at her watch. "You taking off now?"

"Five minutes."

She's already walking away. "See you next week."

≫ ≫

I visit my father on the last Saturday of each month. He's at Wakeman Penitentiary, a low security white-collar prison two hours north of the city. Between Wakeman and Holden there's nothing but farmland, acres of corn and potatoes, cherry and apple orchards, the occasional herd of cows or sheep, and the constant company of manure.

The farther you drive the more the roads narrow, until three lanes turn into two, into one, into an occasionally-paved route to a place no one really wants to go anyway. If you didn't know what Wakeman was, you could mistake it for a holistic resort or a treatment center of some type. It's a single-level sprawling structure in white stucco. The sign at the gate reads *Wakeman* in large letters, *penitentiary* printed in much smaller font beneath it, like a whisper.

A year after my father's arrest, a journalist did an exposé on the prison, detailing how much better the facilities are here than at most inner city schools. Hell, most schools in general. The inmates tend the yards and gardens, dormant at this time of year, the grass yellow and patchy. They have reading groups and meditation, and my dad mentioned that one of the guys was a former inspirational speaker who gives a short presentation every Wednesday after movie night.

I show my ID at the gate and the guard waves me through. It's just a formality; they know me. Like most people, they knew my reputation before I ever showed up.

I park in the half-empty visitors lot and take my time approaching the building. It's an uncharacteristically warm day for the end of February in upstate New York, the late-afternoon sky blue and cloudless, the sun still bright as it begins its descent. I'm wearing a long-sleeve black shirt with a black skirt and combat boots. I'd added a pair of black tights since I was coming to prison, and I carry my denim jacket under my arm. I take one last deep breath before I pull open the door.

Wakeman smells like recycled air and plastic and reheated food. Despite the bright white walls, cheap artwork, and pleasant enough guards, it feels sad. Which, I suppose, is how a prison should feel.

I sign in at the guard desk, and, as he does every month, Officer Hilroy waves me through a metal detector and does his perfunctory swipe with a wand to check for weapons or other forbidden materials. The pockets of my coat are empty except for my license, a five dollar bill, and a tube of lip gloss, all of which I'm allowed to keep. Having passed inspection, Hilroy leads me down the long hall to the visitation room, his thick body shifting from side to side with each step.

"How're things?" he asks, like I might say they're going great. I'd really rather not talk to anyone, but there were different guards when I first started visiting, and they treated me much worse than Hilroy, all sneers and eye rolls and stupid double entendres. Hilroy treats me like I'm human.

"Okay. You?"

"Not too bad. Strange weather today."

"Global warming, right?"

He swipes his badge over a sensor, and the metal doors open to the visitation room. "Polar bears are going extinct."

I thank him as I slip inside. There are a dozen people already here, most of whom I recognize from previous visits. I find a spot that leaves a vacant table on each side, not that anybody cares where I sit. The hum of a vending machine muffles enough of the conversation to make it feel private, while the guard stationed in the corner reminds everyone that there is no such thing as privacy.

I reapply my lip gloss and wait. After a couple of minutes, the heavy green door buzzes open and my dad strolls in, spotting me and grinning widely. Before his arrest, he'd worn suits and ties every day. On the rare occasion he got home early enough to watch TV, he'd wear his suit, loosening the tie just a little. Even now, wearing Wakeman's standard-issue mustard yellow jumpsuit and white Velcro sneakers, he's got that same business-like air. Like we're here to make a deal, not small talk. To discuss a merger, not if I put more money in his commissary account since he wants to stock up on the chicken ramen.

Eleven months after he was arrested, and after a short but

spectacular trial, Kimball Carlisle, billionaire investor, was convicted and sentenced to forty years for his role in one of the largest American embezzlement scandals in history. "Hi, dad," I say.

"Reeses Pieces," he says, folding me into a hug. My mom told me he'd given me the nickname the day I was born. He'd hated "Reese," wanted something sweet and girly, but my mother had her heart set on it, and he loved her, so I was Reese Charlotte Carlisle. Still am, technically.

The guard clears her throat and we break apart, sitting opposite each other on orange chairs, folding our arms on the sticky tabletop.

"You look… dark," he says. He says this every time. "You're like a shadow of yourself." He gestures as he says it, taking in my straight black hair, my pale, makeup-free skin. I used to care a lot more about what I looked like because I wanted people to notice me. Now I don't.

"You look fine," I say. He looks like himself, but smaller. He'd had personal trainers and people who used to come to our penthouse once a month to trim his hair, buff his fingernails, buy him new suits. Without their help, he's withered a little, his skin less tan, his hair more gray, his clothes more…yellow.

"How's life?" he asks. Before the arrest he'd ask me the same question, normally while we shared dinner in his office. Off the top of my head I could name two dozen people who would have killed for that opportunity. They're not lining up to sit with him now.

"Fine. Want something from the vending machine?"

"Whatever you like."

I retrieve the bill from my coat pocket and cross the room to buy a packet of crackers and cheese and some dill pickle chips. I return and we eat in silence. He uses the little red stick to smear cheese product on cracker product and passes it to me. He's the one in prison, but he's still my dad. When people blame me for visiting him, that's all I can think. My mother's dead. My brother's dead. Who else is there?

"Doing anything special today?" I ask after a while. "Did you get that ramen?"

"Yeah," he says, licking dill pickle dust off his thumb. "Eddie B. was pissed. All that was left was shrimp. Everybody knows that's the worst."

"I'll bet." I've never had packaged ramen.

"Anyway, I'm hosting a bit of a party. I think the noodles will ensure a decent turn-out."

"How does that look?"

"How does what look?"

"A prison party."

He laughs a little. "Like half a dozen middle-aged guys sitting on one guy's bed eating dry noodles out of a bag."

"Right."

"We'll have reason to celebrate soon, Pieces."

"I know."

His appeal is coming up in three months. If it goes well, he could be walking out the front doors of the courthouse immediately after, leaving behind all that chicken ramen for Eddie B. and his prison friends. It should go well; I've been paying through the nose for his legal team. Not just his lawyer. His *team*. All of my dad's money was confiscated when he was arrested, his assets sold to pay back some of the money he'd stolen. You'd think that would placate people, but not even close. Despite their best efforts, the FBI hasn't been able to locate the last twenty million dollars, and the treasure hunters of the world—and more than a few lunatics—have been obsessed with it ever since. Because I'm the only Carlisle left to roam the planet, most people are convinced I have the money. Or, at the very least, if I don't have it, I know where it is. If they knew where I lived, they'd see how stupid they are. But they can't find me, so they'll never know.

In the meantime, I'm funding this effort, pretending like everyone else that there's a way out of the mess. That in three months my father's name will be cleared and he'll be free. That's the tiny scrap of hope that stops me from stepping off the roof every day. Maybe, just maybe.

Because the sentencing wasn't a surprise. My dad was guilty, after all. The first time I'd seen him after the arrest he'd told me as much. I would have sworn he was innocent until the day I died if he hadn't whispered in my ear and made me believe.

3

It's nearly dark when I say goodbye to Hilroy and leave the prison. My car is hot and stuffy when I climb in, so I pull off the tights and toss them in the back with my coat, then grab the half-melted chocolate rabbit I've got stashed in the console, break off its ears, and take a big bite.

I hold the severed head in my hand as I navigate my way out of the now-empty lot and back onto the dirt road. This far outside the city you can see the stars starting to appear, the full moon already visible. I crunch through chocolate and rice crisps and turn up the radio, finding an old rock song to keep me company.

Since Doug and Denise's failed date three nights ago, I've been doing my best to convince myself the reason I'd been feeling so tense and antsy had nothing to do with weeks of no human touch and everything to do with this visit. I love my dad, but I hate coming here. It's like going to the cemetery to visit the rest of my family—a sad, unnecessary reminder. Like I'd somehow managed to forget.

I stuff the rest of the rabbit back in the box, licking melted chocolate off my fingers, unsatisfied. A quick glance in the rearview confirms I'm alone, and as I do every time, I press my foot on the gas, harder and harder, until the needle inches well past the speed limit and the car is vibrating and I have to clench the wheel with both hands. My heart is pounding when I reach down to lower the window, letting the night air flood in, whipping my hair into my face, my eyes.

I rarely let myself think about my life before the scandal, when we used to do stupid things just because we could, not because they were the only things that made us feel anything at all. I don't think about parties and friends and clothes and cruises, how we quaked with laughter when the cork exploded out of a bottle of four thousand dollar champagne and broke a thirty thousand dollar chandelier. I don't think about how fast that life flew by and how slowly this one moves, no matter how hard I hit the gas.

The thought brings me down and I ease my foot off the pedal. Plumes of thick dirt swallow the red of my taillights and I slump back in my seat, the thrill gone. Pathetic, but the best I can do. As always.

The truck comes out of nowhere. My headlights cut across the dark front cab when it turns in front of me, emerging from one of the narrow farm lanes that divide the crops. There are no lights, no warnings. Instinct takes over, and I scream and yank the wheel hard to the left. Tires screech their outrage, spinning out over the dirt, the spray of dust and pebbles pelting my face through the open window. The car careens across the road and rattles over a shallow irrigation ditch before stopping short of a row of what might be corn. Right now it's just husks, brittle arms scratching against the doors in greeting.

I clutch my chest and gulp in too much air, reaching out with shaking fingers to twist the key from the ignition. I wince and close my eyes when the idiot truck driver decides to turn on his high beams, illuminating the back of my car and nearly blinding me.

"Fucking fuckhead fucker," I mutter, undoing my seatbelt and shoving open the door. Maybe it's the cool air or the terror still pumping through my veins, but my exposed skin pebbles with goose bumps and I wish I hadn't thrown my tights and jacket in the back. I round the car but I'm still half-blind; the truck is right where he stopped, emerging from the invisible lane and pointed straight at me, the glaring light making it impossible to see. The silhouette of a figure starts to approach. It's like a scene from every alien abduction movie, and I'm the newest test subject.

"What the fuck?" I demand, shouting into the night. I use a shaky hand to shield my eyes, but it makes no difference. As the figure nears, I realize it's a man, tall and broad. My already pounding heart picks up the pace. I keep my keys clenched in my palm, as though they'll make an effective weapon, should he decide to attack. Should I decide to fight back.

"You know how fast you were going?" he counters, stopping at the edge of the road, maybe ten feet away. I can't make out more than his outline, and I shift to the side to take away some of the burn of his headlights.

"I had my lights on," I snap, gesturing around us. "How the fuck did you not see?"

He ignores that. "Are you hurt?"

The flash flood of adrenaline is easing, making my limbs

weak, and I want to slump down into the grass, another unsatisfactory ending to another unsatisfactory day. All the build-up and none of the payoff. I should have gone to that hotel room. I should have let whatever was going to happen, happen.

"I'm not hurt," I mutter finally. "Turn off your lights. They're blinding me."

"I thought you wanted them on."

"That's the law, genius."

I run a hand through my hair and turn back to my car so I can leave this miserable field.

"Do I know you?"

I stop mid-stride. I'm only halfway turned around, that precipitous moment where I can climb into my car and drive away, or turn back and have this conversation. *Yes, I'm Reese Carlisle. Yes, I was at the prison visiting my criminal father. No, I don't know where the money is. No, I didn't kill my brother.*

"Who do you think I am?"

He takes a few steps toward me and my muscles tense, preparing to run. Right. Like I'm going to lead him on a chase through a corn field. I stopped running years ago.

"Denise," he says.

Everything freezes.

Only Doug knows Denise. And I can't think of a single sane reason Doug would be parked along a dark country road on a Saturday night, accidentally scaring the crap out of me.

Except… he doesn't sound like Doug.

He comes closer and I shift away, moving the glare of the headlights from my front and his back to right in between, and I see who it is.

The stranger.

There's no jacket, no Rolex. He's wearing jeans and a T-shirt under an open flannel shirt, and combined with the rattrap old pickup that nearly killed me, he looks like he belongs here. Here. Not at Verre Plein. Not in that hotel room.

"You never came," he says. There's no inflection in his voice. He's not angry or annoyed or disappointed. It's just a statement.

"Well, I'm not a fucking psychopath," I reply. Even though thoughts about what might have happened had I gone that night—and not been murdered—have kept me up.

"Me neither." The combination of dark and light make it hard to tell, but he sounds sheepish.

I cross my arms across my chest. "How many cards did you give out that night?"

"Just one."

For some reason, I believe him. He's just some silly farmhand who came into town for the day, maybe a lonely birthday, maybe a sad anniversary. Just trying to make himself feel better. I can relate to that.

"Well," I say, clearing my throat. "I should—"

"You changed your hair."

The words stick on my tongue. I force myself to think. Denise. Dental assistant, divorced, dogs. And, three nights ago, a redhead. The one thing I've learned about lying is to stick as close to the truth as you can. And since I'm never going to see this man again, I don't see any problem telling him, "That was a wig."

His brows lift in surprise. "Ah. And now?"

"Real."

"I see."

"Why were you at the restaurant?"

"Just got hungry."

A light breeze rustles the dead corn stalks and I'm reminded again how ridiculous this is. How foolish it is to stand in the middle of nowhere with a stranger and who knows what the hell else lurking in these fields.

I rattle my car keys, breaking whatever spell made me linger. "I have to go." Denise has to get home to feed her dogs. Or prepare for dental surgery. Or something.

"Right." He covers the distance to my car in three long strides. "Let's make sure you're good to drive."

"It's fine."

"I doubt that's true. You tore over the ditch pretty hard." He crouches down and rounds the car, checking…I don't know. The tires, maybe. When he reaches the back tire nearest to where I'm standing, he makes a sound. "Busted," he confirms, tapping the wheel.

"What? I have a flat tire?"

"Yeah. You're lucky it's just the one. Some of these old ditches still have ceramic pipe exposed. If you drive over it the way you did, they're bound to break."

"I only drove over it because you came out of nowhere with your lights off."

He holds my stare for a moment. I'm not taking the blame for this. After a second he stands, just a few feet away. He's at least six inches taller, broad and strong. I should feel afraid, but I don't. I don't know what I feel. Stubborn, maybe.

"I've got some wood in the back," he says, nodding at his

truck. "I'll lay it over the ditch, you drive across, and I'll change your tire."

"Fine."

I get back in my car and watch in the rearview as he retreats to grab a couple of two-by-fours from the bed of his truck. He lays a pair side by side, and I back up to the ditch so he can gauge where to place the next two. There's no way for me to turn around without running over the corn, so I inch my way back over the makeshift bridge, feeling the wood sag beneath the weight. I expect it to snap at any second, but it holds out, and soon enough I'm on the road, parking just ahead of his truck.

I pop the trunk and climb out. I know there's a spare back there, though I have no idea how to change it. I also have no interest. I'd been in two small accidents when I was a teenager, and both times my dad sent someone to deal with the car. I can drive and pump gas, that's it. Fortunately, the stranger knows how to do more.

He grabs a few things from his truck and kicks over a couple of rocks from the edge of the road, wedging one under the front and back tires. He passes me a flashlight before crouching and feeling around the underside of the car, then positioning the jack. I shine the light on his hands, not sure what else I should be doing.

He chews on his lower lip as he works to loosen the lug nuts. "What year is this?" he asks.

"What?"

"The car. What year?"

I don't care about cars. This one is black, I know the license plate number, and I know how to drive it. The end. "I don't know. I got it a couple of years ago."

"Hmm."

He finishes with the nuts and jacks up the car so it's raised off the ground, then stands so he can twist off the flat and fit on the spare. "First date?" he asks.

I stare at him. He's bent to adjust the tire, but only a few inches away. I accidentally shine the light right in his eye and he grimaces. "Ow. Shit."

"Sorry."

He turns his face and blinks a few times. He's hot, in a beer and baseball hat kind of way. He has a heavy five o'clock shadow, the kind I used to whine hurt my skin when the guy I was with kissed me, leaving red patches on my jaw, my neck, my thighs. Now I want to feel it. I'm in the mood for it to hurt a little bit.

He takes the flashlight. "Maybe I should hold onto this." He tucks it under one arm as he replaces the lug nuts, the beam bouncing around the dusty metal.

"I can do it." I reach for the light, but he lifts a hand to block me.

"No, thanks. I like being able to see." He holds my stare, our faces too close, and I'm the first one to cave.

"Suit yourself."

He nods and resumes working. "At the restaurant," he says, after a moment. "That was a first date, you and the charity guy?"

"How do you know he's a charity guy?"

"That story about Africa. With the log."

"I knew you were listening."

"I knew you knew."

Another look and I see that his eyes are very dark. I wonder if he remembers I had brown eyes at the restaurant. They're pale

31

blue now, without the contacts. I used to get a lot of compliments about my eyes. For a while I'd dreamed of being a model, making millions selling mascara.

"Anyway." I kick a small rock under the car. "Yeah. First date. And last."

"You didn't go to his place, either?"

"No. Feel better?"

He smiles.

"How long did you wait?"

He shakes his head but doesn't answer. The visits with my father mark the longest conversations I have in any given month. Already I'm meeting my monthly average with a guy I don't even know.

"Why are you here?" I ask suddenly.

"I'm changing your tire."

"In the middle of nowhere. Why are you out here?"

"Why are you?"

"I asked first."

"I work here," he concedes, nodding back the way he came. "There's a school about fifteen minutes in. It's an extension of Holden College. They have an agricultural program and I was just wrapping up some things. I got a bunch of texts when I was driving back, so I parked to check them. That's why I was stopped. I didn't notice the lights had gone out."

I squint into the darkness, like I might be able to see something. I can't, of course. He could be lying. There could be nothing back there. Or there could be a school, with his name on a door. Professor Something. Master Gardener.

I look at his hands. The cracked knuckles.

I look away.

He could be an escaped convict. Maybe he stole that jacket and the Rolex. He'd paid cash for the meal—maybe he'd stolen that, too. I'd prefer it. I'd prefer his alias to this real person, to his true story. I'd prefer to know I'm not the only liar.

He lowers the jack, tightens the lug nuts the rest of the way, and stands, wiping his hands on his thighs. I need to back up, but I don't. There's a foot of space between us.

"That should do it, Denise."

"Thanks."

"Any time."

"If you turn on your lights and check both ways before entering an intersection, there won't be another time."

He cocks his head slightly. "What if there could be?"

I don't say anything. I don't want to see him a second time. I didn't intend to see him at all. But maybe it's a sign. Maybe it's a giant flashing neon sign saying, here's that chance you didn't take. Take it.

"There can't," I say.

His face falls a little bit. "Right." He bends down to collect the jack and the wrench, and retreats to his truck. He tosses them into the back, the clatter of metal on metal deafening in the quiet.

"Tonight," I say, to clarify. "That's it."

He pauses at the door to his truck, his fingers already wrapped around the handle. Taking his cue, like an honest, decent man. Who changed a tire, got rejected, and dealt with it. "What?"

"Turn off the lights."

He stares at me for a long second, a little bit incredulous, then reaches through the open pickup window and shuts off the headlights. There's a full moon and a blanket of stars overhead, the air cooling rapidly in the dark. I'm in the shadows again. In my element.

"Come here," I say. I remain standing at the side of my car as he approaches, his work boots crunching over the rocks and dirt. He crouches to scoop up the discarded tire and returns it to my trunk, then looks at me. Not for his cue, exactly. But for clarification. Confirmation.

"What do you want, Denise?" His voice is low. I want to hear him say *my* name. Reese Carlisle. To know it and everything it implies.

But I never will.

"Did you want to fuck me? Is that why you gave me that key?"

His throat bobs as he swallows. "Yes."

"I wanted you to. I thought about it."

"You should have come. It would have been good."

"Let's find out."

He glances around. "Right here?"

"Yeah."

"Are you kidding?"

"No."

He exhales. Bemused. Considering. "Are you crazy?"

I hold his stare. "Yes."

Maybe the first sign I'm not the only crazy one out here is the fact that instead of turning around and getting in his truck and driving back to wherever it is he came from, he takes a step forward. There are only a few inches between us to begin with, and before I expect it, there are none. He's taller than me and I feel him against my belly, my thighs, my chest.

He doesn't break eye contact, waiting for me to cry foul, to chicken out, to rethink my proposition. But he doesn't know me.

When I don't move he lifts one hand to the back of my head, sliding coarse fingers over my neck and into my hair. He doesn't close his eyes when he lowers his face to mine, and I can feel his breath on my lips, hear the harsh rasp of my own.

"Still think you want this?" he murmurs.

"Let's find out."

The last thing I see is the tiny quirk of his mouth before he kisses me. There's nothing soft or sweet or searching about the way he kisses, and it's a relief. It says he gets it. He gets that this is one night only, we're not soul searching, we're not bonding, we're not falling in love. This isn't a getting-to-know-you type of fuck. This is getting-off-and-getting-gone. I know the reputation of Fantasy Friends and its like-minded dating websites, but you'd be surprised how difficult it is to find a man who truly just wants a couple of hours, a handshake, and a goodbye. When they meet me—or Hanna or Isabelle or Jacqueline—they transform from the promised one-night stand in the email to Mr. Chivalrous, pulling out chairs, asking questions about my life, my family, my interests.

I can't talk about those things.

It knocks my enthusiasm for the evening down by half, dampens my libido, makes everything that much worse. I normally stick it out. After all, I've gone through the trouble of making a profile, putting on a costume, and showing up.

This—this stranger with his tongue in my mouth on the side of the road in the middle of nowhere—this is the most "real" I've had in months. Years. He's grinding his hips against mine so hard his fly hurts my leg. His hand is rough where it holds my neck, the other squeezing my waist, holding me in place. And I love it. Bruises will extend the experience. They're like leftovers. I can nibble on them for days.

I push him back so I can work my skirt up over my hips. I'm wearing plain black panties, and when I slide my fingers beneath the cotton sides he stops me. "I'll do it," he says, holding my wrist. "In a minute."

I expect him to try to push me to my knees or something, but instead he surprises me by grabbing my ass and hoisting me onto the trunk of the car. He moves between my legs and undoes his fly, though it's too dark for me to see anything beyond the action. He kisses me again, his fingers in my hair, the first time in years I've let someone touch my hair during sex. The first time it's been real.

His free hand skates up the inside of my thigh, making me tremble. The rough scratch of his fingers on the sensitive skin is unbearable, the promise of the trajectory nearly enough to make me come. I try to break away to breathe but he forces me back, nipping my lower lip until it stings and I open for another kiss. I like the idea of this. That he's taking his due. He did me a favor; this is payment. Payback.

It's much better than polite inquiries about how I became interested in cartography.

I pull his hand between my legs, and he laughs against my mouth, the only sound in the night besides our breathing. I try to move my panties to the side but he won't let me, planting my hand on the warm metal of the trunk and returning his fingers to my crotch. He just rests them there, his knuckles rubbing, working the fabric over my heated skin, getting it wet, finding proof that I'm not just a girl who claims to want it. I do want it.

I push up so I can work a hand beneath his T-shirt, the skin of his belly, his hip, his back, hot against my palm. I scrape my nails up so I can anchor us together, using him for balance as I slip my other hand between us, feeling the soft rub of the denim, the smooth cotton of his briefs, then, finally, him.

He hisses when I grip him roughly, tugging hard, punishment for making me wait. He gets the hint and pushes two fingers into my panties, tormenting me.

"Do it," I order. "Hurry."

He buries his face in the side of my neck, and I feel his lips on the delicate skin, his teeth, the suction. He's going to leave a mark. That might be a problem if I had somewhere to be tomorrow, but I don't. There's no one to tease me. No one to pry. No one for anything at all.

Finally, he pushes a finger inside, making me shudder. He knows what he's doing, what he's looking for, and when he finds it he rubs. Hard.

I tremble and writhe against the sensation.

A second finger joins the first, and I shove him away from my neck and fist my hands in his shirt, burying my face against his chest, overwhelmed and consumed. He chuckles and strokes my back with his free hand, a strangely consoling gesture when his other hand is causing so much agony.

"Please!" I feel sweat on my temples and the nape of my neck, my spine damp. "Please."

"Back pocket," he mumbles into my hair, and it takes me a second to realize it's an instruction. He's merciful enough to take that demonic hand away so I can focus, get my bearings, and reach into the pocket of his sagging jeans to retrieve his wallet. The condom is easy to grab and I toss the wallet on the trunk and open the packet. He rolls it on and hooks both arms under my knees, yanking so I have to catch myself on my elbows when I fall back. I'm wearing every item of clothing I started with and so is he, but they're no obstacle when he snags a finger under my panties and pulls them aside. He strokes me briefly, then guides himself in, more gently than I'm expecting.

I drop my head back, watching the sky, the stars, the moon. I feel him. I feel how soft his clothes are against the inside of my knees, the scrape of the hair on his thighs as it chafes against mine, the heaviness of him inside me. He moves slowly at first, but never tentatively. His dark eyes are open and watching, and while I normally keep my eyes closed, this time I can't look away.

He leans in and places one hand on the trunk next to my ribs, giving himself leverage to go harder, deeper. He's moving faster, but still not fast, exactly. The way he's looking at me says he believes me now. He believes I'm the kind of girl who fucks strangers. Who doesn't do next time. And he's making sure I don't forget this one.

He moves harder. Faster. He plants a forearm next to my head. I can smell him; sweat and laundry detergent. No expensive cologne, no hair products. His five o'clock shadow scrapes my cheek and I wince, but I don't complain. I just feel it.

He kisses me, messy and unfocused. He seems like the kind

of man who should be out here, who does things earthy and raw, who has dirt under his nails and knows how to change a tire and fuck a woman and not ask too many questions.

I wonder who he thinks I am.

The question makes me explode. I knew I was close, but I'm still not ready for the tremors that overtake me, transforming into overwhelming waves that make my muscles lock and unlock, my lungs emptying in a startled cry. My hips jerk against his and he groans, the sound deep and heartfelt, as though my orgasm permitted his own, like he was waiting for me.

I hate it when a man collapses on top of me after sex, but when the stranger does it, it's fine. It's like a blanket or a cloak, a kind of camouflage, despite the fact that my legs are spread and he's between them. It gives me time to come back to myself, to study the sky, count the stars, let my heartbeat slow.

Eventually he pushes up. "You all right?"

I nod and clear my throat. "Fine."

He pulls away, turning to tidy up, and I ease off the car on shaky legs, fixing my panties and working my skirt down over my hips. I straighten my shirt and smooth my hair, and when he turns back, I'm me again.

"Thanks," I say.

He wipes the back of his hand over his mouth. "Thanks?"

"Yeah. Thanks." I pull my keys out of my pocket.

"Are you going back to that restaurant any time soon?"

"No."

"You only ever do anything once?"

"I told you. There's no next time."

"Yeah, I heard you, Denise."

"Thanks for changing the tire."

"You're welcome."

There's a four-inch scratch in the paint now, a glaring white scar. I have something similar on my right thigh, but it's twice as long and hurt a lot more.

"Drive safe," he says. The words are a prompt, and I stop ogling the scratch and pull open the door.

"Good night."

I climb in and twist the key in the ignition. My hands are shaking. I'm sure it's just the aftermath of adrenaline. I haven't experienced a spike like this in a very long time.

He waits next to his truck until I pull onto the road. I watch him in my rearview.

He doesn't wave goodbye.

4

I'm at the Food Bank again the following week. Today my shift is from two until eight, and by seven I'm exhausted and all my bones hurt. We received an enormous shipment of cans and I've been sorting and stocking all afternoon. Tuna, green beans, artichokes, fruit cocktail—if it comes in a tin, I've checked the expiration date and arranged accordingly.

"How you doing?" Lyla calls, clopping down the aisle in her heels. I've known she was coming for the past minute and a half.

"Making progress." I gesture at the tower of empty boxes I've stashed in the corner to flatten later. I've got about twenty more to get through before the inventory is fully accounted for.

"I brought you an assistant." Lyla drags Rodney behind her like a kid being escorted to the principal's office. All I know about Rodney is that he's been to prison, he's afraid of mice, and he thinks I'm weird as fuck. I know because I heard him say so. Sound carries in the warehouse, especially when you're listening carefully.

They stop a few feet away, and Lyla elbows Rodney in the side. Today her shirt has a giant tiger face glaring out, its green sequin eyes sparkling in the warehouse light. Duly prompted, Rodney mutters, "You need some help?" while scuffing his sneaker on the cement floor.

I don't *want* help. One of the reasons volunteering here works for me is precisely because I'm left alone. But four of my fingernails have cracked, my palms are burning from the cardboard dust, and my hand slipped when slicing open one of the boxes, leaving a two-inch hole in my jeans. I need help.

"Yeah," I say.

"Good." Lyla glowers at Rodney. "That's what I thought. This place'll be empty by seven-thirty. You two lock up together and leave together. Together," she repeats with scary emphasis. "You got me?"

"Yeah," Rodney mumbles.

There's a pause, then I realize she's waiting for me to answer, too. "Got it."

"Good." She makes a note on her clipboard and totters away.

"What do you need me to do?" Rodney asks, hands stuffed in the front pocket of his oversized hoodie. I'm wearing a hoodie, too. Now that I think about it, Rodney and I are dressed the same: hoodie, dark jeans, sneakers and matching scowls.

"Everything's arranged alphabetically." I nod at the shelves. "Items with the earliest expiry dates go at the front. These boxes are totally random, so you have to go through, check each can, and find the right spot for it."

"Okay."

I use my foot to nudge a box in his direction and stick the box cutter on top before turning back to my work. I hear him slice open the tape and the ensuing rattle of cans, otherwise he's quiet and so am I. When it's quarter to eight and we're down to four boxes, I move to the corner to start flattening the cardboard so we can get it recycled. A few minutes later Rodney tosses the last box into the pile and comes to help, tearing and stomping as needed. It's after eight when we finish, and we're both covered in dust. My hands are dark with grime and the dirt under my nails reminds me of the stranger, fixing my tire. Still a stranger. No name.

I shake my head. Until today I hadn't been able to stop thinking about that night. He hadn't left as many marks as I'd thought, and I was more disappointed than I should have been. Without the bruises as proof of the encounter, it could have been a fantasy, a story I concocted on my lonely drive home from prison.

We wash up in the tiny staff bathrooms and Rodney waits while I turn off the lights and check the doors. It's dark and cold when we exit into the quiet parking lot, my car the only one remaining. The warehouse is in an industrial area, predictably isolated. Desolate, sometimes. No buses come in here, and it's a ten-minute walk to the nearest Holden Rail, the city's commuter train system.

"How'd you get here?" I ask.

Rodney didn't put on a coat, and now he shivers as he huddles deeper into his hoodie, breath hanging in the air. "Rode with Colin."

I look around, just in case. "He left?"

"Yeah."

"You need a ride to the train station?"

"Yeah."

We walk in silence to my car, the February cold especially jarring after the strangely warm day last week. The asphalt is speckled white with frost, the car windows opaque. I pull out my keys and click to open the doors, the taillights flicking on. Rodney gives the car a once-over.

"This is nice."

"Thanks."

"Why are you working at a food bank and driving this car?"

"I don't work. I volunteer."

"Huh." I see him notice the scratch on the trunk, but he doesn't comment.

We get in and wait for the car to heat up, the windows to defrost. I press a button to warm the steering wheel and Rodney snorts.

"What?"

He rolls his eyes.

"Whatever." The area feels lonely and abandoned as I navigate the empty streets, the tires crunching over salt sprinkled on the roads as a precaution.

"Where do you live?" Rodney asks.

"Downtown."

"I figured. Where?"

"Does it matter?"

"You afraid I'll come rob you?"

"I'm afraid you'll come visit."

He snickers and rubs a spot on the window, peering outside. "Why you at the Food Bank, then? If you don't have to be?"

"There are lots of volunteers, not just me."

"Uh-huh."

"Why do you work there?" I ask.

"Cause I have to. Lyla's my mom's second cousin and my mom made her give me this job."

"You couldn't find something closer to home?"

"I wasn't exactly looking hard enough."

I nod. Its remote location was part of what I liked about the Food Bank. Fewer people to interact with. To recognize me.

"I got a brother in prison and a brother in law school," Rodney says. "I guess this is the middle-ground."

"The middle of nowhere, maybe."

"Well. It ain't prison."

"No," I agree. "It's not."

Rodney scoffs as I pull into the parking lot at the station. "Like you'd know," he says, climbing out. "Thanks for the ride."

"Bye."

I watch until he disappears inside, wondering if I should hang around until the train comes. I don't know the frequency of the stops—I'd taken the train a couple of times years ago when I was too drunk to drive and wanted to see how the other half lived, but I don't remember most of the details. The Carlisle family flew first class and had a driver on the payroll.

There are a few other cars and enough foot traffic that I don't feel like I'm completely abandoning Rodney when I reverse out of the lot and turn toward home. Because of the spare tire, the car drives a little weird, but only if you're paying attention. Like the faint bruises and the scratch in the paint, I'd left it on as a tangible reminder of that night. But I know better than to live in the past.

I pass a few darkened car repair shops on my way home, so I

watch until I find one that offers twenty-four hour service and pull in. There are no cars in the lot, but I can see a couple on lifts inside the raised garage doors. I park and tug on a wool hat before walking into the small front area. Enough time has passed that people don't recognize me too much anymore, especially with the dark hair and no makeup, but I still take comfort in my disguises.

The front office is bathed in an orangey glow and smells like cheap cleaning products. A flimsy desk, vending machine, and three plastic chairs occupy most of the floor space, while a middle-aged man with a matching gray moustache and jumpsuit reads a newspaper behind the desk. He folds the paper when I approach.

"Car trouble?" he guesses.

"Flat tire," I say. "There's a spare on there now. I need to change it."

He stands and nods. "Sure. I can help you with that."

I drive the car into the third bay, which is empty, and open the trunk to show him the busted tire. He leaves to confirm they have a match in stock.

"Got one," he announces, coming back with a tire hung on his arm. I'll have to assume it's the right one; they all look the same to me.

"Great."

"It'll only take a few minutes," he says. "You can wait in the office if you want. It's warmer in there."

I stuff my hands in my pockets and retreat to the office, halting halfway through the door. There's a man at the counter, his back to me. He's wearing an army green winter coat with jeans and boots, and he turns at the sound of my approach, eyes widening comically when he spots me.

It's the stranger.

The *fucking stranger.*

He's holding a bottle of motor oil from the rack beside him, and now it slips through his fingers and falls to the floor, bouncing twice before landing on its side. For a long, stunned moment all I can do is stare at it.

"Be honest," he says, eying me warily as he crouches to pick up the oil. "Are you following me? Because I'm flattered, but you're being a little obvious."

Right after my father was arrested, there was this journalist named Larry who used to trail me everywhere, going to extremes even other psycho journalists considered too far. He posed as a gravedigger at my brother's funeral; called claiming to be my father's lawyer; and even hacked into my gynecologist's database to learn when my next appointment was so he could "be there." That was the one that got him arrested.

Despite his efforts to be stealthy, Larry was everywhere. There was no way not to recognize him after a while. And after a certain number of "coincidences," it became suspicious. The stranger isn't Larry, but he's starting to feel like more than a coincidence, too.

"Do you work here?" the stranger asks when I don't say anything. "I need to buy…"

"No," I interrupt. "I don't work here."

"Oh." He takes in my winter coat, torn jeans, sneakers, wool hat. I suppose I could work here.

"Why are *you* here?" I try not to sound paranoid, but I am.

I've thought of little but him for the past week, but now that he's in front of me, alarm bells are ringing.

Before he can answer, the mechanic returns. "All set," he says, wiping his hands on a dirty rag. "You paying cash—?" He breaks off when he spots the stranger. "Or credit's fine," he adds. "Debit. Whatever."

He scribbles the price on an old-fashioned bill and slides it across the counter. I reach for my wallet. I always carry cash, since my credit card says my name. And while maybe the mechanic wouldn't bat an eye at seeing *Reese Carlisle*, the stranger might wonder why Denise is using someone else's card.

I collect my receipt and pull out my car keys.

"Just the oil for you?" the mechanic asks the stranger.

"You know what?" he says. "Never mind." He returns the bottle to the display and goes to the door, holding it open for me to pass through. It closes behind us and I take a few steps before turning.

"Why are you here?"

"Go out with me," he says.

It takes me a second to comprehend. "What?"

"Right now," he says. "Let's get something to eat. I'm starving."

"I don't—I'm not—" I try not to act like a moron who's never been asked out before. I've been on dates. Lots of them. Just not with him. "I can't."

"Why not?"

"I meant what I said the other night. That was a one-time thing."

"Why?"

"Stop asking me questions. I said no."

He tilts his head, almost quizzically, then turns to go. "You're the boss." Behind him, I see his truck parked at the edge of the lot.

"Why are you here?" I shouldn't ask. I shouldn't care. I just need to believe this is a coincidence. As unlikely as it is, I need to believe.

He stops. "I have to change the oil. This place is on my way."

"Your way where?"

"Home." He finally recognizes my suspicion. "Are you worried about something?"

"It seems odd," I say, "that you were at the restaurant, then the road, then here."

He lifts a shoulder. "You were all those places. I wasn't suspicious. I just thought I was lucky."

My mind is racing. I don't know what to believe. I don't know what to do. My brain is saying, *Get in your car and drive away and make sure he doesn't follow you home*. My body is saying, *Do it again*.

"Let's get something to eat," he says, sensing weakness.

He's too nice. He's going to take it personally when I don't want to give him my number or see a movie next week.

"I don't do seconds," I make myself say, even as a desperate part of me tries to plead its case.

"No?" he says. "I think if we'd had more time that night, I could have given you seconds. And thirds."

Whatever protest I'd been about to utter dissolves in the cold air at the mention of that orgasm. That's what I want. Seconds. Thirds. More.

"I live near the restaurant," he adds. "Verre Plein. Come over."

I think about how easy it must be for him. Being himself all the time. No secrets, no lies. He sees a woman he wants, gives her his room key— "Why did you have a key?"

"What?"

"Why did you have a hotel room if you live near the restaurant?"

"Burst pipe in the building. Two floors had to spend the night elsewhere."

Holden City Grand Hotel is not the place a teacher at a farm school would be able to afford. "That's a nice hotel."

"The building paid for it. They should, with what they charge."

The sane part of me, the part saying, *This is too much. This can't be a coincidence*, is turning on the part of me that climbs to the roof every night and urges me to step off. This feels like a compromise. Like inching my toes over the side, but not jumping. Not yet.

"Come on," he says, starting toward his truck. "I don't have a spare key this time, so you'll have to follow."

"We'll see," I say, even though I know I'm going to do it.

He nods, then jogs to his truck. I return to the garage to collect my car, and when I back out into the lot he's idling at the exit. He puts on his blinker to make the turn onto the freeway, and I do the same.

He doesn't drive straight to the city center, like I'm expecting. That's where Verre Plein is, where he lives, where I live. No, he leads us to the east side of the city, popular with artists and hipsters, streets lined with small restaurants hawking food from all over the world.

This is where Denise has her studio apartment.

He parks in a public lot, and I find a spot the next row over. He's waiting when I climb out of my car. "You said you lived near Verre Plein."

"I do. But I told you I was starving and I want tacos. Come on." He doesn't wait, just heads for the sidewalk.

I want to complain, but my stomach leaps at the thought of food, so I follow. The streets are busy for nine o'clock on a Tuesday, restaurants and bars doing good business. He stops at a place called *Rita's Cantina* and opens the door, gesturing for me to go inside. He doesn't ask if I like Mexican, though I do, and the smell of roasting meat and spice makes me forget all my misgivings.

The restaurant is half-full and he leads the way to a tiny corner booth, taking the seat opposite me. The walls are covered with canvas prints of Mexican movies, their hand-painted artwork a bright contrast to the plain walls and tables. A server comes over and I order two tacos and the stranger gets five, then checks with me before ordering a couple of beers, too.

"Five tacos?" I say, sipping my beer. "Really?"

"I've gotta keep up my energy if I'm going to fulfill all my promises."

"All of them? How many are we talking?"

He thinks for a second. "Six," he says, trying to keep a straight face.

I raise my eyebrows. "Oh, wow."

"Not up for it?"

"You're going to have to eat fast if you want to fulfill six 'promises' before midnight."

He sets down his bottle. "What happens at midnight? Do you turn into a pumpkin?"

I said midnight because I want there to be an end time. A finish line. And once we're across, we're done. But instead I say, "The carriage turns into a pumpkin. Cinderella just turns back into herself."

"Oh, yeah? So when the clock strikes twelve you'll still be you?" He leans across the table to look me over. "I guess I can work with that."

I try not to smile, but I can't help it. "Shut up." He's too handsome. He didn't fit in at Verre Plein, not even with the too-small jacket and the fake Rolex. But he belongs here. In a worn old coat and jeans, his fingers as rough and calloused as I remember them. His eyes are green and there's a fine white scar on the bridge of his nose, another at the edge of his eyebrow. He needs a haircut, but I don't imagine he cares.

The server returns with plates of tacos and a trio of salsa, and I squeeze lime over everything and take a bite. The stranger does the same, watching me as he chews.

"So," he says. "Tell me about yourself."

"I thought this meal was just about sustenance."

"I lied," he replies. "Now you know something about me."

"What's your name?" I want to take back the question as soon as I ask it. I don't want to know his name. Correction: I don't want to *want* to know his name. But it's too late.

"Chris," he says. "'Bout time you asked."

"I told you I didn't want to see you again," I remind him. "Your name wasn't important." But it feels important. It feels just as wrong as it does right. I should leave. Stand up and put money on the table and walk out of another date. But I don't move.

"I know what you said." He licks a piece of cilantro off his thumb. "What else do you want to know?"

"Nothing."

"Nothing?"

"Not a single thing."

He laughs. He's supposed to be taking this seriously. He's supposed to be getting the point. He's not supposed to be *normal.*

"I'm serious," I say seriously.

He studies the selection of salsas and chooses the green one. "I know."

I wait for him to say something else, but he doesn't. We eat in silence, and when I finish my meal he still has two tacos left.

"Want one?" he asks, nodding at the food.

I don't want to want anything, but I do.

Wordlessly I hold out my plate. He arches a brow at my abhorrent manners but gives me a taco.

Growing up, we'd had a British nanny, the quintessential older lady who insisted on wearing a uniform every day, though my father told her she didn't have to. She'd given me that same disapproving look a hundred times. A thousand. Scolding me was ineffective. Ten minutes in the time-out chair didn't faze me. But lock me in my room and leave me alone with just my own miserable company? Devastating every time.

Still is.

"All right," Chris says when the food's gone. He fishes out two frail paper napkins from the dispenser and wipes his hands.

"You hungry? Want anything else? Another drink?"

I shake my head. "No."

"Okay." He finishes his beer, watching me. Then he sets down the bottle, gently knocking it against mine, like he's making a toast. Or a promise. "Let's go," he says.

5

His apartment is four blocks east of Verre Plein. My home—my real one—is three blocks west. It's a ten-minute walk door-to-door. We're neighbors.

I drive after him into the underground parkade of his building and down to the second level, where he parks in a reserved space near the elevator and I find a visitor slot along the wall. I climb out and dodge an oily puddle, glistening pink and purple in the fluorescent lights.

The buildings in this area range from very nice to extravagant, and this one is on the nicer end of a very nice scale. Some might call it fancy. A mirrored elevator whisks us up to the ninth floor, making one stop at the lobby, where an older gentleman gets on. He greets Chris politely, then gives me a terse nod as he takes in my hoodie and torn jeans. Once upon a time, I could have bought and sold this whole place.

We exit on nine, and I peer around before following Chris down the carpeted hall. It's quiet and warm and smells like fresh paint. Toward the end of the corridor I notice a missing patch of drywall near the baseboard, pipes visible behind it.

"From the flood," Chris says, gesturing absently as he passes. "They fixed it up pretty quick. And we got some new carpet out of the deal."

"Exciting."

He glances at me over his shoulder, his expression hard to read, then tugs keys from his pocket and stops in front of his door. "Home sweet home." He twists the key in the lock and lets me enter first, reaching past me to flip the light switch.

It's a nice apartment, sparsely furnished, as expected. Since starting my dating game I've been in my fair share of strange apartments, ranging from sketchy to passable to unbelievable. This place falls squarely in the middle. It's spacious, if only because there's not a lot of clutter. The apartment opens into the living room, with an enormous television mounted on the wall a few feet away, a large black leather sectional and matching ottoman positioned carefully in front. Near the far wall of windows there's a dining table that doubles as a desk, a laptop and piles of paperwork covering the surface.

I can make out the shape of a kitchen in the left corner and the shadow of a hallway next to it.

"Can I get you anything?" Chris asks. He crouches to unlace his boots, peeking up at me through his lashes. He's... polite. Normally in this instance the guy offers me a glass of wine, I decline, he gives me what he considers a seductive look, and we get started. No formalities. No pretense.

"No," I say.

"Let me take your coat."

The apartment feels lived in. There's a coffee mug on the end table, a newspaper on the ottoman, a baseball hat hooked on the corner of a dining chair. Potted plants sit in a row in front of the windows and, when he flips on another light, I see an unwashed plate on the kitchen counter next to an open bag of chips.

He's so normal. If he had a dog it would be a golden lab named Buddy.

"Denise?" he prompts. "You want to keep your coat on?"

I tell myself to focus. We've already done it once with our clothes on. I suppose this time should be different. I unzip my coat and shrug out, watching him walk to the table and drape both jackets over a chair. He's wearing a green flannel shirt buttoned over a white T-shirt and faded jeans. I don't think I've ever been with a guy who wore flannel.

"You sure you don't want a drink?" he asks, rubbing his hands together like he's cold. "I'm having one."

I hesitate. I don't want a beverage. Technically I'm only halfway to my two-drink maximum, but I didn't come here to socialize.

"I don't want a drink, Chris."

He pauses with the fridge door open, turning slowly with a beer in his hand. "Right," he says carefully. "You want…"

I check my watch. It's almost ten-thirty. "We have an hour and a half."

He winks at me. "I'll drink fast."

I cross the room and study the view out the window. His apartment faces a street of similar buildings, a checkerboard pattern of light on their faces, winking back at me.

"What were you up to today?"

I turn. He's come out of the kitchen to rest against the counter, feet crossed at the ankles, beer in hand. He gestures to my ratty outfit when I don't answer right away.

"I was cleaning."

"Cleaning what?"

"My car." When the only people you talk to are people you lie to, it comes pretty easily.

"Do you have any friends?" he asks abruptly.

"What?"

"Do you have any friends?"

I haven't had a friend in three years. And if the rate at which they abandoned me is any indication, I hadn't had any for a long time before then, either. "Of course I have friends."

"Who?"

"Why?"

"Because you suck at small talk."

I'm not offended. I'm no better at conversation than I am at seduction. It's hardly necessary when both parties know that the entire evening is just a prelude to sex. There's no need to convince anybody when you're already on the same page. Except for Chris. He appears to be reading another book altogether. "You didn't bring me here for conversation."

He takes a final sip of beer and puts the bottle behind him on the counter. When he straightens, it's like he's unfolding, like he gets bigger, more real, more everything. I don't know why I want him.

I don't know why he wants me.

"Do you have a dog?" I blurt out.

He's about to take a step toward me, but now he stops. "What? No. Why?"

"Have you ever had one? Like, when you were a kid?"

He rolls his lips together, amused. "Yeah," he says finally. "We had a dog."

"What kind?"

"A German Shepherd."

Close enough. "What was his name?"

"Astro."

An iota of tension seeps out of me, like a fishing line being given some slack.

"Why?" he asks, a laugh hidden in the word. "Do you like dogs?"

Denise: divorced, dental hygienist, loves dogs. The alphabet dating game has a few necessary rules. Never bring them home. Don't fall asleep. Stick to the story. "No," I hear myself say. "I don't like anything."

"C'mere," Chris murmurs, almost as though he can hear the warning bells clanging in my brain. He cups my face to kiss me and I try to calm down, will myself to focus. To do this. Mechanical, reliable. Get what I came for.

I press onto my toes and grip the sides of his flannel shirt to anchor myself. The fabric is soft under my fingertips, his chest firm beneath my knuckles. I open my mouth and kiss him harder, but he eases back, fingers curled into my hair, preventing me from following. He has his eyes open, watching, showing, and he kisses me again, slowly.

He doesn't give a damn about midnight.

"I get it," I mutter, twisting my head away.

"Get what?" he asks. His fingers find the hem of my hoodie and draw it up and off, tossing it onto the table. I'm wearing a black T-shirt underneath and now he slips his fingers into the waistband of my jeans and strokes back and forth over the skin above my panties.

I huff and try not to sound petulant. "What do you want?"

"The same thing you want, I think."

"If you wanted what I wanted, you'd be naked."

He laughs, tilting away from me. He doesn't take his hand from my pants, and I feel his knuckles bump against my stomach. "You're funny," he says, wiping his other hand over his face.

"I'm serious."

He's still laughing. "I know."

I pull off my T-shirt, and he goes quiet. Thank God for push-up bras.

"Give me what I want," I say. I take his hand out of my pants and unzip my jeans, shoving them down to my ankles so I'm standing in a black bra and panties. His mouth opens a little bit. I know I'm not perfect. I'm too thin, too pale, too mean, too shadowed.

"Oh," he says softly. Almost unconsciously, he begins to unbutton his shirt, letting it fall to the floor before tugging off his T-shirt. His socks and jeans follow suit, and then we're both standing in our underwear.

He hooks a finger between my bra cups and tugs me in. I feel his other hand at my tailbone, tracing small circles there, dipping under my panties, but not far enough. Then those calloused fingers scrape ever-so-slowly up my back until they're catching on the lace band of my bra. The hand in front slides over my throat to cup my face again, holding me in place for his kiss, but with his eyes now closed.

I relax and kiss him back. I feel the coarse skin of his palm on my spine and the scratch of his chest at my front, and I stand on my toes and put my arms around his neck and do what I came here to do.

"Your hair's soft," he murmurs, pulling back and staring at the strands he's filtering through his fingers. "It's pretty."

Oh, for fuck's sake. "Thanks."

"You're pretty."

There was a time those words mattered to me. It was before I saw my dad in a prison jumpsuit and I buried my brother next to my mother. It was before—

"What happened here?"

The hand at my back drops to my right leg, to the top of the bumpy pink scar that extends eight inches down the outside of my thigh.

"Car accident." I don't know if the truth is just easier to remember or simply harder to forget. I went to my brother's funeral in a wheelchair. They pushed me over the damp grass at a rate so slow I could have crawled to the gravesite faster, but I know that's what they wanted. They moved slowly so the press could take pictures, ask questions. *Were you driving, Reese? There are doubts your brother was the driver. Did you choose the cliff on purpose, Reese? Why would you do that? He was only twenty-one, Reese.*

"Looks painful," Chris says. "Does it hurt?"

"No."

Most men just ignore it. A couple cringed, but most didn't care. They were nice enough not to ask questions, and they didn't touch. I'm over it. A broken femur is the least of my battle wounds.

While I recovered in the hospital they made me see a shrink. He told me about survivor's guilt, but he wasn't trying to help me, he was trying to help *them*. I knew he was reading the papers. Hearing the whispers. He thought I was guilty of much more. He said "survivor's guilt" a hundred times, the emphasis always on the guilt, not the survivor. And maybe he wasn't wrong. Maybe that's why I stand with my toes over the edge of the roof and drive too fast and go home with strange men. And maybe that's why nothing worse has happened. Surviving is my punishment.

Chris watches my face as he unhooks my bra, then leans over to place it on top of my hoodie before returning to look his fill. This much he has in common with the others. They like boobs.

After the infamous crotch shot incident, there came the predictable slew of seedy invitations from porn sites and men's magazines. As though flashing my crotch was the equivalent of a toe in the water, gauging the public's interest. I said no, but even if I'd been tempted, my father would have disowned me. He tolerated a lot, but there were limits. In hindsight it's funny that naked photographs were where he chose to draw the line. As though that were the worst thing a Carlisle could be caught doing.

"What do you like?" Chris murmurs, stroking me.

"Where's your bedroom?"

"Down the hall."

"Let's go there."

I'm normally pretty indifferent about where in the apartment we do this. Against the front door, on the couch, the floor, the bed—it doesn't matter. I'm not sticking around long enough to care. But at the rate we're moving, this will take half the night. Maybe a change of scenery will remind Chris what we came here to do.

"What's wrong with right here?" He steps into me before I can respond. His knees bump my thighs, forcing me back until I feel the cool chill of the windows against my shoulder blades. I shudder, and he laughs and kisses my neck, sucking harder than I expect, making me jump.

"Good or bad?" he asks.

"Good." I exhale shakily and turn so my hair falls over my face, hiding me.

He lets go long enough to urge me to turn around so I'm facing the window. The darkness outside has made the glass a mirror, and in it I can see the shadow of his forearm where it covers my breasts. Then I watch the other hand. He splays his fingers wide, coasting down my stomach with painful slowness. I feel every millimeter, every bump, every ridge, every callus. Eventually the tips of his fingers disappear beneath the top edge of my panties, gliding back and forth until I squirm.

I bite my tongue. I want to rail at him. I want to stomp off. I want to push his hand down and his fingers in and come all over him.

"Open your eyes," he whispers, nipping my earlobe.

I hadn't even realized they were closed. "I was falling asleep," I lie.

He laughs. His teeth glow white in the glass. They match my pale skin, surrounded by his tan, his muscle, his everything. His fingers inch lower, brushing over the damp curls that wait. "Should I stop?"

My breath vanishes. I don't know if it's to prevent me from passing out or begging. "No."

With his hand hidden beneath the black fabric of my panties, I can't see his finger move, but I feel it insinuate itself between slippery folds, seeking and finding entrance. I find my breath just in time to lose it again and slump against him. He only smiles and tightens the arm around my chest, anchoring me.

He's not the first man to do this. But he's the first in a very long time to treat it like an expedition, a curiosity, a sampling of what's possible. The other men had a clear goal in mind; if he weren't turning me on the way he is, I would doubt Chris knows what he's doing.

But he does.

"Push your panties down," Chris whispers. I feel the thud of his heartbeat on my back. Normally, I wouldn't like the imbalance of power, but right now I don't care.

I hook my thumbs under the cotton and shove my panties down as far as I can get them, revealing his hand, the material stretched between my thighs. I keep my face turned, trying to see through my hair until the arm on my chest releases me and comes up to grip my chin, tugging me so I'm facing the glass again.

There was a time I loved attention. I wanted my picture on every cover, every website. I didn't care what they said, as long as they said something. Now I don't want to be seen. I want to be forgotten, ignored, uncared for. And for a long time, I've gotten my wish.

A feeling comes over me, one that has nothing to do with sex. One I try and fail to fight. I do my best to keep my eyes on his hand but they rise of their own accord, locking on his in the glass. He's watching. He's everywhere.

I shatter. I cry out and clutch at him, and he catches me when my knees give way. Everything inside me is lurching and convulsing in endless, artless waves of pleasure.

I realize I'm gasping like I've just been washed ashore after a month lost at sea, and I try to compose myself even though I'm slumped over his arm like a rag doll, rubbing my hands over my heated cheeks, surprised to find them damp. Fuck. I try to be inconspicuous as I wipe my face, and Chris is polite enough to give me some room, removing his hand, making sure I don't collapse when he lets go completely.

I hear him swallow and from the corner of my eye I see him calmly sipping his beer. He lifts a brow and tilts his head toward the hall that leads to the bedroom. "That was one."

≫ ≫

I don't know where I am.

I try to focus, but it's impossible to see. I'm surrounded by blackness. I'm naked and warm and—

Chris snores softly, jolting me out of my confused stupor.

Fuck.

Fuck.

I peer around for an alarm clock, finding one on the far side of the bed. It's 3:02 a.m. I'm furious with myself but refuse to move a muscle until I calm down. Until my eyes adjust to the darkness in the room, allowing me to get oriented. It's a typical guy's bedroom, a king-size bed with a cheap comforter, a few pillows, and a headboard that did serious, cliché damage to the wall tonight. Chris sleeps on his stomach, arms folded up near his head, and faces me, mouth parted slightly, soft snores whistling out. Deceptively innocent.

I make out a couple of nightstands, a dresser, and the outline of a window with a heavy blackout curtain because Chris has to go to bed early on school nights so he can make the long trip to the farm in the morning. He told me that, even though I didn't want to know.

He lied about the six orgasms, though three's not a number I'll complain about. And, despite my best efforts not to beg him to hurry the hell up, I'd heard myself pleading on a couple of embarrassing occasions. He's not one of those guys who's desperate to speed through his sexual repertoire, tossing you around like a contortionist, showing you what he's learned from his favorite porn sites. No, Chris likes to take his time. Draw it out. Build it up. Make it ache.

My heart beats faster, and I tell myself to get a grip. *Don't fall asleep* is a very important rule. It means the guard stays up, it means no pictures on cell phones, no one hunting through my bag.

Shit. Fuck. Shit.

My bag.

When I'm on a date, the bag has the necessities. Cash. Lip gloss. House key. Condoms. No ID.

But when I left the house today, I wasn't expecting a "date." I have my real bag. With *my* wallet. *My* keys. *My* driver's license and credit cards. My *name*.

I order myself to calm down. I'm being paranoid. I don't think he hunted through my bag, but if he did, money's the obvious motivator. And even if he did see my name, there's no guarantee he'd recognize it. Though he'd probably wonder why it didn't match the one I'd given him.

He snorts in his sleep and reaches down to scratch his ass.

No. He's not a snoop.

He's a guy.

I inch out of bed and ease away. We'd abandoned our clothes in the living room, and I find everything and dress quickly in the kitchen light. My stomach growls, and I fill a glass with water from the tap and down it, then snag a handful of chips from the bag on the counter before turning for the front door.

Chris leans against it, wearing a pair of jeans, arms folded across his chest. I let out a tiny shriek, chips shooting into the air.

He rubs one eye, trying to wake up.

I'd left my bag by the door when we came in, and now he follows my alarmed gaze. He bends carefully to hook a finger under the strap, bringing it with him as he straightens.

"I know you don't do seconds," he says, extending the bag as I approach. "Or thirds or fourths, but you can't say goodbye?"

I take the bag and fish out a piece of gum. "You were sleeping," I mutter. I jump when he tucks my hair behind my ear.

"I was tired."

I clear my throat and avoid his stare. "You should go back to bed."

"I wanted to say goodbye."

I meet his gaze. "Okay. goodbye."

"I had a nice time, Denise."

I try not to scowl. "Thanks. Me too."

His chest moves when he laughs. "I'll bet. Let's do this again sometime."

I sigh. "Look. I know I told you I don't do seconds then came here anyway, but I meant it. This was... unusual, but that's it. It's over."

"Why?"

"Because I said so."

He lifts a shoulder. "It doesn't have to be sex. Let's go to a movie. A museum. Hell, let's just go for a walk. I'll buy you an ice cream."

"It's February."

"I know."

I shake my head. "No, thank you."

He's quiet for a second, then he nods before twisting the deadbolt and pulling open the door.

I stare at the carpet in the hall as I exit, trying to remember which way we came from, but Chris leads the way to the elevator bank, barefoot, pushing the button for me.

"You don't have to wait."

He rests against the wall and taps his toes. "I don't mind."

I feel stupid and antsy and hunt around in my bag until I find my car keys.

"Fleischmann's Park," he says.

I freeze, the keys clutched tight in my fingers. "What?"

"Fleischmann's Park," he says again. "There's an ice cream place by the pond, it's open year-round. They have—"

"I know." It takes everything in me not to react. Not to run down the hall and into the stairwell and all the way out to the street. Fleischmann's Park is famous for far more than a fucking ice cream parlor. I jab the elevator button.

"How about Thursday?" he asks. "I've got the day off."

Why would he suggest Fleischmann's, out of every place in the city?

I study him, hoping my suspicion and desperation don't show through, but he's just examining his fingernails, frowning slightly.

The elevator dings as it arrives, the doors gliding open.

"I guess that's a no." His eyes crinkle at the corner when he smiles, unoffended.

Don't do it, I tell myself as I get into the empty car. *Nobody wants ice cream in February.* I stare at the panel of buttons and stab the one for the second level of the parkade.

"I'll meet you at the west entrance," I say, when the doors start to close.

Chris looks surprised, straightening from his slouched stance to grab the doors and hold them open. "Wait."

I push his fingers away. "Don't try to kiss me," I warn. If he tries any romantic bullshit, I'll be sick.

He just laughs. "I was going to ask what time."

I blink. Oh. "Two o'clock."

"All right." He steps back as the doors glide shut. "Two it is. Sweetheart."

WHAT

6

What am I doing back here? My determined stride turns into a less-determined shuffle as I approach the wrought-iron gates that mark the west entrance to Fleischmann's Park. If Holden was originally built as Manhattan's little sister, Fleischmann's is our version of Central Park. Smaller, and with far fewer tourists, it's a sanctuary in the middle of the city, with the requisite pond and boats, gardens, and drug users.

Today it's sunny but cold, my breath just visible in the air. I jam my hands in the pockets of my black parka and peer around, my standard brand of paranoia, even though I'm wearing oversized sunglasses that hide my face. When I first started venturing out in public again, I wore sunglasses everywhere, even indoors. Still, there were times I'd abandon half-full grocery carts in the middle of the dairy aisle to run back to my car and sob hysterically, certain I was having a heart attack. Now I understand that my heart is fine; it's everything else that's wrong.

"There you are."

I turn to see Chris approaching. He has a blue wool hat pulled over his ears and a thick green jacket to ward against the cold.

He's wearing jeans and boots again, and three years ago I never would have noticed him. I saw suits. Cufflinks. Chauffeurs. Now I can't look away.

He smiles like he's happy to see me, like it's nice that I showed up. He doesn't seem bewildered or curious or hateful, like I'm a poisonous snake in a box. He's not waiting for me to strike.

"I said I'd come."

"Do you always tell the truth, Denise?"

"Don't you?"

He brushes a kiss over my cheek, and I feel the faint scratch of his stubble. When was the last time somebody kissed my cheek? It feels familiar. Friendly. Weird.

"You want to head straight for the ice cream?" he asks. "Or do you want to walk around for a bit first?"

"Let's walk."

"Sure. Anywhere in particular?"

"No. You choose." He needs to choose because this is a test. And if he fails, I'm running so fast and so far he'll never find me again.

"All right," he says easily. "This way." He nods to the left, and my heart beats a bit faster as we start down the paved pathway. Despite the sunshine, there are only a handful of other people around, a couple of women pushing strollers, a few joggers, teenagers skipping school to get high.

"I grew up in Montana," Chris offers. "When I moved here a year ago, I didn't know what to do with myself. The buildings. The traffic. The people. I used to come here a lot."

"Why don't you live closer to the school?"

"There's nowhere to live, if you don't actually own a farm, which I don't. Half an hour past where I met you is a prison, and I'm not about to live out there, even if they do have some cheap housing. There are places between Holden and the college, but they're small, and when I moved out here it was to broaden my horizons. I wasn't going to do that in another town with just one traffic light, so here I am."

"Lucky me."

"I keep telling you."

I smile in spite of myself. Yesterday I'd had to drink three cups of tea with honey to soothe my hoarse throat. It wasn't sore from cries of ecstasy, but an unaccustomed amount of conversation. I drank another cup this morning in preparation.

"Right here," he says, pausing next to a large patch of grass with a circle of withered rose bushes in the middle. "Did you know this used to be a sun dial?"

"What did?" I ask. "The roses?"

"The space the roses fill. When they designed the park they had a sun dial custom-made, seven-feet in diameter."

"Where is it?"

"A local pagan cult began using it to conduct 'unwholesome' ceremonies on the full moon, and the city removed it."

I snort out a laugh. "No, they didn't."

"They did too. Cross my heart."

"How do you know this?"

"Research. They tore it out, replaced it with rose bushes, and the sun dial's in the museum on Aiker Street."

"Did you go to check it out?"

"Of course I did."

He pauses at the edge of the pond, a tiny dock with a free paddle boat waiting. It's too cold to tempt anyone to get out on the water. There aren't even any birds swimming. He holds out a hand when I hesitate. "What do you say?"

"No thanks?"

He lifts an eyebrow. "We can walk all the way around if you like, but I can hear your teeth chattering."

"My teeth are fine."

"They're beautiful. So are you."

"Knock it off." I take his hand and get in the boat.

We bob precariously when he climbs in beside me and I grip the side like that'll make a difference. The pond's not terribly deep, and I can see the gray glow of stones through the dark water. It's still and cool as we begin to pedal, my thighs burning almost instantly, unaccustomed to the exercise.

Chris leans back in his seat like this is the most leisurely and relaxing type of activity, linking his fingers over his stomach and studying our surroundings. The pond has a tiny manmade island in the middle that's technically a refuge for rare birds, but everyone knows couples sneak over to have sex when they want to feel daring.

I really hope he's not taking me to the stupid island. I've already been.

He's not. We glide past it, not talking, and eventually my legs stop hurting and just go numb, though it's obvious when I pedal slower, because the boat begins to veer off course and Chris has to match my pace to keep us pointed...somewhere. The pond has a dozen different docks.

"Do you have a destination in mind?" I ask after a while. I

spend ninety percent of the week alone in my apartment; the fresh air and open space is making me twitchy.

"Are you in a rush?" Chris inquires. "You gotta be somewhere by midnight again?" He shoots me a sly look that calls bullshit on my timelines.

"Just wondering."

"We can get out if you want." He nods at a dock about two hundred yards north-west. "It's only a ten minute walk to the ice cream parlor."

I shiver, but it's not at the mention of ice cream. It's doubt. It's doubt that he could accidentally be suggesting that dock. That part of the park.

"Let's go," I make myself say.

We pedal over and Chris ties up the boat and climbs out, crouching down to steady me when wobbly knees threaten to send me spilling into the icy water.

"You all right?" he asks, straightening and rubbing my arms. He peers into my face and I'm grateful for the sunglasses. I don't want him to see my eyes right now. To see them darting around, past his shoulder, to the grassy space behind him. The large wooden signboard reading *Nichols Lawn* in peeling gold script.

"Just fine."

He graciously accepts the lie and leads me up the pathway to the edge of the grass, yellow and wilted at this time of year. "Now, this place is interesting."

"The field?"

"The history. Well, recent history."

My heart beats so hard against my ribs I swear something's going to break. "Wh—what do you mean?"

He misinterprets my stammer as cold. "Do you want my hat? Maybe we should—"

"No," I interrupt. "What do you mean about the history?" I know the history, of course. I haven't set foot here since I was a teenager sneaking out to that stupid island to do stupid things, but I read the news. It's hard to miss the front page when your name's on it.

"Well," Chris begins, thinking he's telling me a story in which I don't prominently feature. "A few years ago, there was this banker who got arrested for stealing lots of money. Like, hundreds of millions. They found a bunch in offshore banks and secret accounts, but there was twenty million they couldn't locate."

Right so far. "That sounds like a lot."

"So people got it in their heads that he'd hidden it somewhere. Of course, the FBI had that same idea, so they searched his homes— I think he had, like, three—"

We had five.

"—but they never found it. So then people started thinking, where could it be? Maybe he buried it." He points at the wooden sign, then leads me across the grass toward a small pavilion. "Nichols was his wife's family. She was a singer, and when she was alive she used to do summer concerts in the park. Right here." He stops in front of the pavilion, cold and abandoned in February. The eloquently carved trim of the peaked roof is rimmed with green mold, the concrete floor playing host to a dozen discarded cigarettes. My dad took me to see her sing when I was little, but she died when Alex was born and I was too young to remember more than the vague idea of her face.

"People decided he'd buried the money somewhere in the park," Chris continues, his cheeks pink with cold. "This place, in particular. And the really determined ones snuck in at night and started digging."

I'd seen the pictures. Nichols Lawn, an entire acre, destroyed. A thousand holes dug by a thousand desperate treasure-seekers, all of whom left empty-handed. My father might be a thief, but he isn't stupid. If he hid twenty million dollars, he wouldn't hide it in a place with a fucking sign on it.

"I remember that," I say. "But it was three years ago. How do you know so much?"

He takes my elbow, urging me back to the path toward the ice cream parlor. The bare tree branches crack in the wind, waving goodbye. "I told you," he says. "I didn't know what to do with myself when I first got to the city. I used to come here and walk around and eat ice cream, and in the parlor they've got a bunch of old news clippings about the treasure hunt."

"Huh." I know the story, but I didn't know the ice cream parlor had the salient details framed and hung on their walls. We enter the small, warm shop and I ignore the ice cream and go straight to the display. The paneled wall of photos feels familiar. I have something just like it at home.

There are front page stories in full color; the destroyed lawn, the yellow caution tape strung up between trees and benches to warn people away. They'd hired security guards to keep watch for months, but the only thing that cooled people's interest was a thousand empty holes. The money wasn't there. For a while, someone would dig a random hole in some equally random place in the park, but no one ever announced finding a chest full of unmarked bills or gold bars or whatever form they imagine twenty million dollars might take. As far as the world's concerned, the money's still out there.

Somewhere.

"They never found it," Chris says when we reach the last picture, dated three months ago. "The money."

There's a stack of postcards available for sale for a dollar apiece. Some feature little treasure maps marking the most likely hiding spots, while others echo the most sensational headlines. *Twenty Million Questions, But Just One Answer! Can You Find It?*

"I know," I say, running the edge of my thumb over a card. "It would have been big news."

"You a treasure seeker, Denise?"

I smirk. "I couldn't dig a hole if my life depended on it."

"Let me buy you an ice cream. Or they have hot chocolate, too, if you prefer."

"I want ice cream."

"Your wish is my command."

Chris turns, and I slip a postcard into my pocket. I shouldn't have to pay for a souvenir that's all wrong.

I unzip my coat and approach the display cases, the glass half-fogged so I have to lean in to make out the flavors. I opt for strawberry ice cream and Chris gets vanilla, and we sit down. The only other patrons are an elderly couple sharing a sundae.

"So where is it then?" I ask, stirring the ice cream in its cup.

Chris takes a bite. "The money?"

"Yeah. What does your research tell you?"

He sits back in his seat and eats his ice cream and ponders it. "Jesus, I don't know. I wish it were in my bank account."

"What would you do with it?"

He shakes his head. "Probably nothing, to be honest. I wouldn't know where to start. You?"

I copy him and shake my head. "No idea."

"No? Really? I think you'd get on a train and travel to the other side of the country in your red wig."

I cough out a laugh. "A train? Am I traveling to 1875?"

He laughs, too, blushing a little, and I stare at him, trying to understand the man who'd left me so wrung out the other night that I'd slept straight through to noon the next day. My body still aches from the things we did. He did.

I can't afford to replay those memories anymore than I can make myself stop. I told myself I'd only agreed to come here today to see if he had picked this place on purpose, if he recognized me, if I weren't the only liar in this pair. But I think I am. I think the only thing we have in common is that we're both lonely, and that's a dangerous thing to share.

"I have to go," I say abruptly, standing. There are two spoonfuls of ice cream left in my cup, but I toss it in the nearby trash and wait for Chris to get up. He looks startled but not completely surprised, and calmly buttons his coat and takes his remaining ice cream to the door, holding it open for me.

"Where?" he asks when we're outside.

"Home."

"I figured. Where's home?"

"Not far. I walked."

"Me too. I'll walk you."

"No, thanks."

He sighs. "Are we back to that? Really?"

"I told you—"

"You told me a lot of things, Denise. None of which have been true."

I'd been trying to shift past him so I could leave, but now I stop and study his face. He's trying to hide his irritation, but it shows.

"I haven't told you—"

"Oh, come on. You had red hair that first night at the restaurant. You told me no second dates, but you came home with me. You said no third dates, but you're here."

"It doesn't matter."

"Are you married?" he asks.

I cough out a laugh. "I'm not married. God."

"Then what's the problem?"

Everybody's looking for something. Money. Guilt. Me. I don't trust anybody, and they shouldn't trust me. You can't play with matches and say you don't like fire.

I fumble for my sunglasses and put them on. "I have to go."

Chris makes a frustrated sound. "Why?"

"Because I don't want to see you anymore. Thanks for the ice cream."

He doesn't say anything when I walk away, and I don't look back.

7

I let myself into my apartment. It's cold and gray and unwelcoming. It's home.

Before I can overthink things—or rethink them—I take the stolen postcard from my pocket and unfold it, carefully smoothing my thumb over the crease the way you touch a scar to remember the wound. I can't be with Chris because he doesn't know me. I can't be with Chris because he *can't* know me.

The card is glossy and black and slashed with fake newspaper headlines, cut and plastered over top like bandages. *Twenty Million Questions, But Just One Answer! Can You Find It?*

Ha.

I shuffle down the hall to the guest bedroom and hesitate only briefly before turning the knob. A museum of miserable memories waits on the other side, news articles so painstakingly collected and clipped and framed that my makeshift shrine wouldn't be out of place in the lair of a serial killer.

The room is narrow, two long walls and two short. The short walls are dedicated to articles about Alex and my mother, pieces discussing their lives and deaths, their tragically brief, creative existences. There's a close-up picture of Alex, his blue eyes too big for his delicate face, the curly dark hair he hated, and his familiar small smile, like he's remembering a joke he heard yesterday and is just now seeing the humor in it.

The long walls are reserved for my father and me, about whom the press has so much more to say. *Liar. Thief. Murderer. Whore.* As far as the world is concerned, we're monsters. But my dad is lucky—his story has an ending. He's in jail, and the world feels like they've gotten closure. But I'm still out here, I'm still free. I'm still fair game.

I take the postcard to my wall and crouch to find a particular article. They're organized by date and grouped by country, a world of hate. I find the one I'm looking for near the baseboard. *Reese Carlisle – Accomplice?* it asks. But the question mark is just a courtesy. They've already made up their mind. The truth isn't even an afterthought.

I tuck the card into the edge of the frame and study the display. The same people who called me a vapid idiot for years now call me a criminal mastermind. I went from too stupid to know the value of a dollar to the brilliant sidekick in a massive embezzlement scheme. If the headlines are to be believed, I helped hide twenty million dollars in overseas accounts, used it to buy stolen diamonds on the black market, and sewed it into the lining of my fur coats, the skins of which were taken from baby animals. None of those things are true, but nobody cares about the truth anymore.

I blink and remember where I am, a whole wall of memories screaming back at me, a helpful reminder. I straighten and wipe my eyes, then leave before I can fall down the rabbit hole again.

The walls in the living room are a stark contrast to the shrine, completely bare with the exception of two large maps held up with thumb tacks and a single red dart. My home décor consists of a map of the world and a map of Holden and its surrounding areas, each riddled with holes from target practice. Most of the country names have been obliterated, but the names don't matter. What matters is how far, how isolated, how random. If my father's conviction is overturned, the world will be looking for him. We'll have to go someplace unknown, where they won't recognize us, won't care.

I retrieve the dart from its current home on the Australian Gold Coast and take a few steps back. I didn't play sports growing up, but I've gotten good at this game and can hit any target I choose. That makes me predictable, though, so I close my eyes, aim at the world map in general, and let fly.

The dart sinks into the drywall with a satisfying thud, and I approach to study my mark. Madagascar. I've hit it before and have already done my research. Madagascar—pepper, vanilla, and lemurs. I like all those things. It has potential.

For a minute I contemplate the maps, their finite places and infinite possibilities, then turn in a circle and take in my dim, lonely apartment. The time on the microwave reads 5:09 p.m., and I groan. It's not even time for dinner and I'm already bored.

I grab my laptop and flop onto the couch, hearing the too-familiar crunch of my cell phone stuck between the cushions. I use burner phones for my dates, but I have one real phone, for which only two places have the number, the prison and the Food Bank. They never call me, but I keep the phone handy just in case, and since I spend a lot of time on the couch, it spends a lot of time in the cushions. I fish it out, check the call display—unsurprisingly, no one has called—and toss it aside before navigating to the Fantasy Friends website. Two minutes later, I close the laptop with an aggrieved sigh. I can't think. I can't concentrate. I can't do anything.

I stand and head for the roof.

≫ ≫

Rodney and I sit across from each other, not speaking. The Food Bank break room is stocked with cheap patio furniture we drag outside in the warmer months. In the fall and winter, it's squeezed into this cramped room, the buzzing neon lights doing nothing to mimic the warmth of summer.

The nylon straps of my seat squeak as I shift, blowing on a forkful of the microwave ravioli I brought for lunch. A can of orange soda sits unopened next to the cardboard container, and the only time Rodney's not staring at his phone is when he's eyeballing my drink. He's been playing some sort of space-shooter game for the past fifteen minutes, a blue binder sitting unopened on the table near his arm. He ate a cold burrito with one hand while he blew things up with the other.

"Well."

Lyla enters, leaning against the wall and exhaling heavily. Today the red braids are twisted into an intricate bun, and her kitten heels are zebra print. That's the only thing that's normal about her, however. She's been trying to deny it, but the flu that's wiped out half the staff has not chosen to spare her, and she's sweating visibly, the hand clutching her ever-present clipboard trembling slightly.

"You okay, Ly?" Rodney asks, stuffing the phone in his pocket and opening the binder as though she's deaf and blind as well as sick.

"I'd be better if you would knock it off with that game and read this thing," she says, covering the short distance to the table and tapping the binder. "How are you going to get into the program if you don't get your numbers up?"

"I don't want to be a chef."

"You don't know what you want. Read the book."

"I will."

"Now."

"*I will.*"

Lyla gives him a warning glare, then grabs a plastic bag of baby carrots from the fridge. She's constantly on a diet but never loses weight. I've given up counting how many apple slices and grapes I've seen scattered around the parking lot "for the birds."

We're quiet until she leaves, and Rodney checks out my soda again.

"You can have it," I tell him, pushing it across the table. "I have water." My voice is rusty, cracking on the words. I haven't spoken to another person since I left Chris last Sunday.

Rodney stares at me for a second. "All right."

He takes the can, pops it open, and drinks.

"What goes around comes around," he says finally.

"What are you talking about?"

He covers his mouth with his fist when he burps. "Lyla," he says, nodding at the empty doorway. "Getting sick like that."

"That's not what that means."

"What what means?"

"What goes around comes around. That phrase is about karma. The flu's just going around. It has nothing to do with karma."

"Say what?"

"Never mind."

He finishes the drink, crushes the can between his palms, and tosses it across the room toward the recycling bin. It bounces off the rim and skips across the floor. He considers it, then relaxes into his seat.

I nod at the table. "What's in the binder?"

"Math lessons. I'm supposed to get my grades up so I qualify for this program Lyla's got set up."

"With a restaurant?"

"With a school. Culinary school. Did you know that was a thing?"

"Yeah."

"Well, I didn't. And I don't want to spend my days baking pies. What are those guys going to say?" He glances toward the door, as though his friends are already outside laughing. Then he asks, "What about you? You got a job?"

I think back to the day I'd returned to Carlisle Gale Investors to clean out my desk. The FBI had already been through; there wasn't so much as a stapler left. Not that I had a particular penchant for stapling, but they'd taken everything when I'd been naïve enough to believe there was nothing left to take. I'd gone in with an empty box and left without even that.

"No," I say eventually. "I don't."

"What do you do, then? When you're not here?"

"It varies." I eat the last piece of ravioli, then stand and drop the container in the trash before taking my fork to the sink to wash.

"You're a real mystery, R.C."

"If you say so."

Rodney crosses his arms. "Well, I don't want to be a chef. What other kind of jobs are there? Give me some ideas."

I lean against the counter. Job prospects were never something I'd considered growing up. I was doing fifth grade math in second grade, and it was simply understood I'd follow in my father's footsteps. Unfortunately.

"Firefighter," I suggest, remembering one of my dates.

He points to one eye. "Bad vision."

"Lifeguard."

"I'm already poor."

"Tattoo artist."

"I don't like needles."

"Well, we're out of options, Rodney."

He laughs, his teeth straight and white. "What do you want to do, then?"

"What?"

"You don't have a job. What do you want?"

"I don't know."

"Uh-oh," Rodney says, glancing at the clock on the wall and standing. "You'd better be careful, or Lyla will sign you up for this chef program."

"I don't think I qualify."

"If I can bake a pie, you can bake a pie."

"You can't bake a pie."

"I bet you I could."

"You could join the army," I suggest. "See the world. You like blowing things up. Or they need chefs, too."

His gaze skitters away. "Nah."

"Why not?"

"I got a record. I went to jail for a year."

"For what?"

"Lifting cars."

"Which prison? Wakeman?"

Rodney laughs like I've made a wonderful joke. "No, not Wakeman," he says finally, wiping his eye. "Wakeman's for rich people. I was in Everett County, down south."

I finish my water and put the bottle back in my bag. "Did you do it?"

He shakes his head. "No. I did a lot of other things, though, so all things considered, a year wasn't too bad."

"A year in prison for something you didn't do wasn't too bad?"

"It's better than five to ten for something I did do."

"Well, who says you aren't good at math?"

"Is there a reason you two are still in here?"

Rodney and I turn to see Lyla in the doorway, tapping her watch. "Get back to work. You know we're short-staffed. You can gossip in your free time." Then she looks between us, perplexed. Like there's no way we'd be spending our free time together gossiping. "Anyway," she says. "Get out there."

"Yes, boss." Rodney picks up the binder. To me he adds, "Stop being a distraction."

"Bring me a pie tomorrow."

Behind his back he sticks up his middle finger. "I got your pie."

>>> >>>

I drive Rodney to the station again, watching him jog inside just as the train pulls up. He lifts a hand in thanks, and I reverse out of the lot and aim for the highway. I had the early shift today, so it's only three o'clock. The whole afternoon stretches ahead of me like the horizon, interminable.

I remember one time in third grade I got in trouble for cutting the head off a friend's doll, and as punishment I was forced to miss her birthday party and sit alone in my room, thinking about all the fun I was missing. It was torture, but I was prepared to stoically stick it out until my father told me that no one would ever invite me to their party again if I didn't know how to behave like someone who deserved to be invited. I had to apologize for what I'd done, the apology like grit on my tongue. But it worked. I had friends again, and I wasn't faced with the lonely torture of spending time with myself.

I mull this over as I drive back into the city and park in the garage two blocks over from my apartment. I make the familiar underground trek back to my building, my footsteps growing heavier as I approach. I don't want to go home. I don't want to be alone. And I'm sure that after the way I left things, Chris doesn't want to be with me either. Once in the elevator, however, I hit the button for the ground level instead of going to my apartment. I'm not exactly known for making good decisions.

I head outside into the brisk cold, but instead of bringing me to my senses, it only makes me move faster. It's seven blocks to Chris's building, and as I walk it occurs to me I don't remember his suite number. We'd taken the elevator from the garage, so I don't even know if there's a doorman.

I reach the building and stop. There *is* a doorman. And now that I'm in front of the towering glass structure, I recognize it. My father used to own two floors here, using them as overpriced business rentals. When we were teenagers, Alex and I were given master keys to the units on both floors and told to "keep an eye on things." Of course, we just used the empty suites to hold parties, then secretly called the housekeeping company and asked them to come clean up after our untidy "renters." Like most residential buildings in Holden, you can only enter if you're a resident, with a resident, or on a pre-approved guest list. Because our units were repossessed, I, of course, am not.

I hesitate in front of the coffee shop next door, well-suited business people flowing past, ignoring me in my skinny jeans and puffy jacket, gray wool hat and sunglasses, grateful to be anonymous. Pathetically grateful no one is witnessing my nervous sweating and shaky hands.

The doorman is keeping a wary eye on me, so I pull out my phone and pretend I'm waiting for someone who actually knows I'm waiting for them. He's not fooled, and because the only phone numbers I have are for the Food Bank and the prison, I send myself a text. *Go home.*

I peer inside the warm coffee shop. If Chris passes this way, I'll see him. But if he comes from the other direction, I won't. Hell, he might be sitting in his toasty apartment right this moment—I don't know. I don't know his last name or anything about him except he once had a German Shepard named Astro.

That's the thing that decides it. I'm going home. I don't even know who I'm waiting for, and he doesn't know who's waiting for him. This loneliness will pass. All the feelings do. I've already experienced the worst of them. The worst of everything. So what if it's three o'clock and that means nine hours until tomorrow, for which I also have nothing planned? So what if this whole fucking world is going to spin forever and I'll spin right along with it, just as aimless?

A cab stops at the curb, and I beeline for it, planning to dodge the man striding from Chris's building and steal it for myself. But I stop, hand extended, when the man getting out of the backseat is none other than the one I've been waiting for.

Startled by my approach, his expression turns wary. Then surprised. Then... I don't know. Something crosses his face, something I can't read. Or too many things to read them all. Anger? Irritation? Alarm?

"Hi," I say eventually.

Chris opens his mouth like he's about to speak, then decides against it. He moves back as someone else slides into the car and the cab pulls away, the silence giving me time to take him in. If he'd gotten out of the cab and walked into his building, I might not have recognized him. Gone are the boots and plaid shirts. Now he's wearing a suit and tie, polished loafers on his feet. It's not a cheap suit, either. The Rolex is back, but I still don't think it's real.

"What are you doing?" I hear myself ask.

His eyebrows raise. "What am *I* doing?"

"Yeah."

"You're the one loitering."

"Why are you in a suit?"

He glances down, as though just remembering. "I had a meeting."

"Why?"

He sighs, like I've managed to both annoy and exhaust him in the span of twenty seconds. "What are you doing here, Denise?"

I don't think I've ever apologized to a man before. To anyone, since third grade, now that I think about it. "I came to apologize," I mumble. "For…the other day. What I said."

"About not wanting to see me?"

The cold that snakes up my legs has little to do with the weather. "Yes. I'm sorry."

Chris sighs and digs his hand into his pocket, retrieving a set of keys. "Don't worry about it."

He turns toward the building.

"That's it?" I blurt out.

He looks over at me. "Did you have something else to say?"

"Well, yeah."

"What?"

"Come get a drink. In here." I point at the coffee shop, curling my hands in the sleeves of my jacket, not sure if I'm trembling because I'm frozen or I'm nervous. I really didn't think this through. What am I going to say if he agrees to come inside with me? In third grade I said, "I'm sorry I cut up your doll, here's another one," and that was enough. But now I don't have anything to give Chris. Nothing to offer, except myself.

He closes his eyes for a second, like he's gathering up his patience. "I don't want coffee."

"So? Have tea."

"I don't want tea."

"Then what do you want?"

He holds my stare, then lifts a shoulder. "I don't know."

"Have water, then."

A pause, then he dips his head, and I think he's trying not to smile. "Are you going to tell me you hate me at the end of this?"

"No. Probably not."

"Probably not?"

"Are you going to do something hateful?"

He falters, just the slightest flinch, something I wouldn't have noticed if I weren't so edgy. If I didn't doubt everybody. But then he says, "No. I'm not," and walks to his building, the doorman frowning as I follow, neither of us certain I should.

"What are we doing?" I ask as we enter the lobby.

"Getting sandwiches," Chris says, calling the elevator.

"They have sandwiches next door. And lots of other places."

"Yes, but mine are better."

"Is that true?"

"Maybe not. But I want to get out of this suit. Not like that," he adds, when I misinterpret the statement as innuendo.

"I knew what you meant," I lie.

We exit the elevator on the ninth floor, and this time I pay attention. His unit is at the end of the hall, 912 scrawled in silver script above the peep hole. Chris opens the door and gestures me in first.

The apartment looks more real in the fading gray light of day. Last time, in the dark, it felt like a stage, small sections carefully lit, showing only what needed to be shown. Today it feels less prepared. There's a cereal bowl on the island, a paperback book splayed open beside it, facedown. There's a sweatshirt forgotten on the couch, a beer bottle on the coffee table. The shoes by the door are scattered, not lined up in pairs. The plants by the window are gone.

"Where are your plants?" I ask, using my toes to edge off my sneakers. I stuff my hat into the sleeve of my jacket and pass it to Chris, who hangs it in the closet.

"My what?"

"Your plants." I nod toward the wall of floor-to-ceiling windows. Last time it was lined with plants, but now the floor is bare. I remember because I can't keep anything green alive in my apartment, and I was impressed that he could. Once, on impulse I bought a Venus fly trap at the checkout at the grocery store and it died three days later, a sad, hungry monster.

He glances at the empty space. "I brought them up to the roof."

"Why?"

"To start preparing them to move outside. What kind of sandwich do you want?"

"I don't know. Why do the plants have to go outside? I thought they were houseplants."

"Are you the one with a degree in Plant Sciences?" Chris asks sternly, leading me toward the kitchen.

"No, sir. I'm not."

He laughs and loosens his tie with one hand while shrugging out of his jacket with the other. I'd never really been one to fantasize about naughty professor role-play, but maybe I'd be open to it.

He pulls out one of the two stools at the counter overlooking the kitchen, then snags the cereal bowl and stashes it in the sink. "Have a seat," he says. "I'm going to change. I'll be right back to make you a sandwich."

He disappears down the hall to his bedroom, and I give the

paperback on the counter a cursory once-over—some faded old western—then get up to pace, releasing some of my nervous energy. Without the plants it feels more like my apartment. Just a box, not a home. There's a closed laptop on the dining table, the case scuffed and silver. Beside it are stacks of papers, some typed, some bearing handwritten notes I can't make out. There are business cards and receipts, but as far as I can tell nothing is related to plants. Not that it has to be, it just seems like he should have a botany book or two lying around. Or a plant.

I freeze when I recognize the logo on one of the papers. It's a donation receipt.

If people donate in person at the Food Bank itself, they get a handwritten receipt from Lyla. If they donate at a satellite location, like a grocery store or as part of a food drive, we mail a typed copy. Chris's receipt is handwritten. I recognize Lyla's loopy writing, the circle she uses to finish her I's instead of a simple dot. *Chris Sherwood*, it reads. *Two hundred dollars.*

I tell myself not to panic. It's nice that he donated. In person. At that location. It's a coincidence. It's just…

"Where'd you go? Denise?"

My heart slams into my ribs before coming to a bruised halt. I feel like my stomach's in free fall, my imagination reeling. My back is to the kitchen, and I picture him watching me with a coil of rope in one hand and a knife in the other, his bedroom transformed into some sort of torture porn set.

"Ah. There you are. What are you doing?"

I turn, my hands clenched so tightly at my sides I can feel my fingernails cutting into my palms.

"Whoa." Chris sees my face and stops mid-step, a few feet

away. He's changed into jeans and a navy Henley, the worn fabric pulling across his chest and biceps. There's no rope. No knife. No evil, knowing glint in his eye. "What's up? What happened?" He looks past me at the laptop, still closed. "You didn't find my kinky porn stash, so what's the problem?"

"You—" The word sounds like a wheeze.

"You need to sit down. You're really pale. When was the last time you ate?"

I drag in a breath through my nose. He looks concerned. Like a guy who just wants to feed people. Maybe this *is* just about a sandwich. Maybe I'm so far from normal I'll never find my way back, even by accident. I blink rapidly. My eyes are stinging, but there's no earthly way I'm going to cry with an audience.

I feel his big hand splay between my shoulder blades, warm and strong, and let him lead me to the stool he'd pulled out earlier, sitting down, legs shaky. The fear of being foolish has made me exactly that.

"I'm fine," I say when Chris slides a glass of water in front of me.

"Drink this, anyway," he orders. "And maybe eat…" He hunts through the cupboards, retrieving a box of mini crackers stuffed with peanut butter. "Eat these while I make you something."

"Who eats crackers?" I turn the box over in my hand; the bright colors, the silly font. "After first grade?"

"You," he says, pointing at me seriously. "Eat some, then tell me what happened." Again, his gaze flicks past me to the laptop. I wonder what's on there. Probably porn, like he said. But maybe more.

Or maybe not.

I eat a cracker. It's too salty and the peanut butter sticks to the roof of my mouth. I eat another one. I like bad things.

I watch Chris's ass as he bends over to study the contents of his fridge, one hand gripping the edge of the door. He's so hot. He's not my type, but I want him. Maybe he's Denise's type. I don't know anymore. I don't know what she likes, besides dogs.

"I've got turkey or roast beef," he says, glancing over his shoulder. If he sees me ogling his ass, he's gracious enough not to preen. "And two types of cheese—"

"Two?"

"That's right."

"Oh boy."

He smiles, the corners of his eyes crinkling. I like the line that deepens around the edge of his mouth, the stubble marking his jaw. He turns back and reaches down to tug open the crisper drawer. "And I have cucumber, tomato, and red onion." He straightens to give me a superior look. "What more could you ask for?"

"Grilled cheese," I say.

"Grilled cheese? What about all my options?"

"I like grilled cheese."

He studies me for a moment. "Okay," he says finally. "Grilled cheese it is. How many do you want?"

"Just one."

He sticks a pan on the stove and turns on the heat, then grabs a loaf of bread from the cupboard and arranges six slices on a cutting board. I watch him butter each piece, then stick three in the hot pan. The sound of sizzling butter makes me feel warm and cozy and at home. Not alone. Not bored. Not hacked limb from limb.

He carves thick slabs of cheese from a block of cheddar and arranges them on top of the bread, then finishes with the second slice. He holds a spatula as he leans against the counter to face me while they heat.

"Eat a cracker," he orders again, nodding at the box.

"I've been eating. I need room for my sandwich."

He crosses the short distance and shakes a few crackers into his palm, tossing three into his mouth at once. "I love these things," he admits. "When I was a kid, my mom wouldn't let me have processed food, and I desperately wanted real peanut butter. When I got to college, I bought my first jar."

"You really know how to rebel." I sip my water. "You're an only child?"

"Yep. You?"

I hesitate. I didn't mean to open this can of worms. Still, I don't want to lie, so I say, "I am now."

"You lost somebody?"

I nod and study a crumb stuck to the front of his shirt, my hand automatically going to the scar on my thigh. "My brother. In the car accident."

"I'm sorry."

"It was a while ago."

"I'm still sorry." Chris turns back to the sandwiches, giving me a second to compose myself—again—and when he flips them over they're perfectly crisp and golden brown. After another minute, he grabs plates and adds one grilled cheese to mine, two to the other, then uses the spatula to cut them in half.

He places the dishes on the counter. "What do you want to drink?"

"Water's good."

He pours himself a glass and tops up mine, then comes to sit on the stool beside me. We chew in silence for a moment.

"Do you always read westerns?"

The question seems to throw him, because he stares at the book for a long moment. He picks it up and considers the cover. "They're okay." He's using a business card as a bookmark, a green diamond peeking out, and he presses the card down with his thumb until it disappears into the pages, like he's embarrassed by his reading material.

"I don't read as much as I should."

"You don't have any botany books."

He taps his temple. "It's all up here."

I snort. "Of course."

He nudges me with his elbow. "I've got books in my office. I don't like people who keep all their work out in the living area, like they're trying to impress their guests. Now eat your sandwich."

I dutifully bite in.

"Verdict?"

I give him a thumbs up. He's only a few inches away, close enough I imagine I can feel the energy from his body, the heat and life. Apart from my "dates," I normally eat dinner alone. Company, companionship—it's become a chore. Like an exercise I stopped doing and lost the strength for. Small talk. Jokes. Anecdotes. I thought I couldn't do it anymore. But here I am. Again.

Impulsively, I lean over and kiss him. The second I do it, I realize I've wanted to do it for a long time. And not just today. Yesterday. And the day before. And the day at the park. Not just because I'm lonely, either. But because, for the briefest moments, he makes me feel human. Like someone who can be tolerated. Even if he doesn't know me, he likes the pieces he sees.

And he's a good kisser.

He kisses me back. His lips are slippery with butter and so are mine, and our noses bump and I can only lean so far without tipping off the stool. Just our mouths touch, then our tongues, and it's not Denise or Shawna or Teresa playing a part, doing what needs to be done to forget everything for a little while. It's just me.

I feel the fleeting brush of his fingers on my jaw, then he groans and pulls away. He pinches the bridge of his nose, turning so he's facing the counter again.

"I can't," he says eventually. "I can't."

The heat that had been stealing through me quickly drains away. And not just the aroused heat, either. All of it. The warmth. The coziness. The silly delusions of belonging somewhere, even for a second.

"Right," I say. There's a roll of paper towels on the counter and I calmly tear off a piece and wipe my hands. "That's fine. Of course." I force myself to take three deep breaths, making sure they don't come out shaky and agitated.

Embarrassed.

Rejected.

I focus on the cover of the book that sits between us. It's a faded hand-drawn picture of a cowboy leaning against a rail as he watches a woman in a purple dress in the middle of a field. *Wyoming Wanderer* is scrawled across the top, breaking up the clear blue sky. I can see the tiny gap in the pages where the business card marks his place, and I want to tear out the last chapter of the book so he never learns how the story ends. So he doesn't get what he wants, either.

Instead I stand and take my plate to the sink, tossing my napkin in the trash. "Thanks for dinner."

"You don't have to go."

"I want to."

I don't look at him, even when I hear him sigh and get to his feet. He comes around the counter with his dishes and when he bends to put them in the dishwasher, I reach for the book. I can't yank out pages while he's here, but I can make him lose his place. Make him feel a little lost and alone, too.

I slide the business card into my back pocket and I'm halfway to the door when the dishwasher door clicks shut.

"Denise," he says.

"Yes?" I open the closet and grab my jacket, pulling on my hat and coat. I use the excuse of tying my sneakers to avoid his stare, even when he comes close enough that I can see his socked feet.

I straighten and reach for the door, turning my back.

"Denise," he says again.

"Good night." I twist the knob, but he presses a hand against the wood over my head, making it impossible to open.

"Let's go on a date," he says.

"I don't like dating."

"I do."

I can feel him against my back, even through the thickness of my jacket. He's careful not to touch me. This invitation isn't sexual. It's an actual invitation for an actual date. There are no wigs and no cautiously crafted email exchanges; no pretenses. He thinks he knows me, but he doesn't. He can't.

"You decide," he says, when I don't reply. "You plan it."

I shudder. "I don't know."

"Don't know what? What to do?"

"I don't know if I want to."

He sighs, but he doesn't sound exasperated. He sounds tired. And I understand. I'm tired, too.

"I'll think about it," I offer, without meaning to. I frown over my shoulder when he doesn't release the door. "What?"

"Give me your phone."

There's no earthly way I'm giving him my phone. It's not like I've got a background image that announces "I'm Reese Carlisle!" but if he sees I have a mere two contacts, it'll scare him away for good.

Perhaps I *should* give him my phone.

"No," I say.

"I want to program my number."

I wish I had a burner phone with me. Then I could text him and we'd both have each other's contact information. But I don't. And I can't give him my real phone number anymore than I can give him my name or address.

"Don't you have a business card?" I ask. "For the school?" I suddenly feel immensely guilty about the card in my pocket. I *stole* from him. He's not going to know where in Wyoming that cowboy wandered.

"It doesn't have my cell."

"Then just meet me."

"Why can't I have your fucking phone number?" He asks the question mildly enough, but there's genuine irritation and bewilderment in his dark gaze.

"Because I don't like to talk on the phone." There. That's true, too.

He rolls his eyes. "Fine. Meet where?"

"Here," I say. "Out front again. Noon on Sunday."

"For what?"

"It's a surprise." It'll be a surprise for me, too, since I have no idea what we'll be doing. Whatever. He seems to like questionable behavior.

He holds my stare for a second, a challenge from which neither one of us backs down. "Fine," he says eventually.

"Fine."

"Should I turn around so you can leave without saying goodbye?"

"Yes, if you don't mind."

He reaches past me to pull open the door. "Want me to walk you home?"

"Of course not."

"Just thought I'd offer." He rolls his lips together like he's contemplating adding something else, then decides against it. He leans against the door frame and watches me walk down the hall to the elevator bank, letting me go. Again.

8

"You're awfully quiet."

"I'm always quiet."

"Nah. You're just always alone."

I glance up from the box of canned corn I'm sorting to see Rodney resting against the wall, considering me as he drinks from his water bottle. Lyla sent him over to work with me when she found him goofing off with his friends. I choose not to dwell on the fact that time with me is considered punishment.

Lyla loomed ominously over Rodney's shoulder for the first ten minutes he spent with me, and we hadn't said much in the hour that passed after she left. I haven't had much to say, preoccupied as I am with trying to plan something for tomorrow's "date" with Chris.

"What do you do?" I ask, straightening and wiping my hands on my jeans. "When you're not here?"

Rodney lowers the water bottle and shrugs. "I don't know. Hang out."

"What do you do, though? Like, in the afternoons?"

"What are you talking about?"

"If you're going to hang out with somebody, what would you guys do?" I've been on dates, obviously. It's just that for the past three years they've been predicated upon a pile of lies that followed the same simple pattern: one week of emails, one fancy dinner, one round of sex, one silent exit by yours truly.

"You want to come along?" Rodney asks. "That what this is? You inviting yourself to hang out with me?"

"No. Of course not."

"Let me ask Colin if he minds."

"Shut up. That's not what I meant."

He pulls out his phone and starts typing a message.

"Rodney!"

He laughs and puts the phone back in his pocket. "What are you up to, R.C.?"

I scowl and study my dirty fingernails. "I'm meeting someone tomorrow afternoon and I'm supposed to decide what we're going to do. But I can't come up with anything."

"You got a date?"

I feel my cheeks heat. "Yeah."

"In the afternoon?"

"Yeah."

"That's pretty PG. You need me to chaperone?"

"You're hilarious."

"Relax," he says. "We can find you something to do. Is this person a guy?"

"Yes."

"You know him well?"

I should, shouldn't I? I've had sex with him. I've been to his home. He made me a sandwich. But I still feel like I'm missing something. Or maybe it's just that I'm holding something back. "Not really."

"You want to get to know him?"

"Maybe."

"You could go bowling. You can tell a lot by how a person plays sports. Does he let you win? Does he whine if he loses? Can he count?"

"Hmm." Outside of hurling balls for the requisite games of dodgeball in elementary school phys ed, the only athletic ability I possess is throwing darts.

"Or go to a movie. You can pick something cheesy and romantic and see if he gets the hint, or you can choose that horror one that's out and jump in his lap when you get scared."

"I don't get scared."

"Of course you don't."

"All right. Thanks."

I resume sorting, and Rodney continues to avoid it. He flips the water bottle up to the ceiling, catching it in one hand when it comes back down. "So what are you going to do?"

I study a rogue can of pumpkin puree. "Not telling. Did you sign up for cooking school?"

"I'm working on it."

"Working on it how?"

"Okay, I'm not working on it. But don't tell Lyla."

As someone who's had years of practice bumping around the edges of the truth, I know there's something he's not saying, and something he wants to. I stop working and sit on an unopened box, fixing Rodney with my best penetrating stare. "Fine, you don't want to be a chef. What do you want to do?"

He tosses the water bottle back and forth between his hands, suddenly shy. "I don't know."

"You have an idea."

He mumbles something.

"What?"

"I said, maybe a video game designer."

I think about how he spends his entire lunch break playing games on his phone and dropping his food on the floor and say, "That's a good idea."

"You think?" He watches me from the corner of his eye.

"Sure, why not? You're obviously terrible at relationship counseling and sorting cans."

"I'm good at everything."

"Have you researched any schools?"

"A little."

"And?"

He shrugs. "And they're expensive. I don't know. We'll see."

"Want me to tell Lyla? Maybe she can reach out."

"Don't you dare."

"She just wants a better life for you. Better than this."

Rodney crouches down to open a box, then thinks better of it and sits on the floor instead. "You work here, too," he points out.

"Yeah. Well." I check the expiration date on a can of baby corn and avoid his stare, but I can feel his eyes. For all my dark hair and dark clothes, maybe I'm not as invisible as I thought.

"Yeah," he says finally. "Well."

≫ ≫

I remember when getting ready for a date meant painting my fingernails to match my shoes and getting my hair blown out. Now it means opening up a new burner phone and punching in a bunch of fake contacts so if Chris asks for my number again, he won't see I'm a friendless loner. I even add a generic background picture of a sunset, like I'm a person who cares about sunsets.

At ten to twelve, I step into a pair of boots and pull on a raincoat, zipping it up to my chin before venturing outside. Most people would bemoan a rainstorm on the day of their big date, but I'm pleased. The rain will keep normal people indoors, where I prefer them.

Chris is waiting just inside the entrance to his building, chatting with the doorman. He spots me, and I lift a hand in greeting, my fingertips pelted with icy rain.

"Hey," he says, coming out. He's wearing jeans and his green jacket, and now opens up a black umbrella, tilting it to shield against the driving rain.

"Hey." Only the oval of my face is visible against the hood I'd had to tie tightly around my head to keep in place.

He doesn't try to be discreet about checking me out. "You look gorgeous."

I look like a pickpocket. "Thanks. You too."

He cracks first, a smile transforming his face. "So what's the plan?"

"It's top secret." I turn away to flag down a cab. There's not much traffic today, but a few yellow tops crawl along the curb lane, eternal optimists. It only takes a second for one to stop.

Chris tugs open the back door and I slide in first, giving the address to the driver as Chris lingers outside to close his umbrella. I push back my hood and drag out my hair from where it's stuck in my collar. "Brr."

He reaches over to snag my hand, rubbing my icy fingers between his warm ones. "You walked over?"

"Yeah."

"Why?"

"Why not?"

He lets my non-answer slide. "Tell me where we're going."

"It's a surprise."

"Give me a hint."

I scratch my chin. "How do you feel about cemeteries?"

He raises an eyebrow. "They're… useful?"

"Then you'll be fine." Of course we're not going to a cemetery, but I still give him a smile intended to be the polar opposite of comforting.

Waterfront Theater is misleadingly named, since the Holden River is about half a mile away and not visible from any angle. My brother Alex, who enjoyed the benefits of wealth as much as he railed against its creativity-killing enabling, would have hated what this place has become. When he took over the abandoned space five years ago, he'd transformed a slightly creepy old building into a whimsical and inspiring haven for local creatives. There are a couple of stages, dressing rooms, a lobby, a small canteen, art studios, and galleries. Alex called it Tiger Wing Hall after the creepy stuffed tiger toy he'd dragged along everywhere as a kid. He'd harangued my father until he agreed to "donate" the money to have the front doors custom-made in the shape of enormous wings painted with orange and black tiger stripes. He loved them until the day he slammed his hand in there and broke four fingers.

The rest of the building exterior would be more at home in a fishing village, with peeling white clapboard and windows that are perpetually fogged, no matter the weather. Still, I'd liked coming here, once upon a time. Alex poured his heart and soul into the place, acting, directing, and managing, making no money but proudly living off his trust fund and offering the world value in other, more creative ways.

I haven't been here since the night of my dad's arrest, though I've kept tabs over the years. Because my father owned the building, it was repossessed with all of his other belongings and resold to make a tiny dent in the amount he'd stolen. It was closed for a short time, then rebranded and reopened as a space for artists, but with a more money-minded focus. Alex had the brilliant idea to let people pay what they thought a show was worth; now admission is fifteen dollars.

The cab stops in front of the awning-covered entrance, the formerly tiger-print doors now painted a shimmering eggshell. The new owners redid the exterior, and it looks more like a tiny home in the Hamptons than a charming arts center. I pay the driver and start to slide across the seat, bumping Chris's knee when he doesn't move.

"What are we doing here?" he asks. His gaze is locked on the building, his jaw tight, fingers digging into his thigh.

"We're going to see a show."

"Here?"

"Yes. It's a theater."

His eyes narrow. I've lied about so many things, it's strange the truth is what makes him suspicious.

"Really."

Now I frown. "Yes, really. You said pick something. I picked."

"You picked this, out of all the places in the city?"

I follow him out of the car and duck under the awning of the building, the pounding rain forcing us to shout to be heard. "You don't like theater?"

He focuses on something over my shoulder. "It's fine."

Wordlessly he reaches over and pulls open the door, tipping his head to indicate I should enter. I do, shuddering as the musty warmth of the lobby envelops us. It's brighter and cleaner than I remember it, and the handful of people milling around are well dressed, their kids wearing raincoats that cost more than mine.

My mother got her start performing here when she was a teenager, and after she passed my father used to bring Alex and me back to show us the series of black and white pictures that captured her art. He hadn't known her at that age, but he loved the idea of her as much as he loved the woman he'd lost. Despite the lavishness of our lives, our countless homes and nannies and drivers, being here in this dingy theater, eating half-stale popcorn and letting our imaginations wander, felt right. It's what brought Alex back, time and again.

As a teenager, I thought I was too old for these types of performances. I wanted to do the things my friends thought were cool. I wanted to wear high heels and go to clubs and flirt with older guys, not watch homespun productions of *The Wizard of Oz* and *A Christmas Carol*. When Alex first broached the subject of reopening the theater, I'd mocked him. He'd ignored me and gone ahead with the plan anyway. Without question, he was the more talented. He got attention for being kind and gifted, if not entirely reliable, his common sense more fleeting than his dreams. I was jealous of his modest success, but I came to his openings, brought friends to the gallery and insisted they buy things. I loved my brother, no matter what they say.

"Do you want to brave it?" I ask Chris, nodding toward the brightly patterned easel with tiny felt puppets indicating the various shows and start times. The afternoon shows are geared toward kids, and already I can feel people glancing at Chris and me, wondering where our children are, and, if we don't have any, what the hell we're doing here.

I turn away slightly, my familiar antsy feelings resurging. I want to sit in the dark theater, in the back row, and go unnoticed. I want to observe, not participate. A children's theater on a rainy afternoon seemed like a safe bet for not getting recognized.

"The twelve-thirty?" Chris pushes a strand of hair off my forehead, the gesture too familiar for someone I can't get attached to.

I shift out of reach. "Yes. *The Power Down Dragon.*"

"Did you know that was playing?"

"No." I can't help but laugh. "Honest, I didn't. I used to come here when I was a kid, and I thought it might be fun to come back. I haven't been in years." When he doesn't say anything, I add, "We can see a movie or something instead. There's a horror movie playing. *Kill Glory 4.* I'll hold your hand if you get scared."

"Let's go learn about energy-saving dragons," Chris says,

unzipping his jacket. "Sounds fun."

"Wait." I touch his arm when he pulls out his wallet and approaches the admission booth.

"What?"

"I'll pay. This is my idea."

"You're not paying."

"I definitely am."

He nods at the bemused attendant. "Excuse us." He tugs me to the side, giving me a mock-stern stare. "You're not paying. I know you do crazy shit like screw guys on the side of the road and not give out your phone number, but this is just too far."

"It's a weird thing for you to take such a strong stance on."

"I'm old-fashioned."

"You screw girls on the side of the road and have a paralyzing fear of puppets. You're nothing if not modern."

He dips his head, lips brushing my ear. "I'm not afraid of puppets."

I turn my face so my breath heats his skin. "I'll give you my phone number if you let me pay."

He straightens, his expression giving away his surprise. "Deal."

"That was easy."

"Was it?"

I return to the booth and buy two tickets, passing one to Chris as we proceed down the dim, narrow hall to theater number three, located at the end of the corridor. It's small, no more than fifty seats that hold the lingering smell of old velvet, the fabric worn to threads in places. The front two rows are already packed with kids, mothers parked on either end, boxing them in. I lead us down the back row, to two seats set dead center.

"This is as far as we can get from the puppets," I whisper.

"I'm not afraid of puppets," Chris whispers back. His whisper is loud enough that the kids hear, and several turn around and giggle. "All right," he continues, settling into his seat and shrugging out of his jacket. He drapes it over the seat beside him and pulls out his phone. "What's your number?"

"Oh, you were serious about that?"

"Were you lying, Denise?"

With only inches between us, the dim lighting and the nostalgia and the wishing for everything I've lost or left behind, I'm terrified. I'm terrified he can see how much I want something. If I want something, he can withhold it. If I have something, he can take it.

"Denise?"

I clear my throat and rattle off the burner number I'd memorized that morning. When he swipes the screen on his phone I recognize the same sunset background I'd chosen for myself.

God.

He *would* like sunsets.

I close my eyes and lean back until I feel my hair snag on the old wooden boards that line the wall, something I remember doing as a kid, even as my dad admonished me to sit up straight.

"You look different," Chris comments.

I crack open an eye. He's putting away his phone but glances over, as though he can sense my movement.

"How so?"

"More..." He drums his fingers on his knee thoughtfully. "Alive."

My other eye pops open. "Alive?"

"Yeah. Less dead." He smiles and touches his cheek. "You've got some color."

I put on blush this morning. "It's cold outside."

"You look pretty."

"Okay. Shut up."

"You're supposed to say something nice in return."

"Oh. You smell good."

"Do I?" He sniffs his pit and I laugh.

"You're the one who wanted a compliment."

"You're as good at compliments as you are at arranging dates."

"Would you have rather gone bowling?"

He considers it. "Sure. Bowling's multipurpose. I can judge your hand-eye coordination. Determine if you're a poor loser. Check out your ass."

"You've seen my ass."

"Not in a week."

"That's your fault."

"I'm trying to be a gentleman. You make it so fucking hard."

Now I laugh, loud enough the kids turn around until I stifle the sound in the crook of my arm. "I don't want you to be a gentleman," I say finally.

"No?" Chris looks amused, watching me like an art film he doesn't understand and is not sure he should like. "What do you want me to be?"

There are too many answers to that question, and I refuse to even let them start circling in my brain. So I take the lame way out. "Quiet," I say, pressing a finger to my lips like a librarian.

The lights dim on the stage and the curtains part to reveal a rather impressive puppet scene. It's an elaborate toy castle, side-sectioned so we can see several rooms inside. A dragon paces back and forth in the stone kitchen, his tiny arms wrapped around his middle.

"I'm so cold," he moans, glancing out at the children in the front row. "There's no power and my castle has lost its heat. What should I do?"

"Fire!" a shrill chorus of voices cries. "Make a fire!"

"Well, obviously," Chris mutters.

>>> >>>

Thirty minutes of dragon-friendly power-saving lessons later, we return to the lobby alongside twenty elementary-aged learners. Compared to the dark of the theater, the dimness in here feels too bright.

"How was that?" I ask, watching the kids race around, invigorated and newly inspired to save energy.

"Oh, wonderful," Chris replies.

"Do you want to watch another show?" I nod at the easel in the lobby. "The admission is good for the whole afternoon."

"Do you?"

"Not especially."

"Thank God. Let's go."

"I knew you were afraid of puppets."

We step outside, the air fresh and cool after the dusty haze of the theater. The rain has stopped and the sky is doing its best to turn blue.

"I'm not afraid of anything," Chris says, lifting a hand to call one of the taxis idling on the far side of the road.

I study him thoughtfully. "All right. Let's see."

"See what?"

"Just wait."

"I don't think I like your surprises."

"I know."

We climb in the back seat, and I deliberately give the driver a street address instead of the more familiar building name. He nods with a notable lack of enthusiasm and steers us back toward the city center. The absence of rain and a hint of sunshine have made people braver, and the sidewalks have resumed their regular bustle.

Downtown Holden is the predictable slew of gleaming metal towers, mirrored façades reflecting each other's success. The bulk of the buildings are banks and investment companies, but there are high-end shops and restaurants designed to dress and feed the city's richest. Three years ago, I was known at all of them. Now I'm pretty sure I couldn't get in the door.

The cab stops in front of the Carone Building, the tallest and most prestigious of them all. "This is us," I say, handing the driver cash and sliding out to the sidewalk.

Chris follows, his expression perplexed. "What are we doing here?"

"Investing. Doesn't that sound fun?"

"Not really."

I smirk. "Come on."

The lobby of the Carone Building is designed to resemble an atrium, with glass-walled greenhouses boasting tropical plants and birds. Behind the information desk is a full-size aquarium with fish found only south of the equator, and the smell of money and luxury is ripe in the air.

After my father's arrest, the city was desperate to wipe away the stench of the scandal. It was only a matter of days before they'd removed the enormous metal signage identifying the Carlisle Gale Tower, and another six months before the Carone name took over. They replaced the polished concrete in the lobby with marble and changed the logo and all its branding, but they couldn't afford to get rid of the fish and birds, so they stayed. A red-tailed Amazon parrot named Abby spots me and squawks a greeting. I wave at her, my boots squeaking as we cross to the second set of elevators. Chris is tense, like he's waiting for someone to escort us out at any moment, but they don't. The first set of elevators is for the people who work here; the second is for those who don't. I press the call button and the doors glide open right away. The car is empty, and we get in, Chris checking over his shoulder, anticipating arrest.

"Relax," I say, pressing the button for the forty-fifth floor, the top. "It's fine."

"What are we really doing?"

These elevators are draped with dingy mats, meant to protect the walls from dents and scratches when laborers move furniture in and out. The cleaning crews use these elevators; so do delivery people. And savvy tourists.

Years earlier, it had been my idea to encourage visitors to take the service elevator to the top floor and climb the final flight of stairs to the roof. Because Holden City isn't a huge tourist attraction, and very few people actually read the fine print in the visitor's maps, not many people make the trip. But it's free and it's totally fine.

We ride up alone and exit into the service hall on the west side of the top floor. The most exclusive office suites are on the other three sides, the hall doors locked to prevent anyone without a passcode from entering. The fire door is at the end of the hall, and I lead the way, pushing it open and climbing the short flight of stairs to the heavy door marked "ROOFTOP."

"Denise, is this—"

There's a faint breeze up here, but the air is light and fresh as I make my way onto the gravel roof deck. When I worked here I used to come up almost every day. Sometimes it was to eat lunch alone to avoid the spiteful stares of my coworkers, sometimes just for the peace and quiet. I've always liked rooftops, and this is the tallest building in the city, offering an unobstructed sightline. I turn to Chris, who looks equal parts impressed and mystified.

"It's fine," I assure him. "It's a tourist thing. Best views in the city."

"I've never heard of it."

"Most people haven't." I nod at the signs that dot the glass railing at regular intervals. *Do not climb on rail. Do not lean over rail. Flash photography strictly prohibited. Do not drop items over ledge. Do not jump.*

The last time I set foot in this building was the day I came to clean out my office. Thanks to the FBI, it was already empty, and I'd been such a mess of confusion and shame that I hadn't really known what to do with the box I brought for my belongings. The suspicious glares of the security escorts made everything worse, and nausea hit me hard. I'd run to the bathroom to hurl up what little food I'd eaten that morning.

And then I got an idea.

I'd inched opened the bathroom door, found the hallway deserted, and darted through the locked door to the service hall, calling the elevator for the roof. The agents only had keys for the elevators so they couldn't follow, and minutes later I was in this exact spot, reading that silly, stern sign: *Do not jump.*

I decided to do exactly that. I climbed over the rail, resting my heels on the two inches of overhang, my sweaty hands clutching the rail as I hung over the city. My father was a criminal. The papers had already indicted me, though the attorney general hadn't and never would. But it didn't matter. Life as I knew it—*my* life as I knew it—was over.

It was the thought of Alex going through it all alone that had me inching my way back over, crouching on the rooftop, and pulling in desperate, heaving breaths I didn't even want. But I couldn't leave him to clean up a mess neither of us had made. He needed me. He'd never had a mother, and though I was only three years older, I'd always done my best to take care of him. Together, we would be okay.

Eleven months later, he was dead.

After the accident, I started visiting the roof of my own building as soon as I was able to climb the stairs. If not for those weeks in a cast, I might have jumped sooner, but I didn't like the visual. When someone jumps to their death they're supposed to break; I'd have a massive plaster cast keeping me together.

No matter how many times that voice inside whispered that I should just do it, take that final step, guilt kept me on the roof. Right on the ledge, that fine balance between life and death, my own brand of purgatory. If I wasn't here to atone, who would?

"You all right?"

I give myself a mental tug back into the present and remember where I am and who I'm with.

"Yes." The word sounds scratchy, and I clear my throat. "Yes. Fine. Do you like it?"

"Yeah." Chris nods and turns slowly to take in the view. "It's amazing."

I walk to the edge and gaze out. Holden is a carefully planned city, with straight, even streets carved in a predictable grid. The Holden River weaves across on a diagonal, cutting through the center and cleaving it neatly in two. There are bright splashes of green where grassy parks struggle to come to life in late winter, and below us cars and people move in slow motion.

"How did you know about this?"

"I…" My mind goes blank for a split second before recovering. "I saw it on one of those tourist maps."

"Wow."

I brush hair out of my eye and squint at Chris, the weak sun glowing over his shoulder. "Is this what you wanted?"

"What do you mean?"

"When you said you wanted city life. Is this what you wanted?"

He scans the skyline again, taking it in. "I guess. You?"

"I've only ever known this." That's not entirely true, obviously. I have four expired passports filled with stamps and visas to prove I've known far more than this city. But it's my home. Or it was. Now it's just as much a prison for me as Wakeman is for my father, albeit with a little less ramen.

"Where would you go? If you weren't here?" I lean against the railing, the light breeze lifting my hair, and raise a hand to shield my eyes from the sun. Chris copies my position, shifting his body so he blocks the rays and I can see.

He rolls his lips, and he's too sexy. Tall and broad and rugged. There are people in this building with purses that cost more than the combined total of all of our clothing. Three years ago, I thought that mattered. Hell, I used to have seven of those bags. A year ago I'd killed an afternoon putting them on eBay and watching the bids soar.

"I'd like to go to Europe," he says eventually. "I know that's typical, but I'd like to see the Eiffel Tower. The Sistine Chapel. That church made of bones in the Czech Republic."

"It doesn't matter if it's typical, if it's what you want to see."

"What about you? Anywhere you want to go?"

Everywhere, I think. Nowhere I've been and nowhere anyone else wants to go. "Maybe a deserted island," I hear myself say, the truth feeling strange on my tongue. "Or some old house in the countryside in Wales or Scotland, where you keep to yourself and nobody cares. Where it's just quiet."

"I'm sensing a theme."

"I'm a bit of a loner."

"So I've gathered."

This is my cue to explain my hermit-like motivations, but there's no earthly way that's happening. "You should be flattered," I say instead. I even tap his arm for cheesy good measure. "I hate most people, but here I am with you."

"Flattered is not the word for it."

"What is?"

He doesn't answer for a long moment, then he cups my face in his hand and lowers his mouth until his lips touch mine, kissing me softly, naturally. Maybe sweetly. Not the kiss of the guy on the side of the road or the one from his apartment; not the kiss of someone who skipped all the first steps and jumped right to the good part. Or what's supposed to be the good part. This is the getting-to-know-you type of kiss, the kind that says I see you and I like you and I want to do this.

I feel myself panic a little bit, because it feels too good. It feels like more than I'm supposed to feel, than he should feel, than anyone should feel. But I can't seem to stop.

I want all of him.

I want none of this.

Oh fuck.

"Where do you live?" he murmurs, nipping my lower lip.

"I—" I blink, disoriented. Disoriented, maybe, but not stupid. A fake phone number's enough for one day. "Your place is closer."

"All right," he says, swiping his thumb over my stinging lip. "Let's go."

9

Chris holds my hand in the cab. I can't remember the last time someone held my hand. He pays the fare when we get to his building, and helps me out of the car like I'm something special. We ride up to his floor with a woman who makes polite small talk about the unpredictable weather, and by the time we reach his door I'm ready to jump out of my skin. This is the most normal, traditional date I've been on in three years but it feels the most dangerous. Like the risks I've been trying to take are nothing compared to this. It's stupid, I know, since I've been here before. I've slept with him before. And I'm still lying to him, so nothing has changed.

But I can't lie to myself.

Something has changed.

He hangs up our coats, and I take off my boots and look around nervously. He'd tidied up. No dishes on the counter, no loose papers gathered around the laptop on the dining table. Beer bottles gone, shoes lined neatly along the wall. I curl my fingers in my sleeves, ridiculously nervous. Marnie and Naomi and Olivia never got nervous. But today I can't muster up any new personalities. All I've got is me.

"You okay?" he asks. He comes a little closer, and instinctively, I shift back, my shoulder blades meeting the door.

I make myself meet his eye. "I'm fine."

"You want a drink or anything?"

"No."

"You want to hang out?"

"Is that what you want?"

He reaches up to catch the ends of my hair between his fingers, rolling the strands back and forth. "Not really."

"Me either."

He kisses me. Not quite as sweetly as he did on the rooftop, now that we're indoors. Now that it's totally appropriate to tear off all our clothes and wrestle each other to the ground to work out all these complicated, alarming…feelings.

I kiss him back, jittery with anticipation, the way it used to feel on Christmas Eve, tense and wonderful and unbearably slow. When I can't take it anymore I make a noise that sounds a bit like a growl, enough to make him laugh, his teeth bumping my lip. I fist my hands in the hem of his shirt and pull it off, feeling the heat of his skin and the scratch of his chest hair and wanting so much more.

"You have to do *more*," I mutter, snagging his hand.

He laughs again. "I will."

"Like, right now."

More laughter. "You're funny, Denise."

"I'm serious." I start to remove my shirt, but he stops me.

"I'll do it."

"When?"

I see the sharp flash of his teeth as he smiles, then he yanks the shirt over my head, unexpectedly swift for a guy who seems to like everything to move at the pace of a dead snail. "Right now."

"Hilarious."

"I got my sense of humor from you." He kisses me again before I can reply, stepping into me fully, our bellies pressed together, his hot and firm against mine.

He slides one hand down my spine to rest at the top of my ass, the other slipping beneath my bra to unclasp it. The straps loosen on my shoulders as he tugs me forward, down the hall toward his bedroom, kissing me the whole way.

The last time I saw his bedroom, it was three o'clock in the morning and I was sneaking out. I could barely discern the shapes of the furniture, identifying just enough to avoid crashing into anything as I made my escape. Now I stop the kissing and take in the room. It's tidy in here, too. The shades are up, letting in the meager afternoon sun, the light glinting off the veneered tops of a dresser and end tables, a plain wooden headboard. The bed is made, the pale blue comforter set off by lemon yellow sheets peeking out the bottom.

There are a couple of framed photographs on the walls. Artwork, pretty but impersonal. Like my place.

"You okay?" Chris asks, lifting an inquisitive brow. The lines bracketing his mouth are deeper, sexier than usual.

"Yep."

"Good." He holds my gaze as he lowers his hands to the button on my jeans, then the zipper, pushing the denim down to my knees before crouching to work it off my legs completely.

He remains kneeling, his face level with my satin panties. "Tell me to take these off," he murmurs, trailing the edge of his thumb along the crease of my thigh, making me shiver.

"Chris."

"Mm hmm?" He leans in and presses a kiss to the front of the fabric, close to where I want it, but not close enough.

"Take them off," I whisper.

He keeps his eyes on my face as he tugs the panties down, fingers circling my ankles one at a time as he lifts my feet. Then I'm naked. Totally, vitally naked. You don't have sex with a bunch of strangers and not get used to it. But this is different. This is daylight. This is no alcohol. This is someone I know.

His face takes on a heavy-lidded intensity I haven't seen before, and he brackets my hips with his hands, stroking into the curls, searching until he finds softer, damper flesh, and nudging it apart. He kisses my legs, each side, higher and higher, his thumbs seeking and opening, stroking and teasing, and by the time his mouth finds me I'm wet and trembling.

"Oh, God," I hear myself mumble. "Please."

He doesn't make me wait this time, urging my thighs apart so he can have better access. He can have everything right now. Absolutely everything.

Chris does this the way he does everything else, with his own brand of slow and steady and rough and sure. I'm melting so fast I have to lean back to brace myself against the dresser, arching my hips to his face. He doesn't ease up when I'm moaning and shaking, my stomach flexing, one hand clutching his hair, making sure this doesn't end until it has to. Until I can't take it anymore. Until I'm covering my mouth to stifle sounds I've never heard before. The orgasm rolls through me, smug and unhurried, proving all the points he's been trying to make. And then, finally, reluctantly, his fingers slow, his tongue just brushing my too-sensitive skin, and all too soon and far too late, he stops.

He sits back on his heels and wipes his mouth on his forearm, and I can't quite catch my breath. My hair hangs in my face, but I don't have the energy to move it. I'm wrung out. I've forgotten whatever reservations I had.

"Wow," I manage.

He raises an eyebrow. "Yeah?"

My heart is bounding around like a loose puppy. "Yeah."

"Hang on a sec."

I really have no choice, so I watch him disappear into the attached bathroom. I hear water running, splashing, then he returns, drying his face with a hand towel he tosses in the hamper. He reaches for his fly, then hesitates. "Still good?"

I try and fail not to smile. "Still good."

≫ ≫

It's after seven when Chris offers to drive me home, of course, and I decline, of course. I can tell he's irked, but he doesn't press. The rain has stopped, and though it's dark outside, it's downtown Holden, which means it's lit up and bustling, because God forbid someone sleep when they could be making money. I keep my head down and my hood up as I walk, just in case. I spent the entire afternoon being exposed and wide open, it's time to get back to normal.

But normal isn't as welcome as I thought, and when I push

open the door to my cold, dark apartment, I immediately miss the warmth of Chris's place. I miss his bed and his couch and his grilled cheese. I miss the old normal, when I had friends and a brother and a father who wasn't a criminal. That we knew about.

I change into sweats and a T-shirt and toss a load of laundry in the washer as I boil water for tea. I check pockets as I add clothes, frowning when I find something in the back pocket of a pair of jeans. A business card. I rack my brain, trying to figure out why I'd have any business cards at all, never mind one for a small Holden City brokerage called Emerald Isle Investors. And then I remember: I stole this card. From Chris. It was his bookmark. He'd never mentioned it missing, so I guess he never noticed he'd lost his place.

I consider tearing the card into tiny pieces and throwing it in the trash, just in case he should somehow ever figure out I stole it, but I don't. Something in the back of my brain is niggling unhappily, trying to make its way to the forefront.

I make my tea and take the card and the mug to my desk and sit. More out of habit than interest I call up the Fantasy Friends website, but immediately close it. My eyes keep sliding over to the business card. Emerald Isle. A green diamond logo.

On impulse I do a search for Emerald Isle, expecting a slew of Ireland listings to pop up. But that's not what happens. Apparently, Emerald Isle is a common name, and there are many places around the world that carry it, including locations in Canada, India and…the United States. North Carolina, to be exact.

If more time had passed between my failed date with Doug and this moment, I might never have thought of his North

Carolina accent as he told his sweetly rehearsed first-date stories. I never would have thought of him at all, again, ever. When I communicate with people through the Fantasy Friends website, I use only the email account generated by the site. It's smarter that way, and easier. It means they see only the things I want them to see, no clues about my actual life. And in our first days of writing, Doug did the same. Until he started replying from his work email. I remember specifically the email signature automatically included with his response, the green diamond I'd otherwise ignored beyond noting Doug's slip up. He should be more careful, I'd thought. You never know who you're going to meet online.

The business card is a generic one for the whole firm, no specific investor name given. But it does have a website, and I call up Emerald Isle Investors and skim the description, learning they're a three-generation brokerage originally based out of North Carolina, though their main headquarters is now here, in Holden City. I try to ignore the anxious thudding of my heart. It's one thing for Chris to have this business card; it's quite another for him to sit three feet away from Doug on our first date.

I click the link for the brokerage staff profiles. It's a small company, only fifteen employees, and Doug is right in the middle of the list. Perfectly average. Doug Winters. I click his bio, doing a double-take when I read about his wife and triplet daughters. I thought I was a decent judge of character, but clearly not. I file away that information and move on.

There are six other Winters on staff. Just to be sure, I click on each name and scrutinize the accompanying headshot, but

Chris is not among them. And why would he be? He works at an agricultural college. He's a gardener. With no plants in his home.

I reach for my tea, but it's cold and bitter and I feel worse after I drink it. I think of the twinges of the well-used muscles in my thighs and the scratchy patches on my chest where Chris's stubble had rubbed. I feel him, everywhere. Too much, now. And not in a good way.

The thing about betrayal is that if you're smart, it only blindsides you once. Then you learn. My father betrayed me. He blew up our entire life. My friends abandoned me, the world reviled me, the newspapers egged them on. Even now, three years later, there are people who refuse to let it go. They think I killed my brother. They think I'm hiding the money. They think I knew.

What they don't know is that three years ago I was a superficial bleached blonde with a black Amex she barely knew how to check the balance on. Three years ago I was stunned and unprepared. Three years ago I'd never fought for anything, so I didn't know how. Three years ago, I was someone very, very different.

This is not a coincidence. My father's deception happened right in front of me and I was blind to it. So now I *notice* things. And instead of seeing red flames of rage, I'm seeing Chris pick up that old paperback when I asked about it while we ate our sandwiches. I'm picturing him using his thumb to push the business card down between the pages and out of sight, like it meant nothing at all.

WHO

10

Who are you? is scrawled across the top of a sheet of lined paper, half of which is stuck to my face when I wake up at my desk the next morning. Unfortunately, the rest of the page is blank. I guess I ran out of ideas.

I sit up, stretch out the kinks in my neck, then peel the paper off my cheek to smooth it out, contemplating the empty space. The questions. The answers. The possibilities. The fact that I don't know who I've been sleeping with says nothing about Chris, and far too much about me. I'd dwell on it, but it won't change anything. I've already had three years to reflect on my own moral failings; it's time to put someone else in the unflattering spotlight.

Chris Sherwood, I add to the page. Then, after a second's thought, I scribble a question mark. *Chris Sherwood?*

I stare at the two words for a long time, then sigh. Fuck. I get up and take my tea cup to the kitchen, sticking it in the dishwasher as I plug in the kettle and wait for the water to heat. The time on the microwave blinks 7:02 a.m. in green, too bright in a world this bleak.

I pace, trying to dredge up everything I know about Chris. Everything he's told me, even though I told him I didn't want to know. His name. His job. He's from Montana. Had a dog named Astro. Lives in an apartment that sometimes has plants in the window, and sometimes doesn't.

The most obvious solution is that he's some type of law enforcement, FBI, most likely, though surely there has to be a law against sleeping with your suspect. A private investigator, then?

The kettle whistles, and I make my tea, returning to the desk to add to my paltry list. Every entry has a question mark next to it. *Teacher? Montana? Plants? Lying asshole?* I don't even have his phone number.

Before the scandal, I could have made a dozen lists like this, a dozen guys I didn't really know, who probably wanted to be with me for the wrong reasons. The money, the attention. But that was different. I wasn't sleeping with those guys, and I didn't care what their intentions were. My name was everywhere. My face. Some other body parts. I had no secrets.

But this is different. Chris is different. I'm different. And, if I'm not mistaken and the business card is more than a crazy coincidence, then he has to want something besides the pleasure of my company, and the obvious answer is the twenty million dollars everybody else wants. The money they're sure I have hidden in the walls. But he can take a sledgehammer to every surface in this apartment—it's not here.

I think back to that day at Fleischmann's Park, when he'd led me right to Nichols Pavilion. I told myself the date was a test and if he failed, I'd run. But I ran for all the wrong reasons. I ran because I believed him, believed he liked me, because it had been so long since I'd believed somebody that I'd ignored what was right in front of me. For three years I've been killing time, trying to figure out what to do, and now there's a gun to my head, telling me time's up.

I could run again, of course. I could move and hide. But I've waited this long for my father's appeal, this long for our shot at some semblance of a fresh start that running away now would jeopardize any chance I have at a normal future. I'll spend the rest of my life looking over my shoulder, wondering where Chris is, what he wants, when he'll find me. And perhaps most importantly, who the fuck he is.

Running is Plan B.

Getting answers is Plan A.

I start my amateur investigation in the most obvious place: the Holden School of Agriculture website. For a bunch of gardeners, they have a surprisingly sleek and modern site, stylized photos of plants and vegetables, slim and happy students. I click on the link for Staff, and scroll through the alphabetized list of names. There are a dozen S names, but no Sherwoods. No Chris. Just to be sure, I read all 110 names in the list. He's not there.

The website appears modern, but maybe it hasn't been updated recently. On impulse, I click on a random bio for someone named Maryanne Whims and find her email address. Maryanne.Whims@financeag.org.

I don't bother setting up private email accounts for my Lonely Hearts personas, just using the site for communicating, but now I create a brand new email address for Denise Reynolds and type a quick message to Chris.Sherwood@financeag.org.

Hey Chris, it's me! Thought you should have my email address! Thinking of you! D

I press send.

Ten seconds later, a new message appears in my inbox: *Message Not Delivered. Email address does not exist on this server.*

I'm not shocked, but whatever bubble of hope was hovering in my chest shrinks considerably. I try again, just in case: Christopher.Sherwood@financeag.org.

Same message.

Same error.

I close the website and type *Chris Sherwood* into a search engine. Not surprisingly, it generates 14,800,000 results. I try to narrow it down with Montana, then Holden City, then investigator, then asshole, but it doesn't help. I might have nothing but time on my hands, but I'm not sifting through fourteen million anything.

My eyes flit to the business card resting on the desk. It could be a total coincidence that Chris was using a card from Doug's business as a bookmark when he sat next to us at the restaurant, just like it could be an oversight that he's not on the school website. Like it was just bad luck that my dad got arrested and my brother died and I became me.

Before everything fell apart, I never would have thought twice about any of this. Things happen for a reason. Life goes on. Live and let live. I was so consumed by my own personal dramas that I didn't bother to pay attention to the things that didn't add up until it was too late and the world imploded.

Well, now I'm not distracted by anything. Now, I stand and go to the maps on the wall, retrieving my red dart from Madagascar and backing up a few paces. This time I aim at the

Holden map. I already know where I'm going, but I throw the dart anyway. I like the sound it makes when it pierces the paper.

≫ ≫

I'm Denise again. I missed her. The auburn wig is clipped back neatly at my nape, and I'm wearing a simple black dress and flats, along with a strand of pearls left over from Alex's costume collection, and my favorite Birkin bag. No matter the business— restaurant, boutique, bank—the first thing everyone in Holden does is judge your shoes and your handbag. If they're expensive enough, you're in. If not, good luck getting a hostess to take you seriously, never mind a banker.

Emerald Isle Investors is located on the second floor of a mid-level building at the edge of the downtown core, just close enough to boast the coveted Holden zip code. The lobby is decorated in muted beiges and grays, with spots of red for color. There's a vase of fresh flowers only just starting to wilt. If I didn't know any better, I'd think it was fancy.

The receptionist who greeted me slides yet another look my way, and I shift in my seat so she can't see my face. I don't think she recognizes me; I know she recognizes the bag. What she can't figure out is what someone with this bag would be doing in this office and not one of the bigger, better firms in the city.

I shift in my seat and try to keep my expression pleasantly neutral, though inside I'm seething. This is day two of my investigation, and yesterday hadn't gone well. I'd made the two-hour trip out to the Holden School of Agriculture with a kernel of naïve hope in my heart, praying that Chris *did* work there, that maybe his email address just wasn't set up yet, that the website hadn't been updated in a while. He doesn't work there, of course. He doesn't have an email. The website is current. I left with a twenty-page information packet and an application form, but no answers.

It doesn't matter how much time has passed, people are still obsessed with the idea of the missing money. It's the one thing in my life that won't die. From time to time a "journalist" will try to check in for an anniversary piece. Or someone working in their backyard will hit something in the ground and swear it's a trunk of stolen money my dad must have buried there when we owned the land. The first half-dozen times it happened people got incredibly excited, and each time it was just a piece of old machinery, churned under the earth when the land was reclaimed for Holden's development.

I know the money's not buried anywhere. It would take a lot of work to dig a hole deep enough to hold twenty million dollars, and anyone examining my father's carefully manicured hands would know he'd never held a shovel a day in his life. Still, it amuses them to look, and it amuses me to see them fail.

I'm feeling slightly better when Doug arrives.

"Ms. Reynolds! Good morning, and welcome to Emerald—." Doug chokes on his words and his friendly smile stiffens as I stand, gripping his proffered hand before he can pull it away. It's ten o'clock in the morning and already there are sweat marks beneath the arms of his blue shirt, the buttons straining slightly over his almost-forty paunch.

"Good morning," I return, smiling brightly.

It takes ten full seconds for Doug to swallow, give my hand a jerky shake, and clear his throat. "You, ah, I—Are you—Is this the correct—"

"Uh-huh. Shall we talk in your office, or is right here okay?" I gesture broadly to the empty waiting area and the all-too-interested receptionist.

"My office," Doug manages, doing his best to regain control. "This way."

He turns and strides quickly down a long hall with laminate wood floors. Evenly spaced, average-sized offices line either side, each desk manned by a similarly hunched, Doug-like investor, mostly male. It brings back memories.

I have to move at a near-jog to keep up with Doug, following him into an office at the end of the hall. It's slightly larger than the others, though just as bland, boasting a view of the coffee shop across the street. He scurries around a large wooden desk like he can hide behind his double computer monitors, and attempts to glare at me, but he's too afraid to make it convincing.

"Tell me everything you know about Chris Sherwood," I say.

Doug blinks.

I don't.

"Huh?"

"Chris Sherwood," I repeat. "Who is he?"

"I—I don't know."

"Then find out." I'm doing my best FBI agent impression now. I've had more than my share of real world experience to draw from.

His jaw drops and he shakes his head like he's trying to wake up from a dream. "What—I—*How?* Do you have a picture or something?" He appears genuinely bewildered, and I believe him. Now the irritation welling in my gut isn't aimed at Doug but the second dead-end I've encountered in as many days. But he doesn't need to know that.

"No, I don't have a picture," I snap, though the woman at the college had asked me the same thing yesterday. How is it that I've been sleeping with Chris for weeks and I don't have a single picture of him? No proof that he exists, that he's not a figment of my overactive imagination? I shunt aside the thoughts and focus. "That night at the restaurant," I begin, breaking off in alarm when Doug covers his face and crumples into his seat like a blow-up doll abruptly deflating.

"Please," he mumbles through his fingers. "I can't do this again. My wife—"

Several framed photos sit on the desk, turned away, their velvet backs inviting touch. I reach over to pick one up, the silver frame surprisingly heavy. Inside is a family photo, taken some time ago, if Doug's more robust hairline is any indication. A smiling family beams at the camera. Doug, his wife, and three identical little girls.

I roll my eyes. I could tell Doug I'm not here to blackmail him—he clearly has some experience—but I don't bother. Maybe he needs the scare.

"He had your business card," I say, doing my best to keep a straight face as Doug's fingers slowly part and he peers out at me like a guilty dog. "At the restaurant. Why would he have your card?"

Doug is incredulous. "Who the hell is 'he'?" Then he gasps. "Wait—the guy from the restaurant—the one you left with… that's…that's Chris Sherwood?"

"I didn't leave with him."

"That's what the server said."

"Well, the server was—" I cut myself off. I wish I could say with all honesty I hadn't seen Chris after that night, but unfortunately, I can't. "That's not the point. It's too much of a coincidence for him to have your card, sit at the next table, and not know you."

"Well, he might know me, but I don't know him!" Doug protests. "Do you know how many clients I have? I'm very—"

Now I don't bother to hide my eye roll. "Do a search," I say, jerking my chin at his computer. "Tell me if he has an account here."

Doug sits up straighter in his chair. "That information is privileged."

I glance pointedly at the photograph. "Is it sacred?"

He huffs, then starts to type. I lean over the desk to confirm he's really searching. He is, reluctantly. We wait as a list of names populates. Three Sherwoods. Two C's. One Christopher.

"Click it," I order.

He does.

A new page loads, he types a password, and the account spread generates. At the top, in red letters—Account Closed.

"What does that mean?" I demand.

"What do you think it means? The account is closed."

"Why?"

Doug uses his cursor to highlight a status box: *Client deceased.* "He's dead."

Now I'm the one who deflates, though I have enough backbone not to show it. "When? How old was he?"

Doug heaves an aggrieved sigh, like he's not the philandering loser in this scenario, and pulls up the bio page. Date of birth: June 11, 1939.

My stomach drops.

It's not him. This Chris Sherwood is not my Chris Sherwood. Or whoever the hell he is.

"Go back," I order. "And click on the other C. And if that's not him, try the other one."

He does as ordered, but neither one is a match.

"Fuck," I mutter. A literal dead-end.

"Who is he?" Doug asks when I straighten and he has room to draw a full breath. "And why do you need to find him so bad?"

"Because," I snap, grabbing my bag, smoothing my skirt, and composing myself as best I can. "He found me."

I don't wait for Doug to answer—or question—and instead stride out the door possessing only half the confidence with which I entered. I don't know why I thought Doug would be in on it. Doug, who can barely cheat on his wife successfully, could hardly be part of…whatever this is.

Because what the fuck is it?

I stab the button for the elevator hard enough I hurt my finger, then hear the receptionist's muffled voice behind me. She shuts up when I turn around, phone pressed to her ear, and I'm pretty sure she's calling security. That, at least, makes me smile, and I abandon the elevator and head for the fire door at the opposite end of the hall.

"Excuse me…" she says, but I ignore her and use my hip to open the heavy door, taking my time as I descend the stairs to the lobby, because they can't really throw me out when I'm leaving anyway. Plus, I've been escorted out of an investment firm before, and it was far worse than anything these guys could do.

I emerge onto the sidewalk, the sun bright but the air icy cold, and I shrug into Denise's trench coat before hurrying across the street to the cafe. I need tea. I need answers. And I've run out of ideas.

I wait in line for a drink, half a dozen people in cheap business suits talking on phones in front of me, all trying to outdo the others with the numbers they spew, just in case someone's eavesdropping. It was the same thing when I worked at Carlisle Gale, always trying to one-up each other, even though we all knew everybody was lying. It was just a matter of who could do it better. Longer.

A guy waiting for a drink catches my eye and smiles, but I don't smile back. Denise has decided to get away from the dating pool for a while so she can refine her bullshit detector and not get conned by any more lying assholes. I don't have to make quite the same effort to remove myself from polite society, but I still need some space. Room to think and prepare so I'm not taken off guard—

My phone rings, the sound so foreign and startling I nearly drop my bag. Because I'm in Denise's costume, I brought Denise's phone. I fumble to retrieve it from my bag and stare at the call display for a second. A gray silhouette stares back, waiting for me to accept or decline, and there's only one person it could be. Whoever he is.

I answer. "Hello?"

"Hey, Denise? It's Chris."

I scowl. He sounds so nice, so normal. So innocent. "Hey," I say, like I'm happy to hear from him. "Where are you?"

"Where—Oh, I'm at work. Why? Where are you?"

"Just running errands."

Now it's his turn to sound surprised, which isn't so surprising if he's been stalking me for who knows how long and is fully aware of my hermit status. "Errands? What kind?"

"The usual. Getting groceries. Banking."

There's a pause, then: "Okay, cool. Did you want to get together tonight? We could grab dinner, see a movie?"

For three years, the mere thought of being in public without a disguise has caused my heart to race so fast sometimes it feels like it's trying to outrun the world. Now, the same overheated, nauseous fear looms, but it's not the world that scares me.

"I can't," I say, before I mean to.

"You can't?" There's a strange note in his voice, but whether it's frustration or disappointment is something I won't even dare to guess at anymore.

"No, I—I can't see a movie," I manage, ducking my head when the smiling man passes by, watching me. "I don't like... them."

"Okay, well, that's fine. Why don't I grab takeout and bring it to your place?"

Fuck no, I think.

"How does Thai sound?" he continues. "Or Indian? Or maybe more tacos? Those worked out pretty well the last time."

The mention of the tacos—and what followed—brings my galloping heart to a screeching stop. I've slept with men I barely knew. Men I didn't care about. Men who were probably lying about their names or their jobs or their marital status. But I didn't care about that, because I didn't care about anything; certainly not myself. And now, somewhat ironically, spending time with a man who's with me for some mysterious, nefarious reason, reminds me that I do care. That there's still a spark of the old Reese Carlisle hiding in these shadows, too stubborn to be extinguished. And she feels decidedly ill at the thought of sleeping with a man who's lying about far more than a wedding ring.

"Are you there?" Chris's voice jars me from my thoughts.

"Yes," I manage.

"Great. Tacos, then?"

"No. No takeout. We'll get drinks."

"I—"

"Do you know Barre None? It's near your place."

Now he doesn't bother to hide his dissatisfaction with the arrangement. Before this, I'd feel bad putting him off. Like it was hurting his feelings. Now I think I'm just hindering his plans.

He sighs. "Yeah. I know it."

"I'll meet you there at eight."

"Fine," he says. "See you then."

I end the call and watch the gray silhouette fade from the screen, disappearing into the unknown ether. *That stupid, lying fuckhead.*

I step up to the smiling barista. "Good morning," she says. "What would you like?"

"Green tea, please. Extra hot."

"Sure thing." She picks up a cup and a marker, scribbling my order on the side. "Your name?"

I hesitate, just for a second. "Denise," I say.

⋙ ⋙

I chose Barre None because it's dark and smug, the kind of place where people go to shun other people, not pick them up. There's no dance floor, no crowd waiting at the bar hunting for drinks and phone numbers. You show up, find a table, order overpriced alcohol, and no one disturbs you.

Except the man you're dating.

Precisely because of the anonymity promised by the bar, I detour from my usual, forgettable dress code and opt for tight pants, stilettos, and a low-cut top. Dressing like myself would get me noticed. I cover the ensemble with a leather jacket and duck through the cold parking garages at a minute to eight, emerging above-ground across the street from the bar fashionably late.

Chris is already inside. I can see him from the doorway, dressed in a gray Henley, hair mussed, nursing a beer. There's not another man in the place with a Henley or a beer, but I don't care about them. I don't care about Chris, either, but it's time we even up our getting-to-know-you scorecards. For the past several weeks, I've mistakenly believed I had the most points, but I think Chris showed up with a full card, and I'm the idiot who's been playing catch up.

I've always been a sore loser.

Three years of hiding haven't improved my manners, and I stroll past the protesting hostess with the same haughty air I always did. But unlike years prior, no heads turn to follow my progress, no phones come out of pockets to secretly film in case I do something scandalous. That's because I'm not dressed to be noticed, pausing for photographs, greeting everyone I want to be seen with and ignoring those I don't. Now I aim straight for the small booth on the left. Leather seats, veneer tabletop polished to a high shine. An overpriced light fixture dangles precariously overhead, casting shadows on Chris's face when he looks up.

He doesn't stand.

"You made it," he says, voice neutral.

It's 8:20.

I slide into my seat. "Of course I did."

"I wasn't sure you were coming."

"Why wouldn't I?"

"You—"

I unzip the jacket and he stops talking. He's seen me naked before, too many times, but the unaccustomed cleavage interrupts whatever lie was coming. I pretend not to notice and don't make eye contact with the approaching server. "Vodka cranberry," I say, as she glides past without stopping.

Chris watches me.

I watch him.

"You look nice," he says finally.

"Thanks. You, too." I think about the gray silhouette on my phone. With the Henley and the shadows, he looks the same. Vague. Unreal. "How was work?" I ask, when he doesn't say anything else.

He sips his beer. "Fine. Busy. How were your errands?"

"Fine. Busy."

The server returns and wordlessly sets down my drink before slipping away. Chris frowns at her retreating form.

"This place," he says.

"What about it?"

"It's so… cold."

"It's Holden. Do you miss Missouri?"

"I'm from Montana. And no. Sometimes."

"Sometimes what?"

"Sometimes I miss the people."

I pick up my glass and watch him over the rim. "What's stopping you from going home?"

He looks thoughtful. "I came to Holden for a reason. I don't know what it is yet, but I'll let you know when I find out."

"Let me know if I can help."

He takes a drink. "Sure."

We're quiet for a minute, ignoring each other the way everyone else does.

Finally Chris says, "How were your errands?"

I don't point out that I've already answered this question. "Good. I was thinking about you."

"Oh yeah?"

"Yeah. I went to the library." That's a lie, of course, but so is everything he's saying.

"I didn't know you read."

"I don't, really. But it's near the museum, so I thought about Fleishmann's and the missing sun dial, and your research, so I went in."

"It's a good story, about the sun dial."

"All your stories are good, Chris."

He smiles, and it's not fair that he can be so attractive and so horrible at the same time. I'm pretty sure I read an article about me with that same quote, some years ago. Anyway.

"So what'd you learn?"

"I was reading about the missing money you mentioned."

"I thought you knew about it."

"I know what's in the papers. I haven't followed the story all that closely, I just know it's supposedly still out there."

"There's no supposedly. They haven't found it, so it's out there."

"Or not."

"How do you figure?" he asks.

"They traced the other two hundred million electronically. Why would there be twenty million in cash? What would someone do with that?"

"Bury it."

I scoff. "That's stupid."

"Why?"

"Because they had a diagram of what twenty million dollars would look like. Assuming it was new bills, tightly banded, it's a minimum of two cubic yards. About the space this booth takes up. Who's going to bury that much money? Wouldn't it just get ruined?"

"Probably. But a desperate person isn't thinking rationally. Carlisle had his fingers in dozens of development projects around the city. He had access to empty lots and digging equipment. It's not impossible. And what's twenty million to a billionaire?"

"A *former* billionaire," I point out.

"Exactly. It's all he has."

"Except he has nothing, because he's in prison."

"He has kids."

"His son died. His wife died. His daughter disappeared."

Chris studies me. "How perfect for her."

My lungs freeze, mid-inhale, and for five terrible seconds, I feel like I'm dying all over again, lying in that field, staring at

Alex's broken body, waiting for my turn. But it won't come. Not yet.

"I didn't mean it like that," Chris says, like he can read my mind. "I just mean, if she knows where the money is, there's no one to stop her from getting it. She could have twenty million dollars, free and clear."

Free and clear. I'd laugh if I could get enough air into my lungs.

"It's been three years," I manage. "She either already has it, or doesn't know where it is."

"Or she's patient."

"Or innocent."

He picks at the label on his bottle. "Do you believe that?"

"That she's innocent?"

"Yes."

I hold his stare. "Yes."

"Fair enough."

I was never one for gambling. Three years ago, everything I felt showed on my face. Now it's the same story, except I don't feel much of anything. Chris, on the other hand, has an excellent poker face. I can't tell if he believes I'm innocent, believes I'm Denise, believes there's money, believes anything.

"Anyway," I say, reaching to take his hand, turning it over to study his palm. It's soft and hard at the same time, years of calluses turning into a smooth bed. "According to the internet, the most popular new rumor is that the money is on Kestrel Island."

"Where's that?" he asks.

"It's the island in the lake at Fleishmann's Park. My—" I cut myself off before I say "my dad." "My research says the island is a bird sanctuary, and Kimball Carlisle was a private benefactor. No one's allowed on the land, so maybe it's the perfect hiding place."

"Why are you telling me this? Do you want to investigate?"

"No. I don't think the money's out there. But if that's the reason you came to Holden, it's worth a shot." I shrug. "Plus, you're a gardener. You're used to getting your hands dirty."

He twines our fingers and turns his wrist so my palm is the one facing up, the skin smooth and clean. "And you're not?"

"Not even a little bit."

Chris is the first one to break our stare, turning his face as he laughs.

"What?" I pull away my hand.

"You're hilarious."

"I am?"

"Of course. You have your hands in people's dirty mouths all day."

Oh. Right. Denise is a dental assistant.

I force myself to look at him, to find something in the grooves around his smile, the crinkles at the corners of his eyes. A roadmap. Something that says I'm right and he's wrong. But I can't see it.

"Do you mind if I do something?" I ask.

He looks surprised. "Okay. What?"

Before he can react, I pull out my phone and snap a picture. The bar is dim enough that the flash goes off, earning me a few unwelcome glares, but I ignore them and study the screen. I captured him perfectly. I might not know his job, possibly not even his name, but I know his face. So someone else might.

He blinks rapidly, dazed. It's the first time in this whole relationship that I've truly caught him off guard. "What's happening?"

I concentrate on my phone, adding his picture to his contact. "I needed a picture to go with your phone number," I say. "How am I supposed to know which Chris is calling?"

He rubs his eyes. "You have a lot of Chrises in there?"

"I have a lot of everybodys. I'm very popular."

"Well," he says, reaching for his phone, resting on the table. "Turnabout's fair play."

I snag his wrist before he can take a shot. "No."

"Why not? You look fine."

"No."

"You look… beautiful?"

"I don't like pictures."

"You just took one."

"Of me. I don't like pictures of me."

"Why? Because you don't show up? Like a vampire?"

"No."

"Then why?"

I'm still holding his wrist, and now I force myself to let go, like it wouldn't be the end of the world if someone took a picture of me, even though it could be. When I wanted to be famous, I was in every picture I could manage, so popular people were sick of me. And now they're starving for news, and the last thing I need is something to remind them I exist, that the monster has yet to be slain.

If I've learned anything in three years of lying, it's to stick as close to the truth as possible, like pacing the perimeter of the rooftop without ever falling off, even if that would be easier for everyone. "I used to be in a lot of pictures," I say. "And now... I don't want to be. I'm different."

The last photos of me were the ones from Alex's funeral. He'd always joked that when he died—at age 101—he wanted a Viking burial, whatever that was, and a flash mob. Instead, he got me in a wheelchair, my leg in a cast, unable to run, though that's all I wanted to do. Instead I kept my head down, refusing to cry. Of course the papers said I didn't cry because I was a murderer, because I'd stolen the money and killed my brother and was a heartless, soulless sociopath. When I got home I dug myself in, built a metaphorical moat, and hid away like any monster would.

Chris doesn't look like he understands, but he doesn't argue. He places his phone on the table and turns it off. The generic sunset screensaver flickers before fading to black. Once done, he holds up his hands in surrender. "Okay. I respect your position. If I were you, I'd be desperate for a picture of me, too."

"Desperate is exactly the word."

"I know." A dimple flashes in his cheek. "Want to get out of here and respect me some more?"

Again, the wave of alarm ripples through me. How beautifully ironic that after years of self-loathing, it's the man who's lied to me most—most recently—who's reminded me that somewhere, deep down, there's a tendril of self-respect slowly unfurling and fighting its way to the surface.

"I didn't dress up just for one drink," I say. If I'm going to go through with this, I'll need courage. It worked all the other times.

157

Chris lifts an eyebrow. "You have to be drunk to sleep with me?"

"Just buzzed."

Now he laughs again, teeth glinting in the muted light. "See, I told you you were funny." But he raises his hand to call the server and orders another round.

"That was easy."

"At least one of us is."

Now it's my turn to laugh, something I hadn't intended to do, something that feels foreign. Strange. Nice. Wrong.

More drinks come, and we take our time. We don't talk about work or money or errands; none of the lies that litter the minefield of our pseudo-relationship. Chris tells me a story about his childhood, when he decided to help his mom by digging up all the beets in the garden so they could have them with dinner, but instead he accidentally dug up the dahlia tubers she'd planted and spent the whole night putting them back. I tell him about the time in elementary school when my dad discovered I'd been charging people five dollars to eat at my lunch table, and he made me donate the money to the school lunch program, which didn't even exist, since everyone who went to the school was a millionaire.

Chris struggles to finish his beer while laughing. "So you've always been delightful."

"That's one way to describe me."

"You ready to go?" He pushes the empty bottle aside, and I nod, even as all the warmth generated by the cocktail and conversation seeps out of me. I reach for my wallet, but Chris waves me off, leaving too much money on the table and standing to help me into my coat. "I meant it when I said you looked beautiful."

"You don't have to flatter me," I say, trying to piece my armor back together as fast as humanly possible. For three years, I've had a very simple mission: do nothing. And now I don't know what to do. Do I sleep with him and keep up the guise? I've done it before, I can do it again. But something in my chest tightens at the thought, begging me not to. It's that spark of the old Reese, the one I thought had been extinguished as she lay at the bottom of the cliff, blood in her hair, the lies that comprised my life sprinkled around me like so many pieces of glass.

I feel the soft press of Chris's fingers on my waist as we weave our way toward the door. It's only Tuesday, but the bar is packed, winter ushering everyone indoors. The cold air is a slap in the face when we get outside, and I shudder, folding my arms across my stomach.

"Where's your place?" Chris asks, glancing up and down the empty street. "Did you drive?"

"I took a cab," I lie.

"Okay." He lifts a hand to hail one, but when a car approaches, I wave it away, keeping my eyes on the ground when Chris turns to me. I don't need to see his face to know he's exasperated. That he wants to come over. See where I live. See if there's any truth to the rumors that there's money in the walls.

"What is it?" he asks. His breath hangs in the air between us, dissipating slowly, like his patience. I've made enough people unhappy to recognize the signs.

"Not tonight," I say finally.

A muscle in his cheek twitches, like he's gritting his teeth, but all he says is, "Fine, we'll go to my place. You okay to walk?"

"Not tonight," I repeat. "Not anything. I had a nice time, but I don't want this to be just about sex." If I weren't so painfully anxious, I'd laugh at the lie. All I ever wanted it to be about was sex. I didn't even want to know his name. And now I *need* to know. I need to know everything.

Chris's eyes widen appropriately at my unexpected attitude adjustment. "That's very different from what you've been saying."

"I changed my mind." My thighs start to ache from the cold and I rock on my feet to keep warm. My fingertips are already numb.

Then Chris smiles and takes half a step back. "I knew I could do it."

"Do what?"

"Make you want more. Lure you in with my charming personality and witty repartee."

"That's not it."

"Sway you with my cooking and good manners."

"You're so off base."

His smile expands. "I know the answer, but I'll ask anyway: can I walk you home?"

"No."

"Not even if I give you five dollars?"

My mouth twitches. "No."

"Wait while you call a cab?"

"No."

"Just tell me you're not married."

"I'm not married."

He studies me for a minute, then lifts a shoulder, giving in. "Okay, Denise. Have a good night. Be safe."

"Thanks. You, too."

We hesitate, because it feels wrong to part like this, like I came here because I don't trust him and I just somehow managed to talk myself into a more serious relationship. And now we can't merely shake hands and walk away like partners in a weird business merger, we have to make it real.

Chris acts first, lifting a hand to tip up my chin, his thumb cold on my skin. He brushes his lips softly over mine, and against all will and common sense, my body presses into him, wanting more, needing more.

But it will never be enough, now that I know it's a lie. My whole life was built on deceit, and when the chips fell, they fell hard. This time I've been forewarned. I can protect myself, in a way I couldn't before. If only I knew what the hell I needed protection from.

I move back, away from him. "Bye."

"Bye, Denise."

The traffic light changes, so I give Chris a quick wave and hurry across, pulling open the heavy metal door to the parking garage. I look back and he isn't following, though he is watching, brows drawn together contemplatively. He nods at me and stuffs his hands in his pockets before striding off in the direction of his apartment. I descend the stairs to the garage, my heels clicking on the concrete like gunshots.

If possible, it's colder in here than it is outside. The entrance to the heated walkways that connect the garages are at either end of the block, at least a hundred yards in each direction. I'm already shivering when I reach the base, intending to walk as fast as I can to the warmth of the tunnel, but something stops me. Call it instinct or intuition, but three years of not trusting anybody has taught me how to trust myself.

I weave through the luxury cars until I find one that's warm, then round to the front, between the hood and the brick wall, and wait, trying to use its lingering heat to stay comfortable. For a long minute, it's just me and the familiar scents of the garages, gasoline and rubber and exhaust.

And then I hear it.

The faint wheeze of the door opening upstairs.

Footsteps descending.

I crouch low, hiding behind the tire, so anyone peering beneath the cars can't see me. In my black ensemble and stilettos, I'm like every implausible cat burglar in every movie. As quietly as possible, I feel in my purse for my phone, turning it to silent.

The footsteps stop.

There's no jangle of car keys, no drunken reveler mumbling incoherently as they try to remember where they parked. Instead there's the sound of someone approaching slowly, carefully. After a second, they stop again, then retreat. I try to peek under the car but can't see anything, so I ease up to peer through the windows, spotting the back of Chris's green jacket, his tousled hair as he swivels his head, looking.

For me.

For several long moments, he doesn't move, and I realize he thinks I drove here, that he's listening for a car to start up, pull away, give him a license plate, a clue. But there are too many clues down here. Too many entrances, too many exits. I wait for him to retreat up the stairs, but he doesn't. He pulls out his phone, presses a button, and waits. I don't need to see my phone to know it's ringing.

When he doesn't get an answer, he mutters something and shoves the phone into his pocket, then turns abruptly and stalks back my way, taking a chance that it's the right direction.

I listen as his steps fade, inching up to see him approaching the door to the heated walkway, where he stops. He turns back, like he's not convinced of his decision, but the sound of the street door opening again and feet clattering down seems to decide for him. In a flash, he pulls open the door and slips through, taking care to close it quietly.

My knees and ankles ache with the cold, but I don't move. From my position, I watch through the car windows as two men emerge from the stairwell. They're both tall and thin, possibly twins, fluorescent light glancing off their smooth white scalps. They wear long dark coats and scowls and communicate wordlessly, a brisk nod sending one in each direction, toward the tunnels.

I make myself as small as I can, pressing between the car and the wall. After a minute, I hear doors slam, then silence. I grimace as I pull off my shoes and my bare feet touch icy pavement, toes curling painfully. The scar on my thigh throbs, reminding me that I've been hurt worse, and I stay ducked low as I dart toward the stairwell, bolting back up to street level and flagging down a passing cab. The driver stops, no doubt hoping a girl carrying her shoes in February is drunk enough to rip off, and I slide in the back, lying flat on the seats, like I'd done so many times in the past. Except this time I'm not fleeing anything as predictable as the paparazzi.

11

It's the last Saturday of the month, so I dress in dark jeans and a hoodie for my shift at the Food Bank, then toss a change of clothes in a bag for my trip to the prison. I grab a frozen pasta dinner from my mostly empty freezer, pretending I'll buy groceries later like a normal person and not a girl who's in a fake relationship with a guy who secretly follows her, with men who secretly follow him.

I call the elevator and wait impatiently. Now that I have a mission, I'm anxious to get it underway. I start to barge in the second the doors glide open, but I'm brought up short when one of Mr. Pedersen's "dates" gets off. My septuagenarian neighbor has no shortage of money or expensive company, and today's visitor is dressed in a miniscule scrap of gold fabric, her hair curled, lips plumped. Unlike me, she dresses to be seen, and like me, everyone's gaze slides right past her. When we lived in the penthouse, the building had a separate elevator for "special guests," so the moneyed residents didn't have to confront the realities of the world. After the FBI raided the place and took everything worth taking—and a lot of things that weren't—Alex and I had to ride the "special guest" elevator back to the ground floor, shouldering our way through the screaming mob so we could get to a hotel to regroup. Alex cried the whole way down.

Mr. Pedersen's date doesn't say anything as she slips past, and I step on for the ride down. I know other tenants have complained about Mr. Pedersen's visitors because I've spent many an afternoon with my ear pressed to the door as management had a "quiet word" with him about his extracurriculars. I could have complained too, but I'm not enough of a hypocrite to judge someone else's sex life.

I take the elevator to the parking garage, pulling my puffy black jacket tight around me as the freezing air pummels my skin. It's crisp and dry, promising snow, and I stride past the parking spot assigned to my suite, occupied by a gleaming black Lexus. I rent the spot to the guy in the next unit, who already owns the maximum three parking spaces. Anyone trying to reverse engineer my address by running plates will find just another investment banker anxious to showcase his wealth.

I hurry through the smells of rubber and gasoline, into the tunnel to the garage on the next block, and down to the second level, where I pay for two spaces. This is where I park my Mercedes. After all these years, it feels a bit like overkill to take so many precautions when coming to and from my apartment, but it's a routine now, and I take comfort in the ritual.

Of course, Chris has seen the car—he nearly crashed into it— but if he ever managed to track it to this location, he still wouldn't be able to find me. These plates are registered to my mother's apartment in the art district. It's been in her family since Holden was first built, and because the deed is in her name, it's one of the few things they couldn't take when they came for my father. It's been sitting dusty and abandoned for years, and if anyone's staking it out, they're in for a long, boring wait.

I make the twenty-minute trip to work, the sky managing to be both too gray and too bright. I pull up my hood as I drive and add a pair of sunglasses, flashing my middle finger at a few traffic cameras for old time's sake. If anything, it'll help me fit in. At the very least, it makes me smile.

There are a smattering of cars in the Food Bank parking lot, and I keep my head ducked against the cold as I hurry to the unremarkable concrete building. The security camera peers down at me, but I know it sees nothing.

I go to the kitchen to stick my lunch in the refrigerator, then make my way up front to sign in before a quiet morning of sorting and stocking. But instead of the usual staff divide of older ladies in front, everybody else in back, the dozen people assembled today are standing up front, mingling uneasily. Lola is there, too, pacing and muttering to herself.

I feel sick. For eighteen months I've wondered what would happen if they found out who I really was, how they'd react, what they would do. And even while my skin flushes hot and my heart pounds too hard, my common sense tells me this reaction is too much. So Reese Carlisle volunteers at the Food Bank. So her father's in prison. He stole two hundred million dollars, not boxes of generic cereal and day-old bananas.

I shuffle next to Rodney, who glances down at me.

"What's going on?" I whisper, my voice still too loud in the cavernous space.

"We got raided," he says from the corner of his mouth. He

keeps his eyes trained on Lola, like he might get blamed for it.

"Why?"

"Beats me."

We've had FDA inspections since I started, both scheduled, both uneventful, neither of which generated this type of reaction.

We continue to stand in an awkward, uncertain silence for another minute, until finally the sound of tires crunching over the frozen pavement interrupts, reminding us there's a business to run. Lola looks at her watch and, seeing the lost time, snaps out of it. Today her braids are thick and purple, shifting around like snakes. If I didn't already think she was scary, I'd be terrified.

"All right. Well, get to work then," she says, less venom in her voice than normal. "We've got work to do up here, and we've got lots to do back there. Salvage what you can, throw away what you can't, and let me know what you're unsure about. And be fast."

We turn to go, but Lola stops us. "And work together," she adds. "Rodney and R.C., Andre and Joanne, Devon and Gayle, Carlos and Susan." Even though Rodney is the only pseudo-friend I have here, I don't think for a second that Lola is pairing us up based on common interests. Quite the opposite—if we're not working with our friends, we'll focus. There's no way anyone in these partnerships has anything to gossip about with their new coworker.

Everyone is wise enough not to complain, vanishing into the warehouse in varying directions. Rodney and I automatically go to my corner, and that's when I finally see what's got everyone so shaken: we haven't been inspected; we've been *searched*.

The warehouse isn't trashed, but it's definitely been investigated. Open boxes of cereal sit on the floor, their plastic-sealed contents intact. Large bags of rice are sliced open, pallets upended, a hundred cases of tomato sauce opened to expose their harmless contents. A large box of melons has been cut down the side, honeydew and cantaloupes spilling onto the floor like oversized marbles.

I was here during one of the other inspections. They came in with their blue and yellow jackets, FDA stamped across the back. Just two guys marching around with Lola and her clipboard, making sure the fridges and freezers were set to temperature, the mouse traps were empty, the expiry dates were in order. A passing grade, a handshake, a goodbye.

This is much, much different.

I turn in a slow circle to take in the carnage. "Did they find anything?"

"Not that I could see," Rodney replies. "We all had to go up front to wait. They were sitting outside when we showed up. Wouldn't even let us back here."

I trail my finger along the open top of a family-size can of baby formula, the chalky white powder sticking to my finger. Ruined. "The FDA did this? Why? Why would they open boxes, spoil things?"

"It wasn't the FDA," Rodney says, as we reach my aisle. "It was the FBI."

My knees lock, my feet skid, and the whole room starts to spin. But it's not Rodney's words that do it, it's the degree of destruction that awaits me. The carelessly dumped boxes, split cans of garbanzo beans and mushrooms and corn leaking all over the floor. Unlike the rest of the warehouse, my aisle has been *destroyed.*

I know because I've seen this before. It happened to my home—all our homes—after my father was arrested. When they took everything just to take it. Computers and ledgers and cell phones, emptying shoeboxes and makeup bags, pouring out bottles of shampoo and conditioner like they might hold twenty million answers.

The FDA wasn't looking for anything at the Food Bank.

The FBI was looking for me.

No, not me. They know where I am. They always have. They just haven't been able to touch me because the district attorney made it clear they didn't have enough evidence for an arrest, never mind a conviction. But something has changed. Something—or someone—has convinced them I know where the money is.

"Reese? You all right?"

Only sheer willpower lets me pull in one breath, then another. I realize I'm gripping one of the metal shelves so tight my knuckles glow white, and I slowly force my fingers to relax. I count backwards from ten. I tell myself everything will be okay. If they'd found something, they'd still be here, waiting for me, like they've been waiting for three years.

But they'll be waiting for a long time.

There's no money in the Food Bank. Not in the cereal or the melons or the garbanzo beans. My dad had no investments here; I'm not even sure he donated. I'd volunteered elsewhere before the scandal, but I only started here a year and a half ago. If the FBI knew about this place at the time of the arrest, they'd have gotten a warrant and searched it long ago.

I think about Chris and his donation receipt. The broken

security cameras. The way he was waiting for me at the mechanic. If he knew about my job weeks ago, why wait until now to do this? What changed?

Rodney presses an industrial-size dustpan into my hand. "I'll sweep, you scoop," he says, gathering stray legumes into a pile.

"It's worse in this aisle," I say, crouching with the pan. "Worse than the rest."

"I know. It's because of me."

My mouth opens, but nothing comes out for five full seconds. Finally I manage, "What'd you do?"

"I told you how I've got a brother in prison, right?"

"Yeah."

"So I was visiting my brother, and he asked if I was going to do that cooking program, and I said no, I think I'm going to be a video game designer. He asked how I was going to afford to go to school when I work here for next to nothing, and I said, 'I got a plan.' And he said, 'Your plan is canned food?' And I said, 'There's money in canned food.' Then bam. This happened."

I try not to stare incredulously. "That doesn't even make sense."

"Why not? They listen in on those visits. And I've already got a record."

"Rodney, that—" There are so many levels on which his reasoning fails, but he's completely serious. Unlike me, Rodney was born with the odds stacked against him. I was born with everything I would ever need, and a million other things on top of that. And yet we've both ended up here. Both trying to figure how to get out.

But I can't tell Rodney the truth, or anything to assuage his conscience, because if Rodney believes his story, his friends believe it, and Lola believes it, and that means no one's blaming me.

"Why would you say there's money in canned food?" I ask, keeping my eyes down.

"Because my mom's friend does canning," he says. "Peaches, radishes, tomatoes—you name it, she cans it. She sells it at the Farmers' Market in the summer, but she printed up some labels and made a website and now she's got a little display at the grocery store, too."

"So you're going to take up canning?"

"No, I was going to steal some of the stuff from here and resell it at a discount. Not anymore, obviously."

"What? Rodney."

He grins. "Just kidding. She needs some help storing her stuff, setting up displays, putting on labels and whatever, and I've been working with her, saving some of my money."

"How much is the video design program?"

"About twenty grand for the year."

"And how much do you have saved?"

"Almost half."

"That's a lot of cans."

"I told you—that's where the money is."

I dump a dustpan full of ruined vegetables into our garbage bag. Opened cans rattle as Rodney sweeps them up, huge gashes in the lids. Even if there was money in canned food, there's no way anyone could have stored twenty million dollars in cans in the Food Bank without it being noticed. Though Holden is a wealthy city, and our location is smaller than many, we still go through a ton of food, and these cans rarely sit on the shelf for longer than a week.

Which means this was never about the search.

You only search when you think you'll find something.

This was a message.

"So," Rodney says, tossing a can in a high arc toward the garbage bag and clapping his hands when he sinks it. "Now you know my big plans. What about you?"

I try not to tense. My big plans, my future—those are not comfortable subjects. Hell, the past and the present aren't much better. "What about me?"

Rodney looks at me like I'm obtuse. "How'd your big date go?"

"Oh. That." It's pathetic, but being asked about my phony relationship is better than being asked about my real life, and some of the tension in my shoulders eases.

"Yeah. That. What'd you do?"

"It was fine. We went to a show. Looked at art."

Rodney makes a face. "Sounds boring."

"You're boring."

"Am not."

"It was a show about the environment."

"Please stop."

"There were dragons."

Now Rodney's laughing. "Okay," he says. "Now I know you're lying. There was no date. No one would ever want to go out with you."

"It's the truth," I tell him. And I laugh, even as his words hit a little too close to home.

≫ ≫

I leave the Food Bank at two o'clock, when my shift ends. There's a lot of work left to do for the clean-up, but we've made progress. I managed to find Lola on my lunch break and ask about the search warrant, but she was flustered and merely waved a stack of forty typed pages in my face, no clue about its specifics. Not yet. But give her time to read through and she'll find my name, or enough of it to connect the dots and realize I'm the reason for this mess. And many others.

I've made the drive to Wakeman so many times it's muscle memory at this point, which is a blessing, since my mind is traveling a dangerous path of its own. It's only when I pass the turn-off for the agricultural college that I realize how close I am. The road is deserted, so I pull off to the side and grab my change of clothes from the backseat, swapping my jeans and hoodie for a white blouse and fitted red pants with matching lipstick. I add some blush and mascara, and study my reflection in the rearview mirror. It's been a long time since I've done this. Since I've tried. Since I wanted someone to see me and remember it.

I stare back at some imagined spot in the distance, where I let Chris fuck me against the trunk of my car. Unlike that night, when I swore I wanted nothing and felt nothing, the memory fills me with something hot and seething, my blood turning to lava in my veins. And though he's a liar and a bunch of other things I haven't figured out yet, Chris is not the one I'm most angry with. I put myself in this position. In *that* position.

I start the car and turn on the radio, flipping through the stations until I find one playing something inane and upbeat, a bunch of rhyming words that don't need to make sense as long as they're catchy. I try my best to let go of my anger and relax; I need to look happy if this visit is going to yield results. I need to look like I'm in love.

The music's not enough, of course, and when I flash a smile at the guard and collect my visitor's parking pass, he flinches, not used to the expression. Neither am I, apparently, because when I park in the half-empty lot and practice my brightest smile, I look like a possessed ventriloquist dummy. I tone it down so I'm not showing teeth, managing to appear marginally less frightening, then put on a pair of black heels and get out. It's cold but I leave my coat behind, taking only my purse. It's tempting just to get back in the car and drive anywhere but here, but that's the coward's way out. Running is Plan B. Getting answers is Plan A. And not only am I here for answers, I finally have a plan.

I square my shoulders. I feel like a boxer climbing into the ring against a far more skilled opponent, knowing everyone in the arena has bet against me. That's where the money is, after all. Still, I stroll inside like I don't have a care in the world, like I'm the Reese Carlisle of three years ago and none of this really matters.

The familiar smells of sweat and antiseptic assault me when I enter, heels clipping on the cheap floors as I approach the desk to sign in. Hilroy glances up as I near, his eyes widening so much at my changed appearance that they nearly disappear behind his fleshy cheeks.

I offer a bashful smile. "Hi."

"Uh… Hey." He looks mystified by my bright and shiny new look.

"I'm here to visit Kimball Carlisle. I'm on the list."

Hilroy shakes his head and refocuses. "Yeah. Yeah, I know. One second."

I take out my burner phone while I wait and study the screen, sending three texts to my real phone. *Miss you already. Can't wait to see you. Love you.* I'll delete them when I get home.

"You checking your bag?" Hilroy asks, sliding over the sign-in sheet and a pen.

"Um, yeah. Totally." I turn off my phone and drop it into my purse, then grab my wallet and fish out a couple of bills before passing over the bag.

He sticks it in a cubby, hands me a chit, and waves me over to the metal detector. I've done this enough that I no longer bother wearing jewelry. The machine is silent, but Hilroy dutifully swipes his wand over my front and back anyway, polite and professional, nodding when nothing registers.

"You look different," he remarks, motioning for me to follow him down the hall. A heavy key ring hangs from his belt loop, dragging his already sagging pants down even farther.

"I feel different," I say, studying my fingernails. "I feel... happy."

"Oh yeah?"

"I met someone."

"That's nice."

I give myself a little shake, like I'm remembering where I am. "I'm sorry. I shouldn't say stuff like that when I'm...here. There's no reason for me to..."

"Nah." Hilroy uses the laminated badge hanging around his neck to swipe us into the visitors room. "It's fine. It's good. Good for you."

"Thanks." Inwardly, I'm groaning. It's been three years since I've been this girl, and it's taking a lot of effort to slip back into my old role.

The room is half-full when I walk in, and while I garner a few stares from fellow visitors and inmates, only the female guard stationed in the corner does a double-take. I sit at our usual table on the left, counting backwards from ten, then a hundred, as I wait for my father to arrive. Finally there's a click as the heavy metal door unlocks, and he comes in, his mustard yellow jumpsuit at odds with his pasty skin, giving him an even more sickly pallor. Still, he brightens when he sees me.

"Hi," I say, getting to my feet.

"Pieces." He hugs me gently, but I'm not the one who's fragile. I can feel his shoulder blades through the coarse fabric, the jut of his cheekbone pressing into my temple. He steps back and takes me in. "You look gorgeous."

"Thank you."

"Very... bright."

"I feel bright."

"Is that right?"

I don't elaborate. "How are you?"

We take our seats on opposite sides of the table, my father's bony fingers splaying across the Formica top, a dozen other oily fingerprints glinting in the neon lights.

"I'm, uh, I'm doing okay," he says, unconvincing.

"What's wrong?"

"Oh, you know."

"Not enough chicken ramen?"

He laughs politely. "Maybe too much chicken ramen."

"You want me to get something from the vending machine?"

"Yeah, sure. Grab whatever you want."

I stand and cross the room, taking the two bills from my pocket and smoothing them between my fingers as I study the selection. I settle on a package of knock-off gummy bears and a tray of peanut butter and crackers. I pay with the five dollar bill, keeping the single in my hand as I collect my change and my snacks and return to the table. I glance at the guard, but she's watching a couple trying to discreetly grope each other near the far wall.

I rejoin my dad and spread our feast on the table, keeping the dollar bill between us. He reaches over to open the crackers, carefully smearing one with peanut butter, then passing it to me. "Here," he says. "I made you something."

My mouth twitches. "You shouldn't have."

He smiles too, then concentrates on his task as he makes another cracker, then lines it with three gummy bears, sitting them in the peanut butter. "Remember when I used to make you ants on a log?" he asks.

"Yeah," I say. "Alex said it was supposed to be flies on a log."

"Nah. It was ants. I know because I collected them from the garden."

I laugh, thinking about his sad cooking attempts, always borne of guilt when the nanny chastised him for letting us subsist on take-out and processed food. Celery sticks stuffed with peanut butter and dotted with raisins was his specialty. Another skill I inherited.

"Weren't you volunteering this morning?" he asks, gesturing to my outfit.

"Yes. I changed on the way over."

"You like that place?"

"I really like it," I tell him. "But something happened today."

He watches me. "What?"

"It got raided."

"Like, inspected?"

"No, like raided. And torn apart. Like our homes. By the FBI."

He stops, mid-chew. "What would the FBI want with the Food Bank?"

"Twenty million dollars."

If it's possible, he manages to go even more still. "Did they find it?"

I think about Rodney, telling me they bug these rooms. The tables. The phones. "Of course not. It's not there."

"Where is it?"

"You tell me." If I thought three years was enough time to let go of the anger I feel for what my father's greed did to our lives, I'm mistaken. For a long time I haven't felt much of anything at all, but as soon as the emotional gates crack open, resentment does its best to shove through.

"Pieces, I—"

"I don't want to talk about this." My eyes fill with tears, not entirely part of the performance.

He reaches over to pat my hand. "I know," he says carefully. "But maybe…we need to."

"Why would we need to?"

"Because I'm in trouble."

I gesture to the prison visitation room. "No kidding."

"Piece—"

"Don't call me that."

He sighs. "Reese. I need some help."

"How much help?"

"A lot."

"The legal team is doing everything they can."

"I can't wait for them much longer. I need money."

"How much? I've been investing what I have. It's not much, but it's something."

"More than that."

"How much more?"

He looks at me meaningfully. "A lot more."

"I told you," I say, my voice shaking. "I told everybody. I don't have *more*. And I don't know where to get it."

One of the tendons in his neck twitches, the way it does when he's angry. When he thinks he's being lied to.

But I'm not the only liar at this table.

"I can give you a dollar," I offer, sliding the bill across.

His eyes narrow. "What?"

I smooth it flat, the paper soft and crinkled. I'd made six of these yesterday, printed them off, crumpled them up, and tossed them in with a load of laundry. Washed and dried, picked the best one. Financial crimes: the Carlisle specialty.

My dad cocks his head, trying to figure out what I'm doing, then slowly reaches over to take the bill, studying it. He turns it in his hand, and before he speaks, I have my answer. They'd televised his court appearances, cameras zooming in on his face, purported experts discussing how to tell when someone is lying. There's the telltale tic near his left eyebrow, the way his mouth tightens, then relaxes. Still, I ask, "Do you know who that is?"

"No," he says, too quickly. He's staring at Chris's picture, printed on the back of the bill, the shot of him from the bar, looking too handsome, too deceitful. We're just a table of liars.

I give him another chance. "You've never seen him before?"

My dad folds the money, hiding Chris's face, and puts it down before picking up another gummy bear. "No," he says calmly. "Who is he?"

I slip the money into my pocket. "He's my new boyfriend."

If it were possible for the table to split in half and open up a chasm between us, that's what the words would do, and it would be a blessing. As it stands, we continue to make strained small talk for the next fifteen minutes, then I make my excuses to go. His hug, this time, is less delicate. This time it hurts.

I stride down the hall to the waiting area to collect my things, heart pounding so hard I swear Hilroy can see it through my blouse. I'm sweating, an uncomfortable trickle running over my ribs before catching in my waistband.

"Good visit?" Hilroy asks, accepting my chit and retrieving my purse.

"The best." I pick up the pen and initial next to my check-out time. I'm not in the mood to smile anymore, to flirt, to pretend. But as I turn to go, I get one more idea. I dig deep, for the old Reese Carlisle, and dredge her up, dirt and bones and no sense of self-preservation.

"Don't tell anyone," I whisper, returning to the desk and biting my lip as I pull out my phone.

Hilroy raises his eyebrows but doesn't say a word as I turn the screen so he can see Chris's picture. Then his brows raise up even farther, right into his hairline. "How do you—"

"That's who I'm seeing."

"You—"

"Can you believe it?"

He's shaking his head, very slowly. "Not really."

I'm struggling to breathe. *Not really.* But it is real, isn't it? Everything that's been happening is all too real. Hilroy recognizes Chris because Chris comes to the prison. And there's only one person at the prison who knows me and where to find me.

"I know it's weird," I make myself say, trying to smile like I'm happy. Like I can even remember how that feels. "But… it's good." I nearly choke on the word.

"Then, uh, I'm happy for you."

I give a little pout and push a bit more. "He's so busy, though. You probably see him more than I do."

Hilroy's tone is almost apologetic. "Sometimes, but he doesn't visit as much, anymore."

My ears ring and my knees turn to putty, nausea welling in my throat. It's the answer I was expecting, but being right doesn't fill me with the same smug satisfaction it once did. I hide my reaction and turn the phone to study the screen, the handsome face gazing back blandly. I look down the hall that leads to the visitors room. Then I nod, letting it all sink in. "That's good to know."

12

I'm extra paranoid on my ride home, turning without warning, slipping in and out of parking garages I know like the back of my hand. I don't catch anyone following me, and it's only when I'm confident no one could have succeeded—even if they wanted to—that I park in my rented spot, heart pounding from the imaginary chase. I dart through the chilly garages until I reach my own block, then jab the elevator call button.

My phone rings, the shrill tone more jarring than a gunshot, and I snatch it out of my bag and swipe the screen without thinking it through. Anyone I might have lost on my convoluted way home could follow the sound, and I need it to stop. It's only when I hear Chris's voice that his photo comes into focus.

"Denise?" he says, when I don't say anything. "Are you there?"

The elevator doors slide open, and I jump in. I press the button for the fourteenth floor and relax approximately one iota. "Yes," I say eventually. "I'm here. I'm just getting home."

"Oh. Where were you?"

"Visiting a friend. What are you up to?"

"Not much. I'm calling to see if you want to get together soon. For a non-sexual date. We could see a movie. Go bowling. Play cards."

"Who could say no to those tempting offers?"

"When are you free? Tonight?"

The elevator stops at my floor and I get off, keys in hand, just as Mr. Pedersen and his latest lady friend emerge from his apartment. He's wearing a shiny black robe and she's in a red halter dress, blond hair twisted in a bun on top of her head. I ignore them and they ignore me, and I let myself into my apartment and lock the door.

"Denise?"

"Sorry," I say. "Tonight's no good. How about Friday?"

"That's a long way off."

"I told you, I'm very popular."

"And I believe you. I'm working Monday—what about Tuesday?"

I press my eye to the peep hole and cringe as I see Mr. Pedersen locking lips with his date, one bony hand gripping her barely-covered ass.

"Wednesday," I say. I don't know what I'm going to do to figure out who Chris is by then, but I'll have to come up with something, and each extra day seems essential for a person with no experience identifying her boyfriend-stalker.

"Wednesday works. What do you want to do? See a movie? I can pick you up at your place and we can go to that old theater on the edge of the town that shows black and white movies."

The last thing I'm going to do is go to any old building on the edge of town where there's nobody to witness whatever Chris plans to do to me. I don't know what he's up to, or who the fuck he is, but this morning's raid and my father's desperation tell me that whatever it is, there's not much time left.

"Come over," I say. "I'll make dinner." I turn away from the peep hole to contemplate my kitchen, knowing the cupboards are bare.

There's a satisfying pause as the words sink in. "You—I—What?"

"I'll make dinner," I repeat. "What's your favorite food?"

A pause. "Roast chicken. With potatoes."

"Is that popular in Maryland?"

"I'm from Montana, and it's popular everywhere."

"All right. Chicken and potatoes. Your wish is my command."

"That's what I like to hear. What's your address?"

"I'll text it."

"Right. And should I bring anything?"

"Just your charming self."

"Easy enough. I'll see you Wednesday, Denise."

"It's a date, Chris."

I end the call and watch his picture disappear, returning to the generic sunset screensaver. Then I think about his phone, with the same picture. Probably a burner, like mine. I think of his apartment. No personal photos. Like mine.

I kick off my shoes and cross to my desk, contemplating the lined paper with *Who Are You?* scrawled at the top of the page, the question still unanswered. I think again of the plants that lined the windows of his apartment when Chris knew I was coming over, the same plants that were missing the second time, the visit unplanned. I watched Alex decorate enough cheap sets to recognize someone staging a scene. Chris's apartment might not even be his primary residence, but the day I waited for him out front, he showed up, not expecting to see me. So maybe it *is* his home, albeit a temporary one. And maybe that's where the answers are.

A high-pitched giggle sounds in the hall, as though Mr. Pedersen and his date are laughing at my desperate, unhinged plan.

>>> >>>

I've been accused of dressing like an escort before, but those were just jealous people and tabloid editors trying to get attention they didn't deserve. The truth is, if you're the right kind of escort, nobody notices you at all. For my one and only attempt at faux high-end prostitution, I wear a fitted black dress that hits at the knee, the front cut so deep it nearly exposes my navel. The thin leather straps that criss-cross the torso are a half-assed attempt at modesty, just as the shiny black vinyl boots are a nod to the cold weather. I choose a honey gold wig with long, loose curls to shield my face, and a pair of oversized sunglasses to hide my darting eyes. All told, I'm wearing fifty-nine dollars worth of clothing, ordered online with expedited shipping and a grimace.

I parade back and forth in front of the full-length mirror in my bedroom, and it's appalling. I'm dressed the part, but I look more like a newborn giraffe figuring out how legs work than a seasoned professional. My stomach is tangled in knots, and I haven't stopped sweating since I put on the dress, its polyester smell making my nose itch.

It's Monday afternoon, the day Chris said he was working,

and two days before our phony dinner date. If today goes well and I find what I'm looking for—not that I have any idea what that might be—I'll toss the burner phone, quit the Food Bank, write my father letters instead of visiting, and vanish all over again.

I dab at my underarms with a tissue, scowling at my reflection and telling myself to get a grip. This will technically be my first time breaking and entering, but the ring of master keys currently tucked in my purse has seen plenty of use. I don't know if I've ever been in this particular apartment illegally, but Alex and I took serious advantage of our keys to the city, so I have some experience strolling into buildings in which I have no business being. If they've changed the locks since reselling the apartments, I'll just stroll back out and dream up a plan B.

I shrug into a dark trench coat, grab my new silver sequined purse, and make sure the hallway is clear before hurrying out and calling the elevator. I keep my head ducked, so anyone who sees me will assume I'm just another one of Mr. Pedersen's special friends.

I ride down alone and cut through two parking garages in record time. At this point, all I'm guilty of are crimes against fashion, but I still jump at the sound of every car door slam and engine starting, convinced my heels clicking over concrete obscures Chris's stealthy approach. I shoulder check a dozen times until I nearly walk into a pillar, then give up the pretense and climb the stairs above-ground, four blocks from his building.

I linger in the stairway vestibule where it's quiet and pull out my burner phone, find my lone contact, and press Call. It rings twice before Chris answers, managing to sound pleasantly surprised. "Hello? Denise?"

"Hey," I say, forcing myself to smile and hoping the emotion translates sincerely. "How are you?"

"I'm great, now that you're calling. What's up?" I can hear noises in the background, muffled ambient sounds, like he's out somewhere, which he's supposed to be.

"I'm sorry to bother you," I say. "Are you at work?"

"Ah, yeah, but I have a minute."

"I'm calling to ask if you have any allergies."

A pause. "Allergies?"

"Yes. Is there anything you can't have? Peanuts? Shellfish? I'd hate for you to break out in hives the first time I cook for you."

"Oh, ah—"

"Or worse," I add. "You could die. One time at work at the dental office we had a patient who didn't know he was allergic to the anesthesia, and he nearly died in the chair. He turned blue and everything. I don't want that to happen to you."

There's another pause, and it sounds like he might be trying not to laugh. When he finally speaks, he says, "No allergies. Thanks for checking."

"Oh, you're welcome. I'll see you Wednesday, Chris."

"See you then. Denise."

I might be imagining the pause before my name, but maybe not.

I put the phone on silent and drop it in my bag, then walk out onto the busy sidewalk and raise my hand for a taxi. Three empty cabs cruise past, steadfastly ignoring me and my vinyl boots, until the fourth one recognizes the hundred dollar bill in my hand and stops. I slip into the back and pass up the money as I give the driver Chris's address. We make the three-minute trip in silence.

I shiver again when I climb out in front of Chris's building and cover the ten feet to the entrance. The doorman holds the door but turns away, not bothering to hide his disgust, and I fleetingly wonder who he'd scorn more: an escort or Reese Carlisle? The thought amuses me, giving me a tiny boost of confidence as I cross the lobby. It's not terribly busy mid-afternoon on a Monday, and I approach the concierge with all the nonchalance I can muster for a first-time cat burglar.

"912," I say, giving him Chris's suite number. "He's expecting me."

There's a sign-in book, but the concierge doesn't pass it over, wanting no official record of this visit. "Have a nice afternoon," he says, staring over my shoulder at a tacky water feature.

Invisible eyes follow me as I enter the mirrored elevator and avoid my own gaze. I select the ninth floor and feel in my bag for the heavy key ring, clutching it in my palm like a weapon. There are two dozen silver keys on it, enough to unlock ninety percent of the city's residential units. It's remarkably unsafe, but when you have enough money, you can access whatever you want.

The elevator dings as it stops. I step into the hallway, and my cheap heels sink into the carpet, muffling my approach. Chris's unit is at the end, and I hold my breath as I pass each door on the way, waiting for someone to jump out and accost me.

No one does.

My hands are sweaty, fingers trembling, as I stop at his door and force myself to knock. If he answers, I'll pretend it's a kinky new sex game, then get cold feet, make my excuses, and run away. If he answers, we're both caught.

The three sharp raps echo in the hallway, but no sounds come from inside the unit. No television, no footsteps, no voices. I knock again, just in case, but again I'm greeted with silence. Glancing around carefully, I slip the first key in the lock, and turn.

It doesn't move.

I tug out the key and try the next one. No luck.

The third.

The fourth.

I'm sweating profusely, hot drops slicking down my sides.

The eighth key works.

The click of the lock turning is deafeningly loud, vibrating up my arm. I stand frozen for several long seconds before I twist the knob and push. The door swings open.

I flinch, waiting for a growling Doberman or a gun or even a shout of surprise, but of course none of that happens. Chris doesn't have a dog, and city gardeners don't have guns, and he's at work. I slip inside and lock the door behind me, taking in the familiar space. It doesn't feel like the den of a nefarious con artist or a swindler or a criminal, but then again, neither did our penthouse, and look how that turned out.

The kitchen is tidy, no food or dishes left on the counters. There's a sweatshirt draped over the couch and a jacket hung on one of the dining chairs, but otherwise, everything is neatly ordered. The plants are nowhere to be seen.

I start my search in the bedroom, which, like the other rooms in here, is tidy. The bed is made, dirty laundry piled neatly in the bin, an alarm clock and half-full water bottle waiting on the nightstand. I pull open the closet and see two suits hanging, shirts and ties ready and waiting, in case he needs to get dressed quickly. I peer in the nightstand drawers, but apart from an open box of condoms, they're empty.

A quick scan of the dresser reveals the generic T-shirts, socks, and underwear I'd originally predicted, as well as a few flannel shirts, a Yankees jersey, and a roll of cash wrapped in an elastic band. I figure it's approximately $4000, assuming it's all hundreds. More than the average person might keep in their sock drawer, but this is Holden City, and here it's barely enough to cover a night on the town.

I go through the cabinets in the bathroom, even checking under the toilet lid in case there's a gun taped there, like I've seen in the movies. But there's not. I peer under the bed, then hoist up the mattress, finding nothing more than a stray sock, and smooth the duvet when I put it back down.

I have no success in the guest bathroom, and the kitchen reveals little past the peanut butter crackers he'd confessed to enjoying, an untouched six-pack of Corona, and a steak marinating in a sealed plastic bag.

Ten minutes later, all I've learned is that Chris is freakishly neat, doesn't own plants, and knows how to marinate. I came here not knowing what I'd find, but all I've found are the regular trappings of a rather boring bachelor who doesn't work at the agricultural college.

And that's when it hits me. There's nothing here. No work product. No papers to grade, no text books, no books at all. And the laptop that sat on the dining table on my previous visits is nowhere to be seen. I whirl around, taking in the apartment with new eyes. He might have taken the laptop with him, wherever he is. But if not, then he didn't know I was coming and so had no reason to hide it. Maybe he takes it to coffee shops to draft his evil plans. Maybe he tucks it in a drawer, out of sight. Or maybe, like any boring bachelor, he takes it with him to the couch, resting it on his knees as he jerks off to whatever flavor porn he likes.

The couch sits in the middle of the apartment, facing the large flat screen television mounted on the wall, which makes it easy to spot the laptop wedged between the side of the couch and the end table, like it's waiting to be investigated. I scoop it up, knowing this is my last chance. If I don't find whatever it is I'm looking for here, I'll never find it.

I rest the laptop on the back of the couch and flip it open, hitting the power key and waiting impatiently as it wakes up. The screen comes to life slowly, my heart hammering as I glance at the door a hundred times, expecting the worst.

As though it knows it's torturing me, the screen flickers black, then gray, easing into a murky blue. The little wheel icon spins leisurely.

And that's when I hear it.

Keys jiggling. Metal on metal. The lock turning.

I drop to the floor like a corpse. The couch offers minimal coverage, and I have nowhere to go. If Chris takes six steps into the apartment, he'll see me. Even if, by some miracle, he goes to his bedroom, in the opposite direction, I'll still have to make it to the door without being seen or heard.

The door swings open and he enters, and the world comes to

a screeching halt. I'm completely exposed and pathetically defenseless. All I have is this stupid laptop now asking me for a password I don't know. Even if I could guess, it's unlikely Chris has a folder on his desktop called "Reese Carlisle Plan." What he does have, however, is a sticker stuck to the side of the keyboard, worn and faded, the edge peeling up like he's worried it with his thumb. It's the only sticker on the entire machine, the only sticker in the whole apartment. It's a pair of tiger wings.

Chris hums to himself as he kicks off his shoes, hangs up his coat, and pauses.

I slouch as low as I can, not that it matters. The back of the couch opens onto the entire room. I'm a sitting duck. Very carefully, I close the laptop and slip it back into place by the table. At least if he finds me, he might not know I touched the laptop.

Then, incredibly, I hear his footsteps move in the opposite direction. For a moment there's quiet, then the click of the bathroom door closing. My sticker discovery momentarily turned my terror into shock, but now adrenaline floods back in and I bolt to my feet, clambering for the door and bursting into the hallway, not bothering to worry about noise. I forego the elevator and dash to the stairwell, rocketing down three flights as best I can in my boots, the cheap vinyl chafing my calves.

When I finally pause on the sixth floor landing I'm gasping, thighs screaming. It's hard to tell over the sound of my labored breathing, but I don't think he followed me. I'm alone. I need a minute to regain my strength and process what I found, but I don't dare risk it. Not now. Instead I exit into the hallway, joining an elderly couple as they wait for the elevator. The husband gives me a nod, but the wife stares straight ahead, as though I'm invisible.

We ride down in silence and I drag in great gulping mouthfuls of damp winter air when I reach the street. I shrug into my coat and put on my sunglasses, walking in the opposite direction of my apartment, both out of habit, in case someone's watching me, and because I need time to think. I rack my brain to try to remember if the theater kept any of the memorabilia from Alex's time running the place, any free pamphlets or pins or stickers that Chris might have picked up from our visit. But I know they didn't. The new owners, like everyone in town, were desperate to erase the memory of the Carlisles.

But Chris isn't. I don't know how he knew about Tiger Wing, but he did. That explains his weird reaction to me bringing him there—he's not afraid of puppets. He's afraid of being found out. Because the sticker is not just a decoration, no more than my maps are simply there for the pleasure of looking at them. It's a reminder. A motivator. And the only connection between me and Tiger Wing is Alex.

13

I hate cleaning, but desperate times call for desperate measures. This I know too well. It's why I'm in my mother's apartment, a stuffy one-bedroom on the east side of town. Alex lived here up until a year or so before the scandal, preferring the illusion of living like his creative counterparts. Unlike his artist friends, however, he lived on a trust fund, not tips made waiting tables. When the novelty wore off, he came back to the penthouse. He said it was because he missed my dad's cooking; I said it was because he missed me too much to stay away. Only one of us was joking. Only one of us was wrong.

The bedroom closets hold plastic-draped dresses from my mother's most memorable performances, cartons of heels and ballet flats in near-perfect condition, boxes of hats and costume jewelry. My dad couldn't bear to part with her things when she passed, so he stashed them here, knowing he couldn't very well bring dates home to an apartment that was still a shrine to his dead wife.

The rest of the apartment is normal and unremarkable, if a decade out of date and more than a bit dusty. I haven't been here in years, but we continue to pay the bills, so the power is on but the fridge is empty and there's no cable. I open every window, letting the cold winter wind sweep in to clear the air as best it can.

Tomorrow is my date with Chris, and this is the address I'm going to text him a few hours before we're due to meet. By then there'll be food in the fridge, a newspaper on the coffee table, and a towel in the bathroom, just like a real home. In the morning, I'll buy a roast chicken at the store, mash potatoes, warm up a pie, then slip a few crushed sleeping pills into his beer, handcuff him to a chair, and torture him until he tells me who he is and what he wants and why he's doing this.

Then we'll go from there.

I've been accused of a lot of things, torture not among them, and for good reason. I've never hurt anyone, even if the guilt does its best to convince me otherwise. I couldn't sleep for a week after my father's arrest, and not for a full month after Alex's death. It was only when I went to get my cast removed and the doctor got a good look at me that he prescribed a high dose sleeping pill which, at the very least, would knock me out long enough to help me forget the urge to jump off the roof. I didn't take them, because even if people were willing to let me forget, I didn't want to. I needed to remember. I'd been oblivious to things for too long. Never again.

It takes two hours, but eventually the apartment looks comfortably lived-in. The green velvet sofa faces a wall of bookshelves and a vase of drooping tulips sits on the small wooden dining table. The striped drapes are pulled back to reveal the second floor of the art gallery across the street. A scented candle waits on the bedside table, a box of condoms beside it, the sleeping pills tucked into the medicine cabinet. It smells like lemon and bleach and every surface shines, sanitized to surgical standards.

I have three sets of handcuffs stashed in one of the kitchen drawers, along with a package of plastic zip ties for back-up. There's also a hammer, two knives, and a small blow torch—everything I could buy at the hardware store without drawing unwanted attention. I'm taking my torture tips from the movies.

The rest I'll improvise.

>>> >>>

The next morning, as planned, I visit the grocery store to stock up for my big date. Chicken, potatoes, asparagus, French bread, two bottles of wine, a six-pack of beer. I still get my groceries delivered sometimes, but if something goes wrong with the plan and Chris is found tied to a chair surrounded by a half-eaten meal, I don't want a delivery boy remembering my order.

The grocery store is overpriced but close to my apartment, so I walk home with my bags instead of taking a cab. It's the beginning of March, and the first signs of spring are finally starting to appear. Snowdrops and daffodils fight their way through the frozen earth, wealthy bankers shed their designer winter wear for the new spring fashions, and everything feels briskly, brightly alive.

Except me, of course. I'm dressed in basic black, sunglasses shielding my face, eyes on my feet. I manage two blocks aboveground before anxiety overtakes me and I duck into a stairwell, immediately feeling my nerves ease. I cover the rest of the distance to my apartment underground, then pause and pull out my burner phone, calling up Chris's contact and staring at his picture before sending a text with my mother's address. *See you soon,* I add.

He replies right away. *Can't wait.*

I stuff the phone back into my pocket and use my elbow to hit the elevator button. It arrives quickly, and I get in, traveling alone to the fourteenth floor and entering my quiet apartment. For three years this place has felt like a jail cell, but now it feels like a sanctuary, my paranoia an unnecessary precaution that's finally justified.

I toss my coat on the couch and drop the bags on the floor, then move down the hall to take a shower to prepare for the evening. I condition my hair and shave my legs and moisturize all over—just a woman hoping to please her boyfriend. He'll be happy until the pills kick in.

I have an hour until I leave for my mother's place, so I crack open the cheese plate I bought and make myself a snack, studying my maps as I chew. I admire their myriad holes, my expert marksmanship.

I collect the red dart and toss it at the world map, sinking somewhere into the blue expanse of the Philippine Sea. I approach and peer at it, seeing that I've landed on a miniscule island called Yap. I sit at my computer and look it up. It's part of the Federated States of Micronesia. It has an airport and white beaches and coral reefs home to manta rays and sharks. It does not have an extradition agreement with the United States. It has potential.

I retreat to my bedroom to get dressed for my date. Denise

has worn black on most of our meetings, so I stick with tradition and slip into a little black dress with a fitted top and flared skirt that hits at the knee. For kicks, I wear the same pearls I wore to interrogate Doug, and add some blush and mascara, since Chris liked it the last time. The whole thing takes five minutes, and when I'm done I look like Denise. The only change is in the eyes, and only if you know what you're looking for.

For years, I've been unable to stare at my reflection, sickened by its deceit and disappointment. By Allison and Bianca and Charlotte and all the characters I've played. But today Reese Carlisle gazes back, equal parts fire and ice. Then I smile, and the fury melts away, hidden from view but far from gone.

On my way back to the living room, I pause at the second bedroom, the shrine to my family's failures. I hesitate in the doorway and study the photos, the articles, the accusations. The questions. *So many* questions, most designed to be inflammatory, some edging close to the truth, but never quite close enough. Did you know your father was stealing money, Reese? Did you kill your brother, Reese? Do you know where the money is, Reese?

I shut the door on the memories and draw in a breath. Enough questions. It's time for answers.

I add nude heels to one of the grocery bags, then slip into a pair of sparkly silver flats. My mother's apartment is a twenty-minute walk from here, too far with the food, and I don't want a cab driver to recall picking me up at this address or dropping me off at hers, so I'll walk a few blocks both ways to cover my tracks.

I grab my purse, then balance the bags on one hip as I reach for the door and pull it open.

I stumble to a halt. The hallway warps; fat, thin, fat again. My vision blurs, the lights too bright, then too dim. Sound fades to a distant roar. An errant potato pops out and rolls across the floor, coming to a stop under a blue sneaker.

I look up very, very slowly.

He's wearing the green jacket over a flannel shirt and a pair of jeans. His hands are in his pockets, and he waits patiently for me to meet his eye, my mouth open, useless. The lies gone.

He smiles slightly, but it doesn't reach his eyes. "Hi, Reese."

WHY

14

"You—I—" My mouth is dry. I stare like a moron. How many times had I hoped to hear Chris say my name? But not like this.

He waits for me to finish, but when it becomes obvious I can't think of anything more to add, he shrugs, giving up on the idea. "Am I early?"

I can barely breathe. "Why are you here?"

"You live here."

"I texted you—I told you—"

And then his gaze hardens, just enough that I know it hasn't all been in my head. Somewhere, somehow, all along, I knew. I just didn't trust myself enough to believe it.

"You told me a lot of things," he says, bending slightly to snag the handle of the large black duffel bag he's been keeping out of sight. He straightens and steps toward me, and I hold up a hand as though that could stop him.

"Don't come in here," I order. "Don't even think—" I drop the grocery bags and move back inside. I try to shut the door but Chris just presses past me, letting my hand dig into his chest, showing me how weak I am compared to him, how defenseless.

How this stupid tower has no one to guard it, how I'm the jester, not the hero.

He nudges stray potatoes inside with his feet, then uses his heel to kick the door shut, and for a second I just stare at it, not quite certain how the hell this happened. With the exception of the building manager dropping by to discuss Mr. Pedersen's X-rated visitors, I've never had a guest. I've never wanted one.

I reach for the knob again. I can't be that dumb girl in the horror movie who runs upstairs. I have to try.

"Don't bother," Chris says quietly, reaching past me to turn the lock. "You don't want to go out there."

"Who's out there?" I don't turn around, though I feel him at my back. I feel him, smell him, fear him. Hate him. Chris grips my shoulder and steers me away from the door, leaning back against it himself, blocking the only exit. He considers me, the dress, the sparkly shoes. The shiny hair, the blush, the mascara. The effort.

I'm an idiot.

He takes in the rest of the apartment, sparse and uninspired. The television, the laptop, the balcony. His eyes narrow slightly when he spots the maps, and I know then that he's never been here before. However he found me, it only just happened.

His gaze settles on the crumpled bags of groceries, the roast chicken visible on top.

"I knew you weren't going to cook a chicken," he says.

"I bought potatoes."

"We'll eat them later."

Now it's my turn to take him in, though he looks exactly the same as he always has. Handsome, rough around the edges.

Careless, guileless, determined. I glimpse the duffel bag and swallow. It's full. If he emptied it out there would be enough room for a body.

He laughs as he reads my mind. "Relax," he says. "You're not going in the bag."

"Of course I'm not."

His eyes comb over me. "You look pretty."

"Fuck you. Who are you?"

"I told you my name."

"I told you mine."

"Well, only one of us was lying. About that."

I drag in a shaky breath. I want to cry. And not just because I'm concerned about my well-being, but because this has all been for nothing. Three years. A thousand lies. And the only person I've fooled is myself.

"Who are you?" I ask again.

"Chris Sherwood."

"You don't work at the agricultural college."

"No." He shakes his head once, slightly. "I don't."

"Then…?"

He lifts a shoulder. "Then what?"

I don't know what to do. It's like being in a dream where you need to run, but you can't convince your legs to move. You need to scream, but your voice won't come. I need to do something—but what? What does he want me to do? What does he plan to do?

I take a few steps back, and he doesn't follow. There's only one entrance to this apartment, and he's blocking it. I reach into my purse for my phone, and he doesn't move.

"Do it," he says, when the screen lights up. "Call the police."

"I'm going to."

"What will you tell them?"

"That there's a stranger in my apartment."

"Will you tell them your name?"

"Yes."

"Your address?"

"I don't care if people know I'm here. I don't care anymore."

"You care," he says.

"I don't."

"You wish you didn't. But you do."

I stare at the screen. All I have to do is press three buttons. Say one word. *Help.*

The last time the police came to my home, they didn't come alone. They came with the press. They came with cameras. They came with gossip and stares and accusations. They came until I couldn't take it anymore, until I retreated, until I hid so far and so long that they forgot about me. Until it almost felt safe. Until I could almost make my escape.

I can't escape now. But if there's only one person watching me, that's better than thousands of prying eyes, cameras and journalists. Because if Chris is here for the reason I think he's here, then there's something important I need to do, and I need to do it alone, without an audience.

"You want a drink?" he asks, crouching in front of the grocery bags and contemplating the bottle of red I bought for our date. "This is a good one. Nice choice."

"No. But you should have some."

He smiles a little. "What's your rule on dates? Two glasses with food, right?"

My heart, still pounding, stutter-stops. I use that line on my Fantasy Friends profiles. I say it up front so the men know what to expect. This isn't meet in a bar and fuck in an alley. This is a meal, this is two adults doing what two adults do. It's not as seedy and desperate as it sounds. It's not tragic and lonely and deceitful. It's not me in a costume, pretending my life is fine. It's not. I have rules. I have standards.

I have nothing.

"How long?" My voice is hoarse.

Chris studies the wine bottle and sets it on the table, like we're just saving it for later. Like there'll be a later. Like one of us isn't going to be leaving this apartment in the next two minutes. I'm already a prisoner here, but it's different when I'm not the guard.

"A while."

"And how much longer?"

"That depends."

"On what?" I'm not interested in his games. If the masks are off, they're off. None of this movie villain bullshit. No drawing it out until the cavalry arrives to save the day. There's no cavalry. The only person who might notice I'm missing is Rodney, and that's a long-shot.

"On your cooperation." He gestures to the couch. "Have a seat."

"No."

"Sit." Something about him changes, hardens. But only a little bit, only slightly. Like his disguise fits him so perfectly that when the man beneath shifts, you see it. He's done this before. He's used to issuing orders; used to having them followed. This isn't his first time.

But it's mine.

I sit on the couch and he nudges the coffee table back and sits on it, our knees inches apart. I can smell his soap. See the faint ridges of dirt beneath his fingernails. It's permanent, then. But it's not from digging holes for plants. He's been digging holes for other reasons.

"Let me see your ID," I say.

He's entirely unconcerned as he reaches into his back pocket and pulls out his wallet, the same one he's always carried. He takes out his driver's license and passes it to me. It's a New York state license. The name is Chris Sherwood. The address is down the street.

"Your other ID," I say.

"That's it."

"Who are you?"

"I told you."

"No," I say. "You didn't."

He purses his lips slightly, like he's disappointed in me. Like in this whole situation, I'm the worst person.

"What do you want?"

"You," he replies.

For three years, no one has wanted me. Not for the right reasons. No one has known me; I haven't let them. And now, hearing those words, you'd think it would make everything worse. That it would drive home the fact that no one *does* want me, and maybe they never will. But that's not what happens. Instead, an invisible wall slides into place, separating the past from the present. This is how I feel when I think about my mother; she's something I know about, not something I know.

It's like the bars that separate my father from the world, the dirt covering my brother's casket. It's a barrier. It's distance. It's armor.

If Chris wanted to hurt me, he could have. He could have done it any time. But something has changed. The game is different, the waiting has gone on long enough.

He needs something.

"Tell me why you killed Alex," he says.

I slap him. I don't plan it, so there's no time for him to react or defend against it. I'm stronger than either of us expects. Lifting boxes of cans is a workout. Instinct propels me to my feet, leaping over the edge of the couch, sprinting for the door. I open my mouth to scream, but there's no one to hear.

Chris catches me before I can grab the door. One arm around my waist, the other covering my mouth. I bite, feel his flesh pinch between my teeth. He swears and jerks his hand away, slapping it back to squeeze my jaw so hard I can't open it again. We fall to the floor, the sick smack of bone against wood as Chris's forearms take the brunt of the impact. My knee throbs, and I'm winded, but not crushed.

I fight. What the fuck. This isn't a dream. I can kick. I can punch. The hand on my mouth drops so his forearm presses against my windpipe, dragging my head up. He's somehow gotten onto his knees, one digging into the small of my back, the other leg crossing my thighs, subduing me. Trying to.

"Don't," he says, when I continue to flail. He's not fighting, just holding me, his arm a gentle but effective pressure, cutting off my air supply until I'm weak. Until I'm limp and motionless on the ground, seeing through teary eyes, unable to move.

I've been in this position before, but the last time there was a lot more blood. There was glass. There was pain. There was my brother lying motionless, head turned away as though he couldn't bear to face me after what he'd done.

I couldn't move then, either. It wasn't a dream. It was the ends of my bleached hair stained pink with blood, sparkling with shards of glass like diamonds. It was the screaming agony in my leg, the questions lodged in my throat. The way my brother had looked at me at that very last second before he said my name, then cut the wheel to the right. Hard. Too hard.

"Reese," Chris is saying. "Reese."

He shakes me a little, the pressure on my throat gone, his fingers tangled in my hair like a rein.

"Get off of me," I slur. I try not to gasp in air, but my lungs feel like they're collapsing. The weight on my back eases, and he lets me turn so I can shift onto my side. He straddles my legs, gripping my upper arm tightly. It doesn't hurt, but if I try to move, it will.

He's done this before, too.

"Get off," I say again. My hip squeals where it presses into the hardwood.

"Not just yet," he says. "Tell me about Alex."

"You know everything, or you wouldn't be here."

"He was twenty-one."

Alex's age is public knowledge, but combined with the sticker on the laptop, I know the statement is meant to be more revealing than that. He's not reminding me of Alex's age. He's telling me he knows. He cares.

He wants a reaction, but I don't give him one, keeping my face blank. "I know."

"He was a good kid."

"He was," I agree, though it hurts to say so.

"That's all you got?"

"That's all you're getting."

"It doesn't work like that, Reese."

"Stop saying my name."

"You're going to be hearing a lot more of it if you don't cooperate."

"Yeah? From who?" This is all he has, I realize. My name. Not my secrets.

"Those people you think forgot about you…they haven't."

"They don't care anymore."

"They'll always care."

The wood floor digs into my cheek when I speak. "You're wrong. You're the only one who cares." I flop onto my back, looking up at him. We've been in this position before, but now there's nothing sexual about it. The invisible barrier is there, the same one that's separated me from the world for so long. The one that reminds me he's someone I thought I knew but didn't.

"What are you thinking?" he asks.

My eyes dart over to the duffel bag. "What's in there?"

"My things."

"What things?"

"Clothes. Toothbrush. Pajamas. The usual."

"Are you going somewhere?"

He reaches down to brush hair away from my forehead. "No."

The words sink in. *"No?"*

"That's right." He gestures around the apartment. "I wasn't

lying about this part," he says. "I did want to see where you lived."

"What took you so long?"

He smiles. "You don't make things easy." The smile fades, and he considers me, gaze flitting past my temples, my mouth, my chest, my hands. "You're not what people say."

"No kidding."

"I don't know if that's a good thing."

"I don't care if you think it's a good thing. I want you to go."

"I'll bet. But I'm not going anywhere, and neither are you."

I think about my maps. I may not know where, but I'm definitely going.

"I didn't kill Alex," I say. I've said it before, a dozen times, but no one believed me.

Chris's green eyes are dark when he stares down at me. "You had a reason," he says.

"I didn't." The trial ended, and four days later the guilty verdict came in. They announced it on the radio while we were on our way to the theater. Alex was driving. He took a different route because the media was staking out every square inch of the city, waiting for us to make a mistake. That's what he said. *We have to go to the theater, Reese. We need to take this route to avoid them.*

But maybe he was avoiding Chris.

What I told the police and the doctors and everyone after was that the news had been too much for Alex to bear and he'd lost control of the car and steered us off the embankment. That a year of suspicion and doubt had culminated in a conviction that left us with nothing and nowhere to turn.

What I left out is how the embankment wouldn't have been there had we taken the normal route to the theater. There wasn't even really a reason for me to go with him, except Alex said he was worried about me, that I'd lost my friends and my roots were showing, and I needed to get out of the house. He insisted I get in the car.

When they announced the verdict he'd turned to me. And for the first time I saw in Alex's face the same thing I'd seen mirrored in mine when my father told me the truth. A horrible understanding.

And a terrible decision.

"Reese," he'd said.

⋙ ⋙

Chris declares himself hungry and proceeds to reheat the chicken, warm the bread in the oven, and boil the potatoes. He lays everything on the table in front of me and gives me a paper plate and a spoon. I can't get better utensils because I've been handcuffed to the chair for the last half hour. These aren't the shiny new handcuffs I left at my mother's place. He brought his own.

He puts my frozen apple pie in the oven, then returns with a wineglass for himself and a plastic cup for me. "Red or white?" he asks. "Lady's choice."

"Freedom," I choose.

"Red it is," he says.

My stomach lurches hungrily, but I stare sullenly at the food Chris piles onto my plate.

"When did it begin?" he asks casually.

213

"You first."

"That's a long story."

"Apparently I have a long time to wait."

He arches a brow. "Not really."

I pick up my spoon and saw at a piece of chicken until I get a bite-size piece free. I put it in my mouth and chew. I know Chris is waiting for me to start talking, but I've been silent for three years, I know how to hold my tongue. And if answers are the only leverage I have, I need to keep them to myself until I figure out exactly why he wants them.

"I saw you," he says eventually, buttering a piece of bread. "On a date."

"I already know this."

"Not that date, another one. Before. Your name was Amelia."

Amelia. Aspiring actress, animal lover, archery enthusiast.

"You were blond," Chris adds. "The guy was a construction worker."

Last Halloween. We went out for dinner at a jazz bar. He tried so hard to impress me. A nice guy, more muscles than brains. All I was looking for. But he was looking for more. He'd been on a lot of bad dates. He thought I might be different.

"I remember," I say.

"I like this color better." He gestures to my hair, and I flip him off with my un-cuffed hand.

He smiles. "I'd been trying to find you for a while. I knew you were in the city, since you visited your father. I followed you home as best I could, but you're pretty good at getting lost in the crowd. So I waited. And then, one night, I saw you."

"You knew it was me."

"Sure. You had a blond wig; I'd seen enough pictures of you as a blonde to recognize you."

I eat some potatoes.

"I followed you guys back to his place, searched the address, found his name, found him online. Found the Fantasy Friends profile; found you."

"That was six months before we met."

"Yeah, well. You shut down the profile. I spent a lot of time on that site before I could track down your new one."

"I hope you made some friends."

He smirks.

"And then?"

"Then Denise messaged Doug. For a while, I'd tried to contact you through my own profiles but you never responded. I hacked Doug's account, so when he replied I could keep track of your messages. I found where he worked and followed him to the restaurant on date night."

I think about the fake Rolex, the suit jacket that was just a little too small. Both of us in costume.

"Did you really think I'd come back to your room?"

He sips his wine and studies me. "I don't know. You've exhibited some… risky behavior."

All those dates, those men, those chances. And this is the one that really fucks me.

"What were you planning to do if I showed up?"

He shrugs. "Whatever you wanted me to do. Same as what happened on your car a few nights later."

"Why? Why not… You could have…" My mind is whirling. I don't know what he could have done. Random sexual encounters were the only encounters I had. "What about your job? It has to be against the rules to… do that."

He butters another piece of bread. "This *is* my job."

I flinch. That hurts. Even though I'd gone into this thing saying it was never going anywhere, it stings to know that it was never going anywhere for him, either. At least Doug tried to call again. So had the construction worker.

But Chris made sure we met again. And again. He knew something they didn't know.

He knew me.

The piece of chicken I'm chewing tastes like sawdust.

"Aw, come on," he says, nudging me under the table with his foot. "You were lying, too."

"I'd rather be the only liar."

"Just try to be the best one."

"What are you waiting for?" I blurt out. "Why not just… do whatever it is you came here to do? If you only wanted answers about my brother, you got them. You can go. Why are you still here?"

"Because it's not over."

"What's not over?"

He gestures between us. "This."

"*This* is definitely over."

He laughs. "Too bad, but that's not what I meant. You know what closure is, Reese?"

"Of course I do."

"I don't. I haven't slept through the night in three years. I was a shitty—" He clears his throat. "I wasn't very good at my job. I got too close to your brother. I liked him, and I betrayed

216

him, and now he's dead. And I want answers."

"Answers and closure aren't the same thing."

"I'll be the judge of that."

The scar on my leg itches. I scratch it with my chained hand, the metal rattling against the wooden chair. I see Chris notice, watch where my fingers touch the bare skin of my thigh.

"Are you done eating?" he asks.

"Yes."

"Good. Time for bed."

I sit up straight. "What?" I know he brought an overnight bag, but the realization that he actually intends to stay is jarring.

He finishes his last piece of bread and stands, fishing the tiny handcuff key from his pocket. "Let's go."

I shove the chair back. The legs screech across the wood as I pedal hard with my bare feet, having foregone the flats at the start of dinner. "Don't do this."

"You'll be fine," he assures me. "It's a little early, but you can have a book if you want." He grabs the back of the chair to keep me in place, then snares my cuffed wrist as he twists the key in the lock. I get up only because he's got my arm pulled up behind my shoulder blades, and if I don't move, it'll break.

"Which one's your room?" He nudges me down the hall, my legs barely moving, forcing him to dig a knee into my thighs to propel me forward. "This one?" he asks, stopping in front of the first closed door.

"No!" I say, too late.

He shoves open the door to the Carlisle family museum, and I feel him stop close behind me. "What the hell is this?"

He forces me into the room, though it has nothing to do with me and everything to do with his own morbid curiosity. I hear him suck in a breath as he surveys the walls, the art, the hundreds of clippings, carefully trimmed and framed and hung. He's silent as he takes it all in, stopping in front of my wall, the pages about me, the ones that criticize, theorize, vilify. *Murderer?* they ask. *Thief,* they say more confidently. *Liar,* more certain still. *Whore!*

"Reese," he says. There's something in the way he says it, something sincere. Like he's concerned, though he can't be. He's leaning over me, trying to see my face, and I hang my head so my hair flops past my cheeks, shielding my eyes. I'd done this that first night at his apartment, hidden the things I couldn't hide otherwise. The things he'd been looking for.

I scan the framed pages that make up the row of photos along the baseboard. There's me at Alex's funeral, wheeling across the soft grass, heart breaking as they heckled me. There's a close-up shot of my face, eyes wide and dry. They hired experts to read my expression, my body language. They—the court of popular opinion—came back with a unanimous verdict: Guilty.

Shame keeps my eyes glued to the ground. "Do whatever you want," I tell him. "I don't care."

15

I'm confused when I wake up, one hand stretched awkwardly over my head. Memories trickle in like the faint rays of morning light pushing through the blinds and slicing across the floor: My brilliant plan, the knock at the door, the questions, the answers. The failure.

It's Thursday. I have nothing to do on Thursdays. No one to wonder about me. No one to call and ask if I'm alright. This is part of why I never got a pet. I didn't want the indignity of being the lady whose body was found half-eaten by her Maltese.

I peer under the covers to confirm I'm still wearing the dress I put on yesterday, then spot the alarm clock, now perched on the dresser on the far side of the room. Chris took everything off the nightstands, and even removed the drawers in case I had any secret weapons. Unfortunately, I hadn't had the foresight to stock my bedroom with guns and knives and lock picking tools.

It's almost seven o'clock and I have to pee. "Chris," I call, my voice a croak. I clear my throat. "Chris!"

If this were a movie—a good one—I'd have found a way to break off the zipper of my dress, use part of it to pick the lock on the handcuffs, and the other to fashion a weapon to maim Chris when he entered. As it stands, I'm lying in the same prone position in which he left me when he unlocks the door, yawning into the back of his hand.

"You're up early," he remarks.

I have to pee badly, but a pressing new issue has arisen. "Why is there a *lock* on my door?"

He runs his fingers through his hair. It's sticking up on one side, flat on the other. If I hadn't just learned he was nuts, I'd think it was cute.

"It's to keep you inside," he says. "So you can't come out in the middle of the night and maim me."

I try not to look scheming. "Where did you sleep?"

I use the guest room for my shrine, and since I never have guests, I didn't bother getting a pull-out couch. The one I have is more for appearances than comfort.

"On the floor in front of your door," he says. "Curled up like a dog."

"Good."

"I slept on the couch, like a normal person."

"Don't get ahead of yourself."

"It's good to see you've maintained your sense of humor."

"And men. I have to pee. Hurry up and uncuff me."

He pulls the key from his pocket and reaches for the headboard. "Don't try anything."

I don't. My bladder is screeching, and the worst I could do right now is pee on his foot. I get up and start for the en suite, but he stops me.

"Use the one in the hall."

"What? Why? My stuff is in this one."

"Exactly."

I don't keep weapons in the bathroom, and my motives here are purely sanitary, so I proceed down the hall, Chris's fingers looped lightly around my cuffed wrist. I stop in shock when I see that the doorknob is missing from the bathroom door.

"Where the fuck is the knob?"

"Jesus, Reese. Language. It's not even seven."

"Where's the doorknob?!"

"It's gone, obviously. In you go." He nudges the small of my back, and I stumble into the bathroom, wincing at the too-bright light. I hardly ever come in here, but I know there was hand soap and a roll of toilet paper. Now there's just a folded wad of paper on the edge of the counter. Even the toilet paper holder is missing. I wouldn't know how to kill someone with a three-inch plastic spring, but I'm bitter to learn that the option has been taken away.

"Are you going to listen while I pee?" I ask, eyeballing the hole in the door.

"Yep." He leans against the wall on the opposite side of the hall. "I get off on it."

"I wouldn't be surprised."

He winks.

I stomp inside and shut the door, which makes very little difference since the two-inch hole removes any illusion of privacy. I turn the cold water tap all the way up and do my business, washing my hands and drying them with the small towel Chris was kind enough to leave behind. How many people has he held prisoner before? And where are they now?

I stare at myself in the mirror, mascara smudged around my eyes, my face pale. I look like I normally do, and suddenly that's a bad thing. That's a girl nobody sees and who nobody's supposed to see. It's a girl nobody will miss.

Chris pushes open the door. "Come have breakfast. You'll need your energy."

"I don't eat breakfast."

"Then starve." He herds me down the hall and cuffs me to the chair again, then rounds the island into the kitchen and opens the refrigerator. He'd seen it last night when he put away the food, but now that he's hungry, it finally dawns on him that my cupboards are bare.

"Why don't you have any food?"

"I don't cook a lot."

"But it's empty."

"Well, I wasn't expecting a hostage situation."

He shoots a vexed look over his shoulder. "I told you my story," he says. "Why don't you tell me yours?" He snags the remaining half of last night's bread, hunts for butter, finds none, and aims another irritated glare my way.

"Sure," I say. "One night I was driving home from visiting my father in prison, and I met this guy on the side of the road. He'd staged the whole thing like a stalker, and I fucked him because I didn't care enough about myself not to. Fortunately, he cared enough to continue stalking me, and now I'm held hostage in my own apartment."

"It's not stalking. It's investigating."

"It's delusional. You're a criminal."

"So are you."

"Am not."

"Are too."

He takes the seat opposite and cuts off slices of bread. There was an old jar of jam in the cupboard, and he smears two pieces and passes me one. I said I didn't eat breakfast, but I eat what he offers anyway, since I'm not sure when my next ration will be. If ever. The bread's already a little stale. As far as last meals go, this one's a disappointment.

"You know where we're going today?" he asks.

"Prison?"

"No."

"The agricultural college you work at?"

"Wrong again."

"Back to the theater so you can face your fear of puppets?"

Something passes over his face, so quickly I might have missed it had I not been waiting for it. He may know something about me, but he has no idea what I know. "Were you dating my brother?" I ask abruptly.

He does a double-take, bread halfway to his mouth. "What? No."

The reaction is believable, but I overreact anyway. "Yes, you were! This is some sort of sick romantic revenge! You were stalking us both! You twisted fuck!" I leap up from the chair, my wrist firmly cuffed to the side, and position it between us, as though Chris will view it as an insurmountable obstacle.

"I'm not—"

He comes at me and I swing the chair with everything I have. It thumps against his thigh and he curses as he tackles me. My wrist wrenches painfully when the chair skids sideways, and we land with Chris on top again. My breath lost, again. I kick at his shins as hard as I can, and he swears some more and twists my arm as he kneels on my legs. I try to blink away tears of pain and frustration, but I can feel them catching in my eyelashes and searing my cheeks.

"Help!" I scream as loud as I can.

"Fuck! Shut up!" As he'd done last night, he covers my mouth, but this time he's prepared and squeezes my jaw tight so I can't bite.

I squeal behind his fingers and try to buck him off, but it's no use. He's bigger and stronger and he's had a lot more practice. "Would you stop?" he snaps, flipping me onto my back. My left hand is stuck up over my head, attached to the stupid chair, and he snags my other one when I take a swing at him.

"I hate you," I sob, his face blurry through the tears.

"I know," he says. "I hate you, too."

⋙ ⋙

The same blue pickup that nearly killed me the first day we met is parked in a corner spot on the second level of my building's garage, a guest parking pass displayed on the dash. Chris steers me into the back seat, my feet and hands bound. He said it wouldn't have come to this if I'd behaved myself, but I'm not sure that's true. The fact that he's walking with a slight limp makes this mistreatment only slightly more bearable.

I'm still in last night's dress and flats, but he'd scrubbed my face clean with a wet cloth after he tied me up, and let me swish toothpaste in my mouth so I felt slightly more human. Then he'd gagged me, ruining the illusion.

He covers me with a blanket, in case someone should peer in the back seat, and I twist around until the blanket's covering only the lower part of my face. If I don't exert myself I can breathe okay through my nose, but I have to lie on my side so I don't crush my hands. I tip my face so I can look out the window.

I know we're outside when I see the gray sky and the hazy sun. I can make out the upper levels of some of the buildings as we navigate our way out of downtown, marking our progress toward the east side of the city and the freeway. After that it's just sky and question marks and I fall asleep.

Chris wakes me with a hand on my foot, uncoiling the rope from around my ankles. I keep my eyes closed as I feel his rough hands massaging the blood back into my feet, thumbs bumping over the ridges left from the knots. I wait to see if he does anything more, anything worse. The dress stops above my knees, and I feel it bunched there, ready to be lifted. But he doesn't try.

"Reese," he says, shaking my leg. "Wake up."

I pretend to come to, squinting at him. From this angle, I can see sky but no buildings, a little more blue peeking between the clouds. He pulls me so my legs dangle over the edge of the seat, then grips my shoulder to lift me to a sitting position.

"You snore," he remarks, undoing the gag.

"Liar." I peer past him, then glance up and down the freeway in both directions. Nothing. No traffic. No witnesses.

I recognize this spot. It takes help fourteen minutes and twenty-eight seconds to arrive at this location. I know because that's what Agent Trapper, the lead investigator on our case, told me the 9-1-1 records showed. He said we'd gotten lucky and a farmer had driven past, noticed the destroyed guard rail, and called for help. I guess Agent Trapper and I have different definitions of "lucky."

"You know where we are?" Chris asks.

I shake my head, just to be difficult.

If he thinks this is going to traumatize me and make me confess, he's more delusional than I suspected. I've come back to this spot a few times. This section of the road is farmland on one side, and a sharp rock embankment on the other, dropping fifty yards before shearing off into more grass. There was a guard rail here when we went through, and I remember seeing newspapers with pictures of the shorn metal, the gaping hole. They replaced it, made it sturdier. More difficult to kill someone. I've climbed over the new rail and sat on the edge of the cliff, watching the tall grass sway beneath, calling. I sat here and thought about what happened, what I'd seen. I touched the scar on my leg and tried not to believe. Up or down. The choice is easy when someone makes it for you.

Chris helps me stand but leaves my hands cuffed behind my back. We walk to the front of the truck and stop near the rail, peering down. The view is the same as I remember it.

"Alex died right there," he says, pointing to some vague place below, as though I'll ever forget it.

I don't say anything.

"He texted me that morning and said he was worried about you. I thought he was concerned for your safety, but now I think he was afraid. Worried about what you might do to him."

I scoff but don't reply.

"He told you the truth, didn't he?"

I glance over. Chris's face is hard, pensive. There's a stoicism there, too. A tightness in his shoulders, but a forced ease in his posture, the way he's leaning against the metal, his hands gripping the edge. It's personal but it's not. Like us.

"You tell me," I say finally. "I don't know what's true."

He meets my eye. "He told you about the money."

My breathing stops for a split second, enough for Chris to notice. Enough for me to force air out and back in and pretend it didn't happen.

Alex didn't tell me about the money.

My father did.

"No," I say.

"Yes," he says.

"Alex didn't know what my father was doing."

Chris nods. "He did."

"He didn't."

"You knew, too."

"I didn't."

"He was helping him."

"No."

"And so were you."

"You're grasping."

I watch his hands uncurl from the rail.

"Alex didn't know anything," I tell him. This is what I told the police. Something tells me he's already heard it. The story I practiced. The story I want so badly to believe. "He just wanted to run the theater. He didn't want to believe my dad did what they accused him of doing. But when the verdict came back, it was too much. We were in the car and he lost control."

"You're lying," Chris says.

"I'm not."

He grips my chin and makes me face him. "He knew about the money, because he's the one who lost it."

I try to jerk away but I can't. "That's not true."

"Why do you think he needed my help?"

"I can't think of a single reason."

"Because he knew he was in trouble."

"No. He wasn't. They only arrested my father. If they had something on me, they would have arrested me, but they didn't. Same for Alex."

"Then why did you kill him?"

"*He* was driving, you asshole!"

"Why did he take this route? It's twice as long to the theater!"

I try to turn my face but he won't let me. He's inches away, watching my eyes, watching everything. I've kept this secret for far too long, from everyone but myself. There are some things you can't deny, no matter how hard you try.

"Because there's a cliff," I say finally, my voice breaking at the admission. Like saying it out loud is what makes it true.

Chris scowls. "Why would he want to drive past a cliff?"

I feel tears on my lashes. "To kill me."

≫≫ ≫≫

They thought it was the lifestyle I missed. My father, my brother, my friends. The homes, the cars, the jewelry. They thought the worst had been done, that all the tangibles were gone, and I was bereft. They were wrong. Seeing Alex's eyes the second before he twisted the wheel was what did it. Seeing that the one person I had left—the one person I thought had always loved me—

wanted me to die, broke the last part of pre-scandal Reese Carlisle and left only shadows in her wake.

Chris doesn't want to believe me but I know that he does. He made me look at him, but only because he wanted to see, not be seen. But I saw.

He shuffles me back into the truck and agrees not to gag me if I promise to be quiet. He ties my feet again, but I don't care. I don't care about anything. The admission leaves me spent. It's humiliating, admitting to the man who fucked you for answers that yet another person you thought cared about you, did, in fact, not.

He climbs into the driver's seat but doesn't start the truck. I stare at the back of his chair, the scuffs on the worn leather, feeling itchy tears drip off the side of my nose. "Are you done?" I ask eventually. "Is this over?"

I'm aware there's no blanket. That we're at the top of a cliff I've already been tossed off once.

I hear him open his mouth, the soft snick of sound as his lips part, then he's quiet again. He starts the truck and drives us back to Holden in silence.

I could probably fight when we get in the elevator. He untied my feet and freed one of my hands, cuffing it to his, so I can't make a run for it. But no one gets in the elevator as we ride to my floor, and I no longer care enough to try to run away. We enter the apartment and flop onto the couch, oddly normal if not for the handcuffs. He even offers me gum, but I decline. He folds a piece in half and chews.

"What's this all about?" he asks, gesturing to the maps pinned to the wall.

"Target practice."

"I know, you know."

"Of course you do."

"About Madagascar and Australia and Yap."

I stay silent.

"I looked at your laptop last night. Your big travel plans. They sound nice."

I swallow.

"How are you going to pay for it?"

"I had a job before all this. I know how to invest."

"Your own money?"

I say nothing and stare at the wall.

"Why the map of Holden?"

I shrug. I feel him watching me, but I set my jaw and refuse to return the stare. After a second, he uncuffs himself and attaches the empty shackle to my ankle, hobbling me. "Seriously?"

"Yeah."

He approaches the wall and carefully unpins the map of Holden City, then walks over to the window and uses his gum to fasten the map to the glass. Pinpricks of light shine through the holes; hundreds of random constellations.

He rejoins me on the couch and studies the scene. "What are you planning here, Reese? What's the pattern?"

"Your guess is as good as mine."

"I don't think you do anything randomly. Not before the scandal, not after. I looked into you. You made yourself famous. You worked for that."

"I was an idiot."

"I thought so, too, at first. But it turns out you're not."

I glance down, my cuffed hand and ankle casually resting on top of my knee like I've chosen this position. Like any of this is my choice. I can see the edge of my scar poking out beneath the hem of my dress. This stupid dress. His stupid compliments.

"I want to change my clothes."

"You can change before bed."

"Why not now?"

"Because I said so." He pulls out his phone and calls up a picture of a tall bald guy in a black pea coat. "You know him?"

"Know" isn't the right word, but I think I recognize him. He's one of the guys who followed Chris into the parkade that night.

Still, I say, "No."

"How about him?"

A picture of the other guy I saw in the parking garage the night Chris followed me. "No."

"Johan and Davor Litski," he says.

"So?"

"Alex's friends."

I snort. "I doubt it." My brother's friends were quintessential struggling artists. They wore vests and pork pie hats and jeans with paint stains. They all had hair.

"Maybe 'friends' isn't the right word."

"What's the point of all this?"

"Did you know about the gambling, Reese?"

I sigh. "Who gambled, Chris?"

"Alex."

"You're wrong."

"I'm right. When we started investigating your father, we

needed a way in. Your brother was our way."

"Who's 'we?'"

A muscle in his neck ticks. "Don't worry about that."

"Oh, okay."

"We looked at you too."

"You got a real close up."

"Three years ago."

I frown. "Did we meet?"

"You and me?"

"If you were so tight with my brother and his bald friends, we would have met."

"You think you'd have noticed me back then? Liked me? With your blond hair and your manicures and your high heels?"

"I was blond, not blind."

"Would you have noticed?" He sounds sincere, like he really wants to know.

I look him over. Two days' worth of stubble, the flattened nose, broken more than once, probably well-deserved. The worn Henley, non-designer jeans, rough hands. "No."

He sinks back into the cushions, satisfied. "We never met."

"Why not?"

"Because we couldn't find anything on you."

"There's nothing to find."

His lips curve into a humorless smile. "There are twenty million things to find, Reese."

I gesture to the map on the window, infinite possibilities mottling the paper. "Well, good luck."

16

At some point, I fall asleep. When I wake up, I'm sprawled on my stomach on the couch, my hand cuffed to the coffee table, a blanket covering my legs. The sun is still up, and I can see the green lights on the microwave glowing 6:01 p.m. I yawn and inch my way to a sitting position, turning to find Chris playing a game on my laptop a few feet away.

"Why are you still here?" I mumble.

"We're roommates, remember?"

I catch a whiff of my breath. *Yikes.* A hank of oily hair hangs against my cheek. It's hard to believe I showered twenty-four hours ago in anticipation of a big date/torture session, and now I'm hunched at an awkward angle to accommodate my shackled wrist.

"I want to take a shower," I say. "And not be handcuffed anymore."

"Sorry." Chris strolls over, unfairly attractive and clean in jeans and a white T-shirt. "You can't be trusted."

"*I* can't be trusted? You hypocrite." I try to imbue the word with venom, but I have neither the energy nor the appropriate level of hypocrisy.

Chris crouches next to the table, out of kicking range, and unfastens my hand. "You can take a shower if you want. I'll order pizza. What do you want on it?"

"A gun and a lock pick?"

He tugs me down the hall to the knob-free bathroom. "Have you ever shot a gun?"

"No. You?"

He lifts a brow but neither confirms nor denies, just unzips my dress and unfastens the back clasp on my bra. "You want a hand with the rest?"

He did that so fast I barely had time to register what he'd done. No more than my back is bared, but I clutch the fabric to my chest like a maiden. "No!"

"Okay. Pull your arm out of the sleeve, then put it over your head."

"Why?"

"I told you, I don't trust you." He doesn't wait for me to obey, just pulls the left side of the dress down and works my arm out of the fabric, then does the same with the bra strap. I'm still clasping the material over my breasts when he seizes my left arm and cuffs it to the shower rail. "Can you reach the tap?"

I can't even close my gaping mouth. "This is ridiculous!"

"You're the one who tried to bite and run. Twice."

"You're the hostage taker! *You're* the bad guy!"

He reaches in to turn on the water. "You've got five minutes."

"Twenty."

"Six. Use them wisely." He walks out before I can argue further.

For a long moment I don't move, just stand beside the tub

while my hand goes numb in its cuff, staring at the slowly rising steam.

"Six minutes," Chris calls through the door.

"Get away from the peep hole!"

He laughs, but I can't tell if he's watching or not, and I can't reach the door to check. I get in the tub, dress and all, and pull the curtain shut behind me. It's got a cheery rubber duck pattern, a holdover from my bathroom growing up, one of the few things that wasn't confiscated when the FBI raided our homes. The stupid smiling ducks make me want to cry. Hell, they make me want to bawl my head off. I sniffle and shimmy out of the dress, watching it absorb the puddle of water at my feet before belatedly realizing I'll have no dry clothes waiting when I get out.

I step under the spray and scrub at my face, trying to convince myself I'm not crying when really I am. My shoulders shake so hard I have to hold onto the shower rod to avoid falling down, and I turn my face into the water and hope it absorbs my sobs. This is so ridiculous. Everything about my life now is even more preposterous and laughable than it was three years ago. I have nothing and no one and no hope, and the only person who knows or cares where I am keeps gouging open a wound I thought had healed.

"Hey."

I squawk and lose my footing, dangling from the rod like a lame acrobat until I find my balance. I see Chris silhouetted on the other side of the curtain, making no move to peer behind it. He may be a liar and a kidnapper and probably something more sinister, but a Peeping Tom he is not.

"What are you doing in here?" I demand, my voice shrill.

"Bringing you a towel. What do you want to wear? Pajamas? What do you sleep in?"

I've fucked this man. Had dinner with him. Watched a puppet show. And he doesn't know what I like on my pizza or what my pajamas look like. I'm hesitant to say I *deserve* this, but I could have done things differently.

"Get me sweatpants and a T-shirt." I wipe my nose with the back of my hand. "They're in the bottom drawer of my dresser. Underwear in the top. Don't choose anything sexy."

"Aye-aye. Pizza's on the way."

I wait until I see his shadow disappear, the door softly thudding shut, though I don't know why he bothers since it doesn't lock and he's coming right back. Perhaps it's just an ingrained sense of Montana decency. Assuming he's even from Montana.

He brought in shampoo, conditioner, and a bar of soap from my en suite, and after some fumbling I manage to get my hair lathered up.

"Hey," I call, when I hear Chris come back.

"What?"

"Are you really from Montana?"

"I am."

I squeeze my eyes shut and rinse my hair, and when I emerge from under the water he's gone again. The six minutes probably work out to be more like twelve, and I'm pretty sure it was the tears that bought me the extra time. Whatever. I'll take what I can get. Which, now that I'm standing, shivering, cuffed to the rod and without hot water to keep me warm, is not much.

He'd placed the towel and clothes on the toilet, but when I

try to pick up the towel with my foot, my leg the only limb long enough to reach, all I succeed in doing is knocking everything to the floor. I yank the shower curtain closed again.

"Chris."

Silence.

"Chris?"

"What?"

I jump. He's on the other side of the door.

"I can't reach the towel."

"I put it on the toilet."

"I know. It fell."

I hear the door swing open but he doesn't enter.

"What?" I demand when nothing else happens. I'm cold and handcuffed and naked and somehow his inaction manages to make a terrible situation exponentially more annoying.

"What are you doing?" he calls. His voice is distant enough that I can tell he's still at the doorway.

"Freezing to death," I snap. "Can you pass me the towel?"

No movement.

I roll my eyes. "Please?"

"Show me your other hand."

"What? I—Oh, for fuck's sake." I stick my other hand up over the rod and extend my middle finger. "Satisfied? Do you feel safe?"

His shadow approaches and dips, then he folds my fingers around the towel. I yank it over and dry off as best I can, but it's difficult to wrap a towel tightly around your head with one hand. I know Chris is waiting on the other side, probably to pass me my clothes, and I sigh and give up. My hair is as dry as it's going to get, so I stick out a hand and ask for underwear. He gives me a plain gray cotton pair, and I awkwardly pull them on, my feet slipping on the porcelain. The fabric sticks to the rivulets of water trailing down my skin.

"Bra," I say, then hesitate.

I feel the scratch of lace against my fingers as he passes it to me. There's no way to get it on with my hand shackled to the rod.

"How—" I begin.

He sighs and I see him grip the side of the curtain.

"Don't come in!"

He stops. "I've already seen it, Reese."

"That was different. This is different. Everything's different."

"The only difference is nobody's lying."

"It's still different and I'm still handcuffed, genius. Just undo the cuffs. What could I possibly do in the fucking shower? Blind you with shampoo? It's designed *not* to do that." It's true. I'd read the back of the bottle with some hope.

There's a pause as he considers, then he reaches around the curtain, grips my arm tight enough to hurt, and uncuffs me without letting go. He pulls the curtain open so I'm standing in front of him in my damp panties, back turned, bra clasped in my hand.

"Hurry up," he says gruffly.

"Let go for a second. I'm not going to do anything."

He releases me reluctantly, but I feel him behind me, tense.

I pull on the bra, then he passes me the T-shirt and sweats without making me turn around. I use my moment of two-handedness to dry my hair in the towel, then finger comb it. I don't look great, but I feel a little more human than I did bound and gagged in the back seat of his truck.

My stomach rumbles, reminding us both there's pizza waiting, and he leads me to the living room. The haze outside has parted to reveal a sky tinted with the glowing purples and oranges of sunset, a pretty vista for a not-so-pretty day.

"Let's eat on the balcony," I suggest.

He snorts. "Let's not."

"I'm not going to jump off."

No comment.

"Or try to push you."

A dubious look.

"I'm pretty sure I'll be handcuffed, anyway."

He doesn't agree to the balcony, but he does open the doors, drag the dining table closer, and shackle me there. At least I can feel the breeze. Stick out my tongue and taste the freedom.

He'd opted for the basics on the pizza, but I'm too hungry to complain about boring pepperoni. He takes a bottle of beer for himself, pours me some in a paper cup, and we eat and drink silently.

"Have you ever done this before?" I ask eventually. I focus on freeing a piece of pizza clinging to the box with a tenuous piece of cheese.

Chris reaches over to pinch off the string and doesn't pretend not to know I'm referring to his hostage-taking hobby. "No," he says.

"It seems like you have."

"Not quite like this."

"But similar?"

"In a way."

"Did you like Alex?"

He'd been concentrating on his own pizza, but now he lifts his gaze to mine. Those green eyes, so fathomless. Like there's no depth, no deception. Or too many depths, too much deception.

"Yes," he says. "He was a nice kid." The lines at the corners of his mouth are deeper, sadder.

"I know." I sip my beer and watch the sun sinking over the horizon. "Do you like my dad?"

I feel his stare on my cheek.

"No," he says.

"But you talk to him."

"From time to time."

"More often than I talk to him?"

"Depends."

"Are you a police officer?"

"No." Chris pushes back his chair and goes to the kitchen for another beer.

"Were you? Ever?"

"No."

"Law enforcement?"

He sits back down, cracks off the cap of the bottle, refills my cup, then drinks. His non-response says enough. I suppose I already knew.

"But you're not now," I say.

Again, no reply.

"Why can't you go home?"

His mouth curls slightly and he takes another sip of beer. I watch his throat move. "Dumb and Dumber," he says.

"What?"

"Johan and Davor. Your brother's friends."

"They're your roommates? Are they not nice?"

"They never empty the dishwasher."

"Assholes."

"At least they don't bite."

"Assholes."

I'm rewarded with a sliver of real smile.

"Alex told me you were funny," he says, after a bit.

I want to ignore him, deny him, pretend I don't care, but what comes out is, "He did?"

"Yeah. I thought he was full of shit. I saw your pictures. The magazines. The websites. Your pink car."

I laugh at the memory of the Maserati. It feels like a different lifetime.

"I thought, there's no way that girl's funny. There's no way she's smart enough to do what we think she's doing."

"What did you think I was doing?"

"Laundering your father's stolen money to pay off your brother's gambling debt."

I shake my head. "Nope."

"That's where I'm getting stuck, Reese. Because you are funny. And you *are* smart."

I rattle my chained wrist. "Obviously."

"But there's no trail. No connection between you and the money. Not the stuff they recovered, not the stuff that's still missing."

"If you're not law enforcement, how did you get them to raid the Food Bank?"

"What are you talking about?"

I'm sure he knows, but I remind him about the not-so-health-and-safety-oriented inspection. The more I speak, the deeper the crease between his brows gets.

"I had nothing to do with that," he says.

"I thought we were done lying."

"Of course I looked at the Food Bank," he says. "But that was a while ago. Before we met."

I think about the receipt I saw in his apartment. Then I think about the first night I drove Rodney home, how he and I had to stay late to lock up because someone had messed with the security cameras.

"I'm not as smart as you think I am," I say. "But I'm not that stupid, either. If I had twenty million dollars, I wouldn't take it to work. And I wouldn't bury it, either. How big would that hole have to be? I can't dig a hole." I know this from experience. "Plus it's impractical," I continue. "Eventually I'd have to go back and dig it all up, hoping it hadn't composted. I'm not digging a *second* hole."

"So where is it?"

I hold up my hands, palms smooth, innocent. "Beats me."

"I think you're lying."

I pop the last bite of pizza into my mouth. "I'm disappointed."

"The pizza's fine."

"In you. Everybody wants the money. I hoped you were different."

"You've gotta have a plan, Reese. You're too smart not to."

I jangle my shackled wrist. "The plan's not working."

"You don't have enough money to last another three years

cooped up here. You're not working, you're taking care of your father, thinking about travel—where's the money come from in this scenario?"

"You saw my research. Yap is cheap. Get it?"

"I take back the funny comment."

I finish my beer. "I have to volunteer tomorrow. I know you think no one cares about me, but they'll notice I'm missing. They'll call. Come over."

"They won't come over. You gave them a PO box as an address."

Dammit. That's true. "They'll still call."

"I've got your phone. I'll handle it."

I open my mouth, then close it. Chris has my burner phone. I toss those things away after every date. Lyla has my real phone number, same as the prison. And, if I'm lucky, that phone is buried in the couch cushions where it always is.

"I want to go," I insist. "I like my job."

"Sorry, that's not how this hostage thing works. You don't get to socialize."

"Then what happens next? We're 'roommates' indefinitely?"

"Just tell me where the money is and this all ends."

"I told you I don't know. I had nothing to do with the scheme. I didn't know my brother gambled. I still don't believe you. I think Johan and Davor are your brothers. Dumb, Dumber, and Dumbest." I tick up three fingers, counting off the members of a happy, dumb family.

He rolls his eyes. "Why would Alex try to kill you?"

I flinch. I've asked myself the same question a thousand times, but it's my first time hearing it out loud. The first time someone asked the right question. And if he's asking, it's because he believes there's a chance I'm not a murderer.

"To avoid this," I mutter, swiping crumbs into a napkin and crumpling it in my palm. "So I wouldn't have to face the fallout."

"He didn't think you could handle it."

I shrug.

"Bullshit."

I look at him, surprised.

"You can handle it," he says. "How you're going about things is a little fucked up, but you're dealing. Alex tried to kill you because it's a better fate than falling into Johan and Davor's hands."

"Why would that happen?"

"There are twenty million reasons, Reese. Do we really need to list them?"

"I don't have the money!"

He slams his palm on the table. "You know where it is!"

"I don't!"

"You're lying. You graduated at the top of your class. Your top two clients at Carlisle Gale were among their best. You know your shit. If someone needed to hide money, you're the person they'd turn to."

"Did it ever occur to you that maybe I didn't *want* to be a criminal? That maybe my dad knew it and kept me in the dark?"

"Yeah. It occurred to me. And then he got arrested."

My heart stops. "What do you mean?"

"I mean, he didn't see the arrest coming, so he had to scramble. And, if you weren't part of the plan before, you became part of it."

"No."

"Yes. Alex was the problem. You were the solution, Reese."

"You're looking for something that doesn't exist. Flattering me isn't going to make it real."

"You know you were the first person he called when he was arrested? Not his lawyer, not your brother."

I swallow. I do know that.

Chris leans in. "He never spoke to Alex after the arrest."

"Alex was ashamed of him."

"No. Alex was ashamed of himself."

I try to see my brother as Chris saw him, but I can't. Alex was light. He was happy. He was unburdened. He was a butterfly flitting through the sky until its wings tangled in a web. Then he was gone.

But my memories of Alex don't mesh with the expression on his face in those final seconds. Despair. Determination. Dead. I always thought murder-suicide was a strong reaction to the news of the verdict, but I never considered an ulterior motive.

"Prove it," I say.

For the first time, Chris looks uncertain. "Prove it?"

"Prove that Alex was who you say he was, not the brother I knew."

"And then what?"

"Then I'll help you find the money."

17

The next morning, I'm tidied up and fed and cuffed to the coffee table, watching a house-hunting show while Chris takes a shower. He won't tell me where today's excursion will take us, but if it involves getting out of the apartment and getting answers, I'm a willing victim. Perhaps it's Stockholm syndrome, but whatever motivated Chris to agree to my offer intrigues me. He cares about this. Not me, I know, but the situation. Alex, maybe. The money, definitely. He wants answers, and so do I.

The couch cushions vibrate at 10:32 a.m. It takes a second to register the sensation, then it hits me: My phone. My real phone. I was supposed to be at the Food Bank at 9:30—it must be them.

I crane my neck to peer down the hall, but Chris isn't lurking there, anticipating another failed escape attempt. The shower is still running.

I feel between the cushions for the phone, squeezed into its familiar spot. I can ask for help. Tell Lyla to send the police. Give her my real address. Entertain my second set of visitors in three years.

But that would mean more headlines. More attention. No

trips to Madagascar or Australia or Yap.

And no answers.

But do I really want those answers? What if Chris is just biding his time, keeping an eye on me while his "roommates" search for the money he's convinced I have? What if they get fed up and start lopping off body parts as an incentive? I'd be upset if they cut off my hair, never mind my arm. What if this is my one opportunity to put an end to things?

My fingers fold around the phone and I press it to my ear. "Hello?" I say, my voice low.

"R.C.?"

I straighten. I was expecting Lyla, but it's Rodney.

"Yeah," I say. "Hi."

"Where are you? You were supposed to be here an hour ago. Lyla's worried."

I stare at the muted television. A retired couple tours a condo with ocean views and palm trees. They're in Antigua. It looks nice.

I glance at my maps.

I hesitate.

"I'm sick," I hear myself say. "I overslept. I'm sorry."

"Are you coming in?"

The question makes me want to cry. What if I never go back? What if this is the last time we talk? What if the one sorta-friend I made in all these years never knows the truth?

But I have too many what-ifs and not enough answers.

"No," I say. "I'm really sick."

"Oh. Okay. I'll tell Lyla."

"Tell her I'm sorry," I add.

"She'll be all right. What goes around comes around, remember? She probably infected you."

I smile a little. "Yeah. Probably."

"You mind if I have your soda, then? The orange one in the fridge? It's been there a while, and I want it."

"Sure, Rodney. You can have the soda."

"Cool. See you next week." Having gotten what he wanted, he hangs up.

I stare at the darkening screen and weigh my options. It's not too late. Three buttons. 9-1-1. The phone's registered to this address. They'd have to send someone to check on me. I wouldn't even need to say anything.

"I'm surprised."

I squawk and jump in my seat, wrenching my cuffed arm and wincing as pain sears my wrist.

Chris calmly crosses the room and plucks the phone from my hand. He's wet from his shower, wearing sweats slung low on his hips, a towel over his shoulder. His hair is dripping, rivulets of water running over his broad chest. There's a faint bite mark on his left pectoral, right above the heart. I did that a week and a half ago, when things were much, much different.

I slump against the cushion and stare up at him stubbornly. His eyes are dark, his mouth a flat line. He's angry, obviously. But if he heard the call, he knows I didn't do anything to jeopardize his whole hostage scheme. My heart is thudding, but I keep my expression bland. For three years, I haven't cared about much of anything, and now that I do care, I'll do anything to protect it. To protect myself.

For a long moment he considers me, then comes to some sort

of internal conclusion. He sits on the coffee table and rests his elbows on his knees, passing my phone between his hands. "Why didn't you tell them?"

"Because I want answers."

"So do I."

"Well, we have lots in common."

"You'll get your answers. You got any other phones stashed around here?"

"No." He'd already found and confiscated my bag of burners, but he looks doubtful.

"They're going to be suspicious," I say. "They'll know something's wrong if I don't show next week."

"It's early," Chris points out. "Let's just see how today goes."

≫ ≫

I behave myself in the elevator. Chris cuffs our wrists together and holds my hand against his side, tucked beneath the edge of his jacket. We ride down with a neighbor from the floor below, and he doesn't notice a thing.

I don't try to get his attention.

The parking garage is quiet as we approach the pickup, and I balk when Chris opens the back door and nods for me to climb in. "Why can't I sit in the front?"

"Because you're a hostage," he stage whispers.

"This isn't funny."

"I'm not kidding. Get in." He grabs the coil of rope from the floor. "Hurry."

"No."

He raises his brows. "No?"

"No! We're working together now. You're going to show me Alex was a gambler, remember? I'm not trying to escape."

"I worked with liars for ten years, Reese, and you're one of the best. If I didn't know who you were when we met, I still wouldn't. Hell, I still don't. Get in the car."

"You're awfully righteous for a guy who lied just as much as me."

"Not that much."

"The same amount."

He grabs my free hand, cuffing it with the other behind my back. Before I can fight, he's boosted me onto the seat, dumped me on my back, and looped an arm around my calves so he can bind my feet.

"Stop!" I protest. "That's not necessary."

"I'll decide what's necessary."

"What do you think I'm going to do with my fucking feet, Chris? Drive the truck?"

I'm angry, but I'm also frustrated. And sad. And confused. And when he picks up the dirty gag from the floor, I panic. I kick hard, my feet smacking his chest when he reaches in to pull me to a sitting position. That thing is not going in my mouth.

"No!" I try to keep my voice down so I don't justify his mission. "Don't gag me. I'm not going to scream."

"Stop fighting."

But I don't. I can't. I thought the last three years were apathy, but they weren't. They were build up. For this. Whatever this is.

I flop onto my back, even though it hurts my arms, and I kick with my tied feet as hard as I can. The back seat is so narrow it's essentially a tunnel Chris can't enter while I'm kicking, and when he finally manages to pin my legs to the seat and climb on top of me, I forget my promise and open my mouth to scream until he slaps his hand over it.

"Would you stop?" he snaps. Too much of his weight is on me, and it's hard to breathe. I feel tears leaking out the corners of my eyes, and I know the second he feels them because he hesitates.

The man doesn't like to see women cry.

"Please don't," I whisper against his hand. "I won't say anything."

His jaw tenses. "I have to."

"You don't."

"Don't take it personally."

I clamp my lips shut when he tries to slide the dingy scrap of fabric over my face. "It's very personal!" I say through my teeth.

"Don't make it hard, Reese."

"I won't," I mumble. "Just don't gag me."

He sighs. He turns his hand, and we can both see the shine of my tears on his fingers. After a second, he relents. "Am I going to regret this?"

"No. I promise."

He raises a brow. "Well, that means a lot."

In the end, Chris covers me with the blanket but leaves my head free, mouth un-gagged. In return, I'm silent for the trip across town. Even if I wanted to say something, I wouldn't. I can feel the tension radiating from the front seat, and I'm sure any smart remark would result in us turning around and me being frog-marched back to my cell. For three years, I've considered my apartment a sanctuary, but I was wrong. It was a bubble, an insulator, and I no longer want to hide away from the world. I thought I knew as much as there was to know about my family, but if what Chris says is true, I knew nothing about the two men in my life, the only ones I've ever loved. Now I want answers, no matter how damaging. Secrets are what got me into this mess.

I watch the skyline pass. We're traveling east, toward the art district, the shiny buildings turning into slightly less shiny buildings. Chris said Alex was a gambler, and Holden has two popular casinos, but they're on the west side, where the city's wealthiest denizens prefer to socialize. Right now we're about two blocks from my mother's apartment.

We circle the block three times. I squint against the sun that peeks through the clouds at intermittent intervals and monitor our progress via the rooflines. Terrific parking is something Holden boasts about; Chris isn't hunting for a spot. He's making sure he's not being followed.

We finally park on a side street between two towering office buildings. They reflect each other's mirrored windows and make me dizzy. Chris turns off the truck but doesn't move, and after a minute or two he gets out and rounds to the front. I see the top of his head swivel, no doubt wary of pedestrians who might question why he has a bound woman in his back seat, and I assume the coast is clear when he opens the door and grabs the rope around my ankles.

"No kicking," he warns.

I nod obediently, which does nothing to reassure him, if his frown lines are any indication. With my feet free, he leans in to grab my shoulder and pull me to a sitting position. I smell his soap, see the damp spots that linger in his hair from his shower.

He meets my eyes for a second, then sighs, pausing as he reaches into his pocket for the key to the handcuffs. My heart starts pounding. I wondered if I would be uncuffed for this excursion, because if he's taking me someplace where it wouldn't be an issue to see a cuffed woman being led around, I'm in even more trouble than I suspected.

Chris freezes when a businessman strolls by, talking loudly on his phone, but I don't make a sound. A single ounce of tension leaves his shoulders when the man is gone, but it's not enough to convince him to produce the key. Instead he leans in so his lips are next to my ear, one hand gripping the space between my neck and shoulder. To anyone passing by, it might look romantic, but it's not. It's borderline painful. Thus far he's been careful not to hurt me, so I know this isn't a threat. He's worried.

"You have to behave when we're in there, Reese."

"I know. I will."

"You try anything, and you'll regret it."

"You can uncuff me," I say. "I'll be good."

He leans back so we're eye-to-eye. The hand on my neck slides up so he's cradling my jaw. "It's not just me who needs this money, Reese."

"I know," I say, even as I'm filing away his choice of words. *Needs*, not wants.

"Johan and Davor are not guys you want to meet."

"I believe you."

"They're not guys I want to meet again."

"I get it, Chris. Just uncuff me."

He tightens his grip on my jaw when I jerk away, and my

gaze flits back as I try to wrench my face free. I can't.

"I know where you live," he says quietly. "I know how to find you. And I know how to find your father."

A sick feeling claws through my belly. I know my father lied about his connection to Chris, but he's still my dad. He's still the only person in my life who didn't cut off all communication with me after the scandal, even if that communication is closely monitored by the state.

I want to kick Chris. I want to knee him in the crotch and watch him writhe on the street. But I squash those urges and stare at him, letting him see my sincerity. "I just want answers."

"And then you'll get the money."

"I'll talk to my dad. He has to know where it is."

I hear his throat bob as he considers this. He's on the fence about whether or not he believes I genuinely don't know where the money is, but he obviously has no other options because after a second he nods tersely and frees my hands. I sigh with relief and rub my aching wrists. Chris watches the gesture. I think he feels bad. Despite his threats, he'd rather not be doing this. He *needs* to do it.

He helps me out of the car. We're where I expected we would be, about half a block away from the main street of shops and services for the area. This place rides the edge between the old and the new, evidenced by the mix of high-end suits and torn blue jeans, expensive cars, and dented pickups that help us blend in.

When I used to come here it was normally with a cab or a driver, so it's only when we round the corner to the front of the glass tower that I realize where we are exactly. The Chopin

Lounge is a high-end piano bar with a celebrity chef and an even more famous bartender. After midnight, they clear away the tables and bring in a deejay, the atmosphere a sleek blend of class, sex, and money. I'd come here a few times, but I know Alex was a big fan.

It's a few minutes after eleven, and the place is empty, still in the midst of preparations for the early lunch crowd. A young hostess in a starched white blouse approaches, her practiced smile faltering a bit when she takes in my jeans and T-shirt and Chris's only slightly more respectable jeans and black button-up.

"Table for two?" she asks, picking up leather-bound menus.

"Yeah," Chris says, peering over her shoulder, distracted. "In the back. Is Angela here?"

"Um…"

"Tell her I'm here."

"Who, exactly?"

"She'll know."

When the hostess hesitates, Chris takes the menus and nudges me through the lounge to a corner table at the back. He takes a seat facing the front of the restaurant, and I take the one opposite, glancing around to catch the hostess's judgmental scowl.

"I think you're supposed to wait to be seated," I whisper, flipping open my menu.

"Don't read the menu," he snaps, closing it. "We're not here for lunch."

"Then why are we here? I'm hungry. Who's Angela?"

He shifts around, looking agitated, so I give up the attempt at conversation and take in our surroundings. The walls are covered in dark gray fabric, the ceilings high, good for acoustics. Along the wall midway through the room is a small stage with a white baby grand piano positioned in the center. The tables are round and high, paired with tall chairs upholstered in white. Everything is muted so as not to detract from the well-lit bar along the back wall, three shelves of overpriced alcohol designed to open wallets.

I hear the muted murmur of the hostess as she speaks on the phone, then her voice brightens as she greets new customers. Chris stiffens, but it's just a trio of indistinguishable businessmen being led to a reserved table by the front window. The thirty floors above the restaurant are high-end condos and penthouses, and many of the residents have permanent reservations in the lounge.

"Alex used to come here," I offer, just to say something. "It was a short drive from the theater. He liked this place."

Chris nods, distracted. "I know."

"Have you ever been here after midnight? It turns into a club. Alex liked the music. And the tequila. Maybe too much. My dad had to come pick him up a few times."

Despite the money and his hectic schedule, my dad did his best to be a hands-on father. He wouldn't send a driver to collect his drunken child from a club in the middle of the night; he'd do it himself. It wasn't just Alex. He'd picked me up a few times, too. And in the morning he'd squeeze us a glass of fresh orange juice and admonish us to make better choices, advice I clearly should have heeded.

Chris scowls at his watch, and finally the doors that lead to the kitchen swing open. He jolts at the snapping sound, then relaxes slightly as a tall, stick-thin woman in a patterned red satin dress enters. Her black hair hangs over her shoulder in a thick braid, her fingernails and stilettos the same glossy ebony. Chris stands, so I do, too, watching as she grips his biceps as she kisses both his cheeks, leaving behind a smudge of blood red lipstick.

"Long time," she says, easing into the third chair as Chris and I re-take our seats.

"Yeah," Chris says, eyes on the front door. "How've you been?"

I look suspiciously at the door, too, but the only people coming in are an elderly couple asking for directions.

"Just fine," Angela replies. A waiter glides over with a tray of shot glasses brimming with clear alcohol. "Sake," she explains.

"It's eleven o'clock," Chris counters.

She shrugs and picks up her shot, downing it easily. Chris doesn't touch his, so I don't touch mine. His edginess is rubbing off; I don't know what's coming, but it's making me antsy. And he keeps eyeballing the door.

"This is Reese Carlisle," Chris says, nodding at me.

I forget to breathe for a second. It's been a long time since I've been introduced as myself, and I'm not sure how I feel about it.

Angela turns, her eyes lined with thick dark pencil. They widen as she gives me a second look, something I don't think she would have deigned to do had my name not rung a bell. I meet her stare with a bland gaze of my own.

"Huh," she says, fingering the end of her braid. "Interesting."

"Tell her about Alex."

Numbness floods me, the body's first line of defense. This is what I came here for, but now that the moment has arrived, I don't know if I'm ready for it. I don't want to know that my brother wasn't the person I thought he was. I already went through this with my father. And with Chris. Enough.

"I liked Alex," Angela says, after a moment. She trails a nail around the edge of her empty sake glass. "He was fun."

I don't reply, just watch her drawing circles.

"He was... generous," she adds, in a way that clearly says "generous" is not the right word. Could he really have been twenty million shades of *generous*?

More lunch people come in, and every time they enter Chris grows more and more tense. I eye the sake contemplatively.

"And he was addicted."

I look up from the drink. Chris already told me, but still I ask, "To what?"

"He liked to gamble."

"How would you know?"

She turns to Chris, and they exchange some unspoken promise. "Because I'm a dealer."

"What?"

More diners arrive, and Chris presses his hand on the table, hard enough the sake glasses slide half an inch in his direction. "Just take us back," he says. "She's not going to tell."

Angela smirks. "Who would believe her?"

I want to kick her, but I feel Chris's warning stare before I see it, so I keep my feet to myself. Angela stands and strides toward the kitchen doors, and I look at Chris and roll my eyes so hard I almost fall off my chair.

"Play along," he orders.

"Can I have the sake?"

"No." He pushes me after our guide. "Hurry up and follow."

The kitchen is long and sterile, bare walls and polished steel countertops. A handful of prep cooks work silently, their white jackets pristine. It smells like garlic and warming oil, and my stomach rumbles.

Angela's skin-tight red dress guides the way like a beacon, and we follow her through a door on the opposite side of the kitchen. The small glass inset has a tattered paper sign taped to it that reads *Deliveries Only*, but ten steps down a dim, narrow hallway is a set of intricately carved double doors that almost definitely don't lead outside. There are no windows. A large man in a dark suit stands to the side, and, with a murmured word from Angela, he retrieves a key from his pocket, opens the doors, and moves back.

Before the scandal I would have sworn up and down that I knew every nook and cranny of this city's party corners. And I would have died before I believed that Alex knew of something cool from which I was excluded.

But I never knew about this.

Never had a clue.

A cavernous space extends in front of us. The walls are again covered in fabric, but this time it's a deep, muted red that helps Angela blend in. There must be a hundred different tables in play, roulette and craps and poker and games I can't identify. The room is full but quiet. The gamblers range in age from young to exceedingly old, mostly male with a few women sprinkled in, all races represented. Everyone is dressed well, except Chris and me. The air is cool and, when I inhale, I feel a strange surge of energy. I think of Vegas casinos and the pumped-in oxygen that keeps gamblers awake and spending.

"Do you play?" Angela asks.

I shake my head.

"Only with other people's money," she remarks. "Smart. This way."

I open my mouth to point out that I was a financial advisor and dealing with people's money *was my job*, but she's already weaving her way through the room, expecting us to follow.

"That was my job," I mutter to Chris. "I wasn't playing."

"I know," he says reassuringly. "Of course."

He's still tense, eyes darting around, scoping out the room. Only a handful of people appear to have even registered our arrival, and none of them care.

Enormous stacks of chips and cash exchange hands as we make our way to the far side of the room. There's another set of doors here, and a single door on one of the side walls. I only notice because I see Chris taking it in, like he's mapping the space.

Somewhere in the last hundred feet, my heart starts to pound. A small part of it holds out the naïve hope that Alex will appear, fresh martini in hand and not dead at all, just secretly gambling for the past three years. But the larger part, the broken part, knows that's not what I'm about to find at all.

There's a poker game in progress at a table near the double doors, but after a quick word with the dealer and some extra chips added to the stacks, the game and its players move to a nearby station. Servers in tiny dresses arrive with trays full of complimentary champagne. No one seems to care that it's not even noon.

"Have a seat," Angela says, nodding at the recently vacated chairs. She stands in the dealer's spot, looking at home.

I sit and Chris sits, and I have no idea what to expect. I don't like gambling. I didn't before the scandal, and nothing has changed. It takes too long and it's boring. The odds are stacked against you. I don't see the point.

"That was Alex's favorite chair," Angela says. She cuts open a new deck of cards and starts to shuffle. Her fingers fly across the shiny rectangles, and the whisper of paper cuts the air. "I was his favorite dealer."

"Was he your favorite player?"

She watches the cards. "They're all my favorite."

I hope this isn't Chris's idea of proof. "Great."

She places a card in front of Chris, face up. King of diamonds. "That was your father's seat."

My father didn't gamble, either. He'd play a few games here and there to be sociable. But Alex. Together? That's impossible.

I think about those late night phone calls, him shuffling out the door in khakis and a polo shirt, not bothering with his standard suit and tie. "I'm going to get your brother," he would say. I never asked from where. Alex was a club kid—there were lots of options. But when I pictured him in a club, it was the one on the other side of the kitchen. The one where drugs and men and women were the lure, not money. We had lots. Too much.

Chris runs his finger over the edge of the wood. It's a thick table, varnished to a shine where it's exposed beneath the felt, and in front of me is a carving. *A + C*, one on top of the other, joined by a plus sign, similar to the Carlisle Gale logo. I'd seen Alex write this before—he used it as his signature at the theater.

My father didn't leave his initials, but I can picture him here. I can see him accepting a drink—*just one, Reese, we have to keep our heads when we're dealing with money*—one eye on my brother.

"How is Kimball?" Angela asks, flipping over the jack of diamonds next to the king. She gets no points for subtlety.

I open my mouth to respond, but Chris beats me to it. "He's fine," he answers. "It's prison."

"I should write more," Angela says, rolling her lips. "But I don't."

I try not to gape. *This* woman writes *my* father? In *prison?* Apart from his lawyer's sporadic and handsomely paid drop-ins, I was under the impression that I was the only person in touch with him. He's certainly the only person who's spoken to me over the past three years. But Angela writes him letters. Chris pays him visits. He collected my brother from this gambling room when he wasn't joining him. What the fuck was going on? I know I was self-centered, but I thought I knew what was happening in their lives, too. The embezzlement was supposed to be a secret, but this? Everything?

"Hey." Chris rubs my back. "Just listen." To Angela he says, "Tell her about Johan and—"

"Davor?" Angela rolls her eyes. "Dumb and angry," she says. "More money than sense." She glances at me. "No offense."

I straighten in my seat. Chris's palm settles more heavily between my shoulder blades, but I don't know if it's meant to be reassuring or to hold me in place. I had money *and* sense, if not a whopping amount of awareness.

"They're sharks," she continues absently. "Loan sharks and

other things. That's how Alex started paying when he ran out of money."

I think of the two hundred and twenty million my father stole. Is it even possible to lose that much?

"He didn't want to involve your father, and your father didn't want to be involved. But after they broke his fingers—"

I slammed them in the Tiger Wings, he'd said. *Tiger wings! I'm so embarrassed, Reese. Can you believe that?*

And I could.

I believed everything.

"...still owes lots," Angela is saying. "They've been trying to get someone on the inside to work your father, but they haven't succeeded. I heard they might have gotten someone in there recently. I don't know. Have you spoken to him?"

I think of our last visit. How frail my dad was. How he winced when we hugged. I was so preoccupied with my brilliant fake-money scheme that I hadn't paid enough attention to what was right in front of me.

"How much?" I hear myself say.

Chris puts a hand on my arm. "Reese."

"How much does he owe?" I'm picturing Alex's face when he steered us over the embankment. How much were our lives worth?

"About a million," Angela replies coolly. "Plus interest."

"How much is that?"

"After three years? Closer to two."

"That's bullshit."

She shrugs, one bony shoulder piercing the sky. "I'm not involved."

"That's bullshit, too."

Her eyes narrow, and she reassesses me. Before the scandal I didn't care if people underestimated me. I didn't care if they thought I was stupid. It was easier that way. Dismiss the bleached hair and the sparkly heels and the crotch shots—fine by me. But now? Now I'm really not in the mood.

"How many other people do they finance?"

Chris is stroking my back, and now he squeezes my shoulder. "Reese."

I shake him off. "If they keep you in business, you don't care how dumb they are. You care where the money is. And so do they. That makes you part of the problem."

Angela's eyes flash angrily, and she opens her mouth to speak, but Chris stands and cuts her off. "Don't do this," he says.

"You're an idiot," I counter. "Do you really think she didn't tell your 'roommates' where to find you the second you walked in the door?"

He grits his teeth. "Shut up."

I point at the carving. "A first grader could have done this. Is this really the best *proof* you could come up with?" I swipe at the jack and the king. "I don't know where your money is, asshole." I point between them. "You, and you, and Dumb and Dumber can go fuck yourselves. Or each other. I don't care."

A few people have turned, their interest piqued by the commotion, but Angela merely studies a display panel on the table, unimpressed by my impressive outburst. "They're here. Two seconds."

Chris's eyes widen. "What? Two? You—"

"I didn't call them," Angela says, sounding bored. "They

must have followed you. Find a way to blend."

He grabs my hand and pulls me to a standing position just as the doors we'd entered through swing open. I catch a glimpse of two tall bald guys in suits before Chris presses me into the corner and drops his head to mine. I squirm and shove at his chest.

"Don't," he murmurs, snagging my hands and squeezing them so hard it hurts. Past his shoulder I see Angela saunter over to greet her allies.

"What are you doing?" My heart thumps against my ribs. I'm sure he can feel it.

"This happens all the time in here," he says, one hand gliding down my back to cup my ass. "Just play along."

I twist my face away when I feel his stubble graze the corner of my mouth. How many times have I made out in the corner of a dark bar or club? How many times did I not care about the man I was with? When was the last time I cared about myself? Now. I care now. It may be too late, but I care.

"Don't," I say, my voice rough. "Don't kiss me."

He inhales, the sound catching. "I won't," he says. "But you need to pretend."

"I'm always pretending."

"I know the carving isn't proof," he says. "And I don't care if you believe Alex had a gambling addiction. I care if you believe the threat is real."

"Your roommates are real. I see them."

"I'm not making this up, Reese. They've been looking for you just as long as I have. You're lucky I found you first."

"I feel lucky."

"Stop. If Angela can't get them out of here, you're going to need to run. They probably have people outside. If you don't see them, it doesn't mean they're not there. Don't lead them back to your place."

I wait for him to crack a smile or tell me he's kidding, but he's dead serious. There's something in his eye that says this is for real. And he's not playing the hero, not offering to save my life. He's telling me to save myself.

"Where will you be?"

"Same as you. Making a run for it. But we have to split up."

"Doesn't that just make *you* safe? If they think I have the money?"

"Nah. They're pretty mad at me, too."

"Why?"

He doesn't have time to answer. There's a shout, then a loud bang, then Chris is shoving me toward the closest set of doors. Angela was predictably useless. "Run!" he shouts. "And don't stop!"

Despite all evidence to the contrary, I'm not an idiot. I run. I check over my shoulder as I pull open the heavy door, spotting the two bald guys reaching inside their jackets. I decide to assume they're reaching for guns instead of waiting for them to prove it, and dart through the door just as something pings off the metal near my head, making me jump. I'm in a long service corridor with at least a dozen doors leading off either side. The concrete floors slap under my feet as I run for the door at the end, the one most likely leading to the back alley. I reach it just as it swings open, another man in a suit coming through. The way he's looking around expectantly tells me he's not an employee finishing up a smoke break, and I barrel into him with everything

I have, knocking him back out. At the last second I see another man waiting behind him. I slam the door and twist the lock, trapping myself inside. My breath comes in desperate gasps, reminding me how unfit I am, how unreal this is.

Screams and bangs echo inside the casino, and it's only a matter of time before Johan or Davor—or both—reach the hallway. I race back and try the first three doors on either side, but they're all locked. The fourth one opens into a concrete staircase lit by flickering fluorescent lights. I jump inside and listen. Beyond the buzzing of the lights, it's quiet. I peer up through the winding stair rails, but no one shoots me.

I hesitate. I've seen my share of horror movies. The dim-witted heroine always goes upstairs when she should go outside. But I can't go out. I can't go in. I can't go down.

A hammering at the outer door cements my plan. I race up the first set of stairs, appalled at how quickly my thighs start to ache. I yank open the door to the first level and squeal and jump back inside when another bald man with a gun comes running down the hall. This door doesn't have a lock, so I run up another flight, the pounding at the ground level door intensifying.

I make it another three floors, my lungs threatening to explode. My legs feel like water. It's humiliating to think I might actually die from a heart attack before they shoot me.

There's a loud crash somewhere below, and I assume it's my friend from the alley bashing his way in. Footsteps thud up the stairs, and though my heart is pounding and my fingers are trembling, I inch open the door to the fourth floor and peek outside. It's empty.

I ease into the hall. I'm at the end, the carpeted floor lined with apartment doors before turning the corner out of sight. There's no way out at this end, so I run until I find a bank of elevators. I jab both the up and down buttons, figuring I'll get in whichever one comes first. History tells me random selection is the least predictable option—that if I don't know what I'm doing, how can anyone else—and I can't think of anything better. When the first elevator arrives I hide around the corner out of sight. The doors open to the empty car and I dart inside and discover we're going up.

I commit to the situation and press the button for the very top floor. The doors are easing shut when the elevator opposite me opens up to reveal either Johan or Davor, the name's not important when they're carrying a gun and pointing it at you.

I yelp and stab the button so hard my nail breaks, the doors closing just as he reaches in. I kick at his fingers and he lets out a yelp of his own, making mine less shameful. Then I'm soaring upwards.

I figure they're watching the numbers so they can travel to the same floor as me, but if I start punching in a bunch of random floors, it'll give them more opportunities to accost me. Thirty-one it is. After that…I guess I'll decide when I get there.

I stand to the side of the doors and squeeze my eyes shut tight when I reach the top floor. I fully expect to be riddled with bullet holes, but when I open my eyes I encounter nothing more than an elderly couple waiting for me to emerge. I get out and they get in.

"Is there rooftop access?" I ask as the doors start to shut.

The man points to my left. I see the numbers climbing on the three remaining elevators and run in the direction indicated.

At the end of the hall is a door marked "Roof Access."

I slip into the stairwell and stop. Somewhere below me, footsteps halt. I'm listening for someone and he's listening for me, and I'm pretty sure we've already met. Hopefully he's as out of shape as I am.

I climb the last flight on my tiptoes, hearing the occasional squeak from below. I guess we have the same idea. Though it's all for nothing when I shoulder open the door to the rooftop and bright sunlight streams in, giving away my great plan. My would-be assailant pounds up the stairs behind me and I hear static and an echo report of "She's on the roof."

The sun has burned through the thin layer of clouds, making everything up here feel exposed and vulnerable. The world is too bright, too surreal. Too quiet. Too open. There are a few barbeques and lounge chairs, small tables and planters—nothing to hide behind and nothing to use as a weapon. I stagger across the empty patio, then drag over a metal bistro table and wedge it under the door handle.

The building on the left is two stories taller than this one, but the one on the right is the same height. Unfortunately, it's about six feet away and, when I creep to the edge and peer down, it's an uninterrupted drop to the alley thirty-one stories below. It also has a recessed roof with a high retaining wall that rises about four feet. Even if I survive the jump, it's going to hurt.

The patio table screeches over the paving stones as someone tries to shove their way through the fire door. *Shit.*

I whirl around desperately.

Shit. Shit. Shit.

They're cursing inside, too, so close I can hear it, feel it, like hot breath in my ear.

Another furious bang against the door, and I know I'm out of time.

For years I've been asking myself the same question as I pace the perimeter of the roof of my own building: up or down.

Now I know the answer.

18

It hurts.

Like, a lot.

Owwwww.

I want to curl into a fetal position and take stock of my injuries and feel sorry for myself for a bit, but the sound of the door banging open on the opposite roof and the stampede of footsteps behind it is strong motivation to move. I roll so I'm pressed up against the retaining wall of the new building, hoping desperately that the four-foot stack of concrete blocks will help me. A scan of my surroundings confirms what my tattered and bleeding hands already know: this roof, otherwise bare, is covered in gravel, much of which is now embedded in my skin. The pain and the position is horribly familiar. I'd lain in a similar way, though with more blood and infinitely more heartbreak, after the car accident, unable to move until someone came to rescue me.

I think it's a safe bet that no one's coming to save me now.

Muffled voices filter across the gap between buildings. I can't make out words, but I figure they're debating whether or not I'd jumped and whether it's a good idea for them to jump, too.

Lucky for me, they opt not to tempt gravity and eventually they retreat and the fire door slams. I don't move. If I were a murderous psychopath, I'd leave someone up there to watch and make sure I wasn't lying right where I am, waiting for me to stand up so they could shoot me.

My hands and knees throb. I lift my head to take in the torn and bloody holes in my jeans, exposing ragged skin. There's a pulsing patch on my chin and, though it's vain, I'm pathetically grateful there was no one around to see my jump. In my mind it was a graceful leap, like a long jump athlete, legs extended majestically as I soared to safety. In reality, the toe of my right foot snagged on the retaining wall, sending me toppling onto my hands and face, knocking the wind and bravery right out of me. Now I hiss as I rotate my wrists and ankles, the joints complaining but not squealing. Not broken.

Fingertips touched to the sore spot on my jaw come away predictably bloody. I wince and close my eyes. Chris hadn't let me bring a purse today, still convinced I have some sort of secret agent gadget just waiting to spring on him. I don't, but I could really use a tissue and a compact. And some money. Because even if I manage to make it off this rooftop and out of the building, I'm still me. Only bloodier and more obvious than ever.

I don't know how much time passes before I hear the fire door on the other roof click shut. Pain keeps me prone and I don't move for another few minutes, eventually pulling myself to a grimacing sitting position. My raw knees screech as I peer over the wall, but the other rooftop is empty. I stay ducked low as I hobble over to the only structure on this roof that might have a door, and find one on the far side.

It's unlocked.

Sure. Now I get lucky.

I pull open the door and pause. No one punches me in the face. No bullets ricochet past. I enter and slump on the top step, rubbing my temples. Everything hurts. And I'm scared. I don't know where Chris is, or if he's alive. I hate that his plan has been semi-successful. I still don't know if I'm convinced my brother and dad gambled together, but I *am* convinced someone will kill me to get to the missing money. Whether their motive is greed or debt repayment is irrelevant. It still means I die, and though I'm a little late to the pro-life parade, I now know for certain I want to be part of it.

I push to my feet and wince as I hold the rail, leaving a bloody streak on the metal as I ease my way down the steep stairs to the first fire door.

It's locked.

Oh, for fuck's sake.

Another flight of stairs. Another locked door.

It takes half an hour and fifteen floors before I find a door that wasn't closed properly. I have nothing to do on the fifteenth floor, no grand plan for how I'll react if I encounter somebody, but it feels like I've been in the stairwell for hours and there's no way I can manage another fifteen flights. I need an elevator.

Like the building next door, this one is filled with exclusive high-end homes. The light sconces probably cost more than Chris's pickup. Ditto the flower arrangements stationed in front of the elevators. Once upon a time I might have appreciated this type of thing, or at least spared the energy to mock it. Now I don't see the point.

I call the elevator and study the fire map on the wall, hoping for some type of secret emergency exit leading to a quiet alley that will whisk me away from all this. There's no such thing, of course, just a basic building blueprint with clearly marked stairwells and exit points. And a gym.

≫≫ ≫≫

Thirty minutes later, I emerge in the lobby in a stolen purple velour track suit, cheap flip-flops, and sunglasses. I couldn't find anything for my hair so I had to pilfer a complementary white hand towel and tie it over my head like a bandana. Now I half-strut, half-limp across the marble floors like I belong here. I spent twenty-five years cultivating this very same level of entitlement. Now it's time for it to pay off.

When I emerge out onto the street I immediately spot two black sedans with the driver's side windows rolled down, dark-suited occupants scanning nearby doorways with serious scowls. They look at me and look away.

I want to go back the way we'd driven in, but the entire block in front of the Chopin Lounge is cordoned off with police tape. Cruisers, ambulances and a fire truck block the road, forcing me to circle the block in the opposite direction. I spot three more suspicious sedans, but in the milling mob of people trying to figure out what inspired the police activity, I manage to go unnoticed. I pass the back end of the side street Chris had parked on, and my heart stutters when I see his blue pickup right where we left it, unoccupied.

I force myself to keep walking, bruised fingers curled anxiously in the sleeve of the velour jacket. The slowly mending flesh on my knees tears itself anew with each step, and my hands feel like they're on fire. The burning palms give me an eerie sense of déjà vu. It wasn't too long ago that I'd stared at the weeping blisters on my hands and wondered how I got there.

I can't believe this is my life. Again.

My stomach growls every time I pass a restaurant, the mouthfuls of water I'd gulped down in the gym bathroom not nearly enough to leave me satisfied. It feels like years, but finally I'm back in my neighborhood, eight blocks from my apartment. The adrenaline that dulled my pain and gave me the energy to keep going has ebbed, and every movement feels like torture. Even the flip-flops hurt, rubbing the space between my toes red and raw, but I'd been so paranoid about wearing anything Johan and Davor and company might recognize that I'd left everything in a trash can at the gym. Still, for all its tackiness, this outfit has done its job. There's not a soul in Holden City who would be caught dead looking at a girl in purple velour.

I duck into a random parking garage, taking the elevator to the third level down. It's dark and quiet, filled with a smattering of cars, and the smell of concrete and gasoline is a comfort. There's no one around so I do my best impression of a burglar and peer into every car I come to until I find one with a dry cleaning bag hanging in the back seat. Locked. I have no idea how to pick a lock, so I move along, repeating the process until I find a car with nothing visible in the seats, but an unlocked door. I pop the trunk and find a gym bag.

Everybody in this town works out, or at least pretends to.

Unfortunately this bag belongs to a man. I don't have a lot of options, so I swap my memorable purple tracksuit for a pair of oversized black gym shorts and a large white T-shirt with a rather offensive saying on the front. I twist it into a knot at my hip, ditch my hair towel, and limp away before someone catches me. No cars followed me in, and maybe I'm being paranoid—which feels justified, at this point—but if anyone outside is waiting for the purple tracksuit to emerge, it'll be too late before they realize she's not coming back.

I trek through this garage and emerge again on the street two blocks later, then repeat the process at the next garage. This time I'm able to exchange the gym shorts for a flowing peasant skirt and a baseball hat.

After another twenty minutes I'm in the garage with my Mercedes. I do two laps in case someone's parked here, waiting, and keep my eyes peeled for any shiny bald heads. I see no one and cautiously approach the car, punching in the alarm code and waiting for an explosion that doesn't come. I don't keep a change of clothes in here but I do have a spare elevator key, so I stuff it in my pocket, lock up, and carry on.

When I finally reach my building, there's a woman waiting for the elevator, so I hide behind a concrete pillar until she gets in, then push the up arrow, hide again, and wait. My heart pounds, but I don't know if it's nerves or exhaustion. It's been a long time since I've had this much adrenaline in my system, and it's hitting me hard.

An empty elevator arrives, and I ride up to the fourteenth floor, my pulse quickening with each rising number. What if Johan and Davor are lurking in the hallway? Loitering inside? What do I do? What *can* I do? I have no money, no friends, and barely enough strength to remain standing.

On impulse, I get off on the twelfth floor and, even though my swollen knees beg me not to, painstakingly climb two more flights of stairs. Anyone waiting for an elevator to open on fourteen will have approximately one second of disadvantage when I come from the stairwell instead. Though I'm just as likely to collapse as attack them.

I utter a silent prayer before inching open the heavy door, but the hall is empty. There are no bullet holes in the walls, and the door to my apartment is intact. I even bend to peer at the lock for scratch marks. Nothing. It's the same shiny silver it's always been. And that's when I realize I have no keys. No way to actually get inside my own home.

I close my eyes, exhausted.

Then I knock.

After a second, there's a scuffling noise and the door is yanked open and Chris is dragging me inside. An impressive bruise is forming on his cheek and his left eye is puffy, but he looks better than me, and he's wearing his own clothing.

He slams the door shut and twists the lock, then pulls back to examine me. He lifts my hands and takes in my torn palms, raises the hem of my new skirt to study my scraped knees. Slowly he straightens to examine my face, the emotions swimming in his eyes mirrored in mine. This is the third worst day of my life. I'm terrified. I'm exhausted. I'm confused. Five minutes ago I thought I had no one, but here he is, waiting.

It's only now that I realize I hadn't allowed myself to hope for this. I hadn't dared pray that he was okay, that I wouldn't come home to an empty apartment. It's an odd wish for a hostage, but he's the first person in a very long time to know me, the first person to laugh at my jokes or hold a door for me or look at me with anything other than contempt or suspicion. Even if it was just an act, it meant something. It shifted something in me. It showed me what was possible, and I'm not ready for that possibility to be over.

He steps toward me and I meet him halfway, a fresh surge of adrenaline fuelling the fire. Everything hurts, but I thread my fingers through his hair and he grips my face. The kiss is rough and desperate. Tongues and muttered curses and promises. My sore head thuds against the wall when he backs me into it but we don't stop, and when he presses a thigh between mine I moan, relieved and bewildered and a million other things I don't have time to name.

The rough tips of his fingers undo the knot in my shirt and scrape the exposed skin beneath. It reminds me of the times he'd done this before, the feelings that touch foretold. Everything I thought it meant and everything it didn't. I want this, but I don't. There are too many lies between us. If I'm willing to fight to live, then I want to live better, too.

"Stop," I gasp, pushing weakly at his chest.

He immediately backs away, lifting his hands. "Sorry," he says. "I'm sorry. I'm sorry."

My breathing is labored and so is his. I touch my swollen lips and feel an ache low in my belly, a new unrequited pain to join the others. I'm too overwhelmed to appreciate the irony of him apologizing for a kiss instead of everything else.

He uses the back of his hand to wipe his mouth, the other adjusting the crotch of his jeans. "I didn't want to, anyway," he says after a moment.

I laugh, the sound rattling around in my chest. "Good," I say. "Me either."

"Great. We're totally on the same page, then."

The laughter fades, but the tired smiles linger when our eyes meet, a kind of resigned indifference that it's *this* page, the most fucked up page in the whole book, on which we should finally meet.

≫ ≫

That night we watch the news. There's blurry security camera footage of us entering the lounge, meeting with Angela, then following her into the back. The cameras in the kitchen and hallway weren't working, so that's where our story begins and ends. There are eye witness accounts of screams and shooting. Someone says there was a fire. They have zoomed in shots of our faces as well as Johan and Davor and their lookalike cronies, too hazy to identify, but obvious if you know who you're looking for.

"It's just a matter of time," Chris says, adjusting the pack of frozen blueberries against his cheek.

"What is?" I switch my bag of frozen corn from my left knee to my right. Chris gave me three ibuprofen and let me take a hot shower sans handcuffs, then cleaned the grit out of my wounds and ignored my cursing as he worked.

"Until they recognize you. It's going to be a big deal, Reese."

"I didn't start that fight."

"It's not going to matter. The news has been slow. You're going to be on the front page."

"There's still some room in the shrine. I'll be fine." I say it, but I don't mean it. For years I fed off the pain of those headlines, used them to fuel my own self-hatred. But now I don't want to read them. I don't want to clip them and frame them and hang them on the wall. I want this to be done. I want to be so far gone I never have to hear my own name again.

The shrill buzz of the intercom startles us until we remember we ordered groceries online for delivery. After sorting through the meager contents of my fridge for anything cold enough to nurse our wounds, Chris declared it necessary.

Now he groans as he pushes to his feet and goes to answer the call, giving permission to send up the delivery guy. He instructs me to wait in the bathroom when the knock sounds, and he's a little mean to the bewildered kid dropping bags inside the front door before being shooed away.

"Wow," I say, coming out of hiding. "That was harsh."

"I'm too tired for another fight."

"You're tired? Do you know how many flights of stairs I climbed today?"

Chris collects most of the bags. I grab the ones that remain and follow him into the kitchen.

"I hope you can cook," I remark, unpacking steak and chicken and vegetables. "Date night was the epitome of my culinary aspirations."

"You bought a pre-cooked chicken."

"I was going to mash the potatoes."

"I can cook. You won't starve."

"That's not the thing I'm most afraid of right now." I contemplate a bag of beets. "Do you actually know how to garden?"

"A bit."

"What about those plants in your apartment?"

He talks around a mouthful of grapes. "I got those from the rooftop garden. Then someone put up a sign asking for the 'borrower' to return them."

For a minute we work in silence, putting away the groceries like any nice, normal couple. Like there's anything nice about us, never mind normal. "We grew corn and potatoes," Chris says, eventually. "On the farm. Beets, too. That story was true."

I glance over. "In Montana?"

"Yep. I'm a farm boy."

"How long have you been in Holden?"

"About four years."

"Did you come to investigate my father?"

"Yes."

"How long did you know Alex?"

"Same amount of time. He was my first assignment."

I watch him dump half a box of frozen chicken wings onto a baking sheet, followed by a full pack of jalapeno poppers. It's strange to think of Alex as an "assignment," but it doesn't feel impossible anymore.

"I'll make you a gourmet meal tomorrow," Chris promises, misreading my silence. "Tonight, this is as good as it gets."

"That's fine."

He puts the tray in the oven and straightens.

I twist my fingers. "Were you in the FBI?"

"Yeah."

"But you're not now?"

"No."

"Why not?"

He takes a breath, like he's steadying himself. His shoulders tighten, then relax. "Same reason you locked yourself away."

"Because you got too many death threats?"

His mouth quirks. "Maybe not the exact same reason."

If I've learned anything over the past couple of days, it's that, whatever fuels Chris, it's not just greed. This is personal for him as well. Whatever happened with my brother, he too was devastated by the scandal and its aftermath.

"Did you like Alex?"

"Yes."

With the groceries put away, I flatten the paper bags and stick them in the cupboard beneath the sink. "Remember when you asked if I would have liked you?"

Chris opens a beer and nods as he twists off the cap. "I do."

"Would you have liked me?"

He thinks, then offers me the beer, which I decline. I plan to take a lot more ibuprofen, and, if his answer is particularly damaging, maybe a lot more still.

"I don't know if I would have liked you," he says after a moment. "But would I have fucked you? Yeah. You were pretty hot."

I cough out a startled laugh.

"Just once or twice," he adds. "To see what it was like."

I laugh harder, bruised ribs aching.

"I'd never been with a glamorous celebrity before I came to Holden. I'm more of the girl-next-door type. Salt of the earth. Kind and generous. You know." He rolls his lips and considers me. "Or maybe not."

"Oh, shut up."

"And I'd never been with a dishonest hermit, either. But you're not that bad."

"This is so nice to hear."

His mouth twitches. "I'm glad I never met you then. Because I never would have gotten to know you now. I never would have heard your stupid jokes or seen your scars or watched you fight. I still saw your you-know-what, though. In those pictures. You've gotta start wearing underwear."

I blush and laugh so hard I can barely stand. I've got no fewer than twenty-five bruises, so many scrapes we ran out of bandages, and a melting bag of corn for my aches and pains. The girl from the crotch shot photos is nowhere to be found. "I'm wearing them now, promise."

"You know your promises aren't worth shit."

I wipe my eyes and straighten. "It's good you waited," I say, gesturing to the mangled skin on my knees. "You would have missed out on a lot."

Chris sips his beer. "You can say something nice about me now."

"I've vowed to stop lying."

That earns me a smile, which is somehow even nicer than all his compliments.

We return to the living room, where the news has given way to a game show. Chris eases onto the couch, wincing but working valiantly to keep his beer from spilling. He'd tended to my wounds but determinedly ignored his own.

"What happened in the casino?" I ask. "After I left?"

He yawns. "Well, as you know, Johan and Davor and ten of

their friends came to do some gambling. They'd put a tracker in my truck, but your building security scrambles the signal, so they couldn't track me beyond the block. As soon as I drove above ground, it was a different story. That's how they found us ahead of schedule."

"That was supposed to happen?"

"Not quite like that. The idea was that you and I would be hiding out of sight while Angela got them talking. I wanted you to know the threat was real. That whatever plans you have for that money, this is never going to end if those guys don't get paid."

"And if I don't have twenty million dollars lying around?"

He arches an eyebrow. "You'll wish you did."

"I'll call the prison tomorrow to set up a phone call with my dad. Visitation's only on Saturdays. I guess you know that."

He nods.

"Are you close? With my dad?"

"No. He thinks I ruined his life."

"You did."

"Well. Sort of."

"So he wasn't embezzling before Alex needed the money? He just wanted to help?"

Chris exhales. "Not exactly. More like he was stealing a little bit here and there, just when it was easy. Things no one would think to look for. But when your brother got into trouble, he needed to pick it up a bit. Problem is, he wasn't very good at it, so once he got in, he just kept getting deeper and leaving bigger tracks."

"Why didn't he tell somebody? After Alex died, why wouldn't

he…" I blink away tears. It's too late to cry, and the salt will burn my wounds.

"Because it's safer in prison. Johan and Davor have to work to get somebody in there, and they haven't had an easy time of it. They're low-end guys, and the guys your father's in with are white collar. It's hard to find a guy who's willing to break some bones in white collar prison, you know? That place isn't half as bad as the place they'd wind up."

"He could have told me."

"He knew you were doing all right."

"All right? I contemplated suicide five nights a week!"

"I meant that you were doing well enough to hide from Johan and Davor, even though you didn't know they were looking for you."

"How would he know that? Because I wasn't missing any fingers?"

"Because I couldn't find you."

"He asked you to look for me?"

"Not exactly."

"Then what?"

"You know why I can't go home?"

"Because your roommates will kill you."

"Yeah. You know why that is?"

"Because you lie about everything."

"Because my cover was that I was part of their game. In order to buy Alex time, I told them we had the money, that I knew where it was. But we ran out of time, Alex died, my cover was blown, and I disappeared."

"Then why would you come back?"

He sighs. "Because of your father. A friend of mine who's at the Bureau told me they got word Johan and Davor had a few guys working their way through the system, and one or two were going to arrive at Wakeman. If they got to your father, we'd never get the money."

"So you *are* FBI."

"No. Then your father called me. He got a letter at the prison. It said it was from you, and the note was harmless. But it was a picture of you arriving at the prison, taken from nearby. Obviously they didn't manage to follow you all the way home, but they knew what you looked like. And he panicked."

"What did he want you to do?"

"Get close to you. Keep you safe. Find the money and keep him alive."

"Did you tell him how you managed that?"

"He can guess."

"Jesus."

"I didn't tell him about your alphabet game, if that's what you're wondering."

"I'm wondering if you told him about the night on the trunk of my car."

"Not in so many words."

I rub my brow. "God."

The oven timer dings, and Chris heads into the kitchen and comes back with a plate of wings and stuffed peppers, setting them on the couch and passing me a fistful of paper towel.

"So that's my story," he says, biting into a wing. "Your turn."

"You already know everything, remember? You stalked me."

"That was research. Fill me in."

"On what?"

"The details. What have you been doing these past three years?"

"Just hiding out. Volunteering at the Food Bank. Mastering the skill of darts."

He looks at the maps, then says, "Tell me about Fantasy Friends."

Something that feels a lot like shame tightens my throat. "What about it?"

"Why'd you do it?"

"To feel something. To talk to someone. Just for a little while."

"I thought you liked it up here."

"Sometimes. But sometimes I just needed someone. Something. To remind me I was…human." Unwittingly, my gaze goes to the hall, as though I can see through the wall and into the shrine, those hateful, hurtful headlines. I see Chris follow the same path and come to the same conclusion.

"Is that what those guys did?" he asks, picking at imaginary lint on his jeans.

"Yeah."

"How many?"

I lift my eyes to his. "I don't know. A lot. I didn't sleep with all of them."

"Were they nice to you?"

"Well, they never held me hostage, so I suppose so."

His smile is tinged with regret. "Did you think I was nice?"

I think about him holding doors. Making me a sandwich. Telling me I was pretty. Smart. Funny. Things I hadn't heard for so long. "I did. But I never really believed it."

"Why not?"

"Because why would somebody who seemed so good be drawn to me? If you were more of an asshole, I would have been less suspicious."

"So how about now? You must be crazy about me after all this."

"You're a nightmare come true."

He shifts so he's facing me more fully. "Where are you going when this is done, Reese? The Outback? Yap? It'll be just the same as up here. Isolated. Lonely. They probably don't have a dating app."

"I'll start one," I reply. "The Yap App."

"It'll never last."

"Then maybe I'll move again."

"Yeah? To where?"

"Oh, let me just give you a copy of my itinerary, abductor."

He laughs. "You know where I'd go?"

"Back to Montana."

"Nah. There's nothing left there for me. I think I'd go to Europe. I've never been."

"I've been. Lots."

"I'll bet. I want to see everything you think of when you think of France. The Louvre, the Eiffel Tower. And I want to go to Scotland and see Stonehenge, and London to see Big Ben. I want to go to Italy and visit the Sistine Chapel and the Trevi Fountain."

He seems sincere. First Montana, then Holden, then the world. Maybe I'm not the only one dreaming of a different life. "The Trevi Fountain? What would you wish for?"

"Good company?"

"That's hard to come by."

"You're telling me. What'd you wish for when you visited?"

"I was ten, so probably a new yacht."

We yawn at the same time, and I laugh into the crook of my arm. It's just after nine o'clock. "Are you going to lock me in my room tonight?"

"Are you going to come out and knife me in my sleep?"

"No."

"Then no."

"No handcuffs?"

He splays his hands wide. "I'd like to say I trust you, but the truth is I left them in the truck, and the truck's part of a crime scene."

"Lucky me." I push myself up, and Chris does the same, limping slightly on the way to the kitchen. "Are you sure you're okay?" I ask, watching him grit his teeth when he bends down to put the empty bottle in the recycling bin.

"Just fine. Anyone who spends more than a night on that couch is bound to have back problems."

"So my plan is working."

He smirks. "Good night."

I take my toothbrush and shampoo back into the en suite, since I'm now free to live freely in my own apartment. I stare at the shadowed circles beneath my eyes, the stray strands of hair that stick out of my sloppy ponytail. Never in my life, not even before the scandal, had I spent a night in with a guy eating chicken wings and talking.

I brush my teeth, spit, and rinse my mouth. This is as good as it gets.

I return to the living room to find Chris arranging a blanket and a throw pillow on the couch. "Hey."

He glances over. "You need something?"

"You can sleep in the bed if you want. No handcuffs. No hanky panky."

He looks surprised, and maybe rueful. "That's all right. Thanks, though. You're a very generous hostage."

"I try." I walk back to the bedroom, close the door, and crawl into bed. I'm exhausted and achy, but I just lay there, staring into the darkness, trying to figure out what the hell my life has become and what I'm going to do about it. Chris. My father. The money.

I thought I had a plan, but I don't know anymore.

The door creaks open. "Hey," Chris says softly.

"Hey."

"I think I'll take you up on that offer."

"I'm on the right."

I hear him fumbling in the dark, approaching cautiously, finding the edge of the bed and working his way around to climb under the covers on the left. His bare leg brushes against mine, and the knowledge that he'd taken off his pants makes me bite my lip in strange frustration. I shouldn't feel this way.

I won't.

"Good night, Reese," he says.

"Good night, Chris," I say.

19

I wake up to the muffled sound of a phone ringing somewhere in the apartment. Beside me, Chris is fast asleep on his stomach, arms folded around his head. I sit up slowly, wincing as my sore muscles groan in protest. That's my ringtone. My real phone. The one Chris took away. Only two places have the number, the Food Bank and the prison. He didn't shut it off, probably expecting that no one would call me and the battery would die, or that he'd be the one to intercept a collect call from the prison, effectively eliminating me as the middle man.

I slip out of bed and limp down the hall as fast as I can, my sore knees wailing. I need to locate the sound before it switches over to voicemail. The ringing is loudest in the kitchen so I start pulling open doors, tracking the noise. I'm two cupboards away when the ringing stops. I stare at the newly stocked shelves and try not to panic. It's probably nothing. I mean, nobody ever calls me, but it's probably no big deal.

Okay, yesterday somebody tried to kill me. It's a big deal.

I yank boxes of crackers and cans of soup off the shelves, grope a loaf of bread, and plunge my hand into a jar of dried pasta. Two cupboards later the counter is a mess, and I'm hopeless. My heart pounds and my hands shake, too many nameless emotions trying to bubble to a surface they haven't seen in too long. Then the ding of a voice message draws my attention to the box of cereal on top of the refrigerator. I yank it down and snatch out the bag, immediately spotting the phone. I dig it out and dust off the bran flakes, then call up the message, but it's just a tinned recording saying I missed a call from Wakeman Penitentiary. No call back number. The one I have in my contacts just sends me to a phone tree that leads to a frustrating series of dead ends. I stare desperately at the phone. I know this is bad. After yesterday and the news that Johan and Davor are close to getting a man inside the prison...

The phone rings, startling me so badly I nearly drop it. I bang my sore leg on a cabinet door and curse, covering my throbbing kneecap with one hand. "Hello?"

"This is Dalton Hilroy from Wakeman Penitentiary. Am I speaking with Reese Carlisle?"

My heart kicks into overdrive. "You are."

"Miss Carlisle, I'm calling to tell you there's been an incident with your father."

Outside the prison, there are a million people who would love the opportunity to hurt my dad. But he's been inside for three years with nothing more to fear than a fading tan and a bland diet. After yesterday's discoveries, I try not to let my thoughts fly to the worst case scenario, but I know I'm being naïve when I ask, "Is he okay?" Best case scenario, he misbehaved and he's been isolated somewhere, left to be tortured by guilty thoughts.

"He's just been moved from the ICU to a special guarded

room. His condition has improved from life threatening to critical. We tried calling you yesterday, but there was no reply."

I brace myself against the counter as shock floods me. Even knowing the answer is not enough to defend against the horror of it. "Was he attacked?"

"I can't discuss that."

My eyes well up with tears that spill over and burn the scrapes on my cheeks. "Critical? Where is he?"

"You can visit him," Hilroy says. "He was transferred to Holden General last night. You'll need ID when you get to the hospital. And you'll be checked for weapons and paraphernalia, as usual."

I hang up and drop the phone on the counter with a clatter. My knuckles turn white as I grip the granite edge and try not to lose it.

"What's going on?"

I whirl to find Chris in the living room, pulling on a pair of sweatpants. He's shirtless, and for a second I just stare at him, the oddly domestic scene so incongruent with our reality. There's a sad, lost part of me that wishes this were real. Wishes this was my life, minus the stolen money and the prison and the lies. Wishes I had somebody who was there when I needed someone, and not because he needs something from me.

"My father…" I try not to be a wimp about it, but my voice breaks and more tears fall. I swipe a hand across my eyes. "My father's in the hospital. They said there was an incident."

"Was he attacked?"

"They wouldn't confirm. But what else could it be?" My vision is starting to blur, but it's not tears, it's panic. Guilt. "I have to go."

"Reese." Chris blocks my exit from the kitchen. "It's not safe. They know what you look like now. The hospital could be a trap. That phone call could be a trap."

I stare at him, disbelieving and believing at the same time. "Then you call," I say, trying to dodge him and only succeeding in being boxed in better. "Call your friend at the FBI and ask him if it's true."

He sighs. "I can't."

"Why not?"

"I'm not exactly doing the right thing here, Reese. I can't tell them I need to know because my hostage is wondering."

"I'm not your hostage anymore. You lost your handcuffs, remember? You're a shitty abductor."

"You're mean in the morning."

"I'm mean all the time," I say. "Ask my friends."

"Be smart about this."

"I can't *not* go to the hospital, Chris. The caller ID said the call was from Wakeman. That's the best I can do. It's not like the hospital switchboard is going to confirm they've got a prisoner on their watch."

"I don't like it."

"I don't care." I push past him. "I know how to hide in this city."

≫ ≫

Denise disembarks at the bus stop in front of Holden General Hospital. She wears her favorite purple scrubs with a cartoon dog pattern, her red hair twisted into a sloppy knot at her nape. Thick-framed reading glasses do their part to mask my face, as does more makeup than I'm comfortable wearing. It takes a lot of powder to cover up bruises.

Two nurses get off ahead of me, and I follow close behind as though we'd traveled together. If Johan or Davor are watching the front entrance, I don't see them, but they don't jump out of the bushes to accost me, either, so I assume my guise works.

Once inside, the nurses peel off on their own agendas, and I approach the admissions desk. "Hi," I say, sliding off my glasses. "I'm Reese Carlisle. I'm here to see my father."

The orderly manning the station sizes me up, unconvinced, even when I pull out my wallet to show my ID. "Hang on," he says, picking up the phone.

I reach over to stop him, and he arches an eyebrow in warning. "Can we be… subtle, please? I'm trying not to attract attention."

"Uh-huh." He turns his back and speaks into the receiver in a voice so low I can't make out the words. After a second he turns back. "Come through here," he says, standing and gesturing through a set of swinging doors.

I walk through cautiously, feeling a little bit stupid in my getup now that I'm surrounded by actual health practitioners. Fortunately, everyone's too busy to judge my deceiving fashion choices, so we wait together until Hilroy appears through a door on the opposite side of the room. He does a double-take when he spots me, then gives the orderly the okay to leave.

"What on earth are you wearing?" he asks as he briskly pats me down.

"I'm trying to go incognito. Is my dad okay?"

"He's alive. Follow me."

We make our way through a series of twisting corridors to a bank of elevators. I start to sweat when we step inside the antiseptic-smelling car, and clutch the handrail for balance.

We get out on the fifth floor, the corridor empty except for two armed guards flanking a nearby door. The walls are a yellowed cinderblock, the floors cheap cork marred with pockmarks. It smells like bleach and medicine and my stomach lurches. When Alex was ten he had his appendix removed here, and spent three days in a private room on the twentieth floor taking pictures of his glamorous new scar. He had a view of the park, cable television, and a private chef. Now the armed guards remain remarkably impassive as I follow Hilroy to the door. They scrutinize me, then shift aside to let us enter.

I stumble to a halt. My father always had the biggest office, the nicest car, the most expensive suit. He was larger than life, the center of the universe. And now oxygen tubes feed into his nose, an IV drips into his arm, and machines beep and hum in a nauseatingly steady rhythm. A thin blanket is pulled up over his waist, and beneath it I see a large bandage bulge around his stomach. But it's not any of these details that hit me hardest. It's how *small* he is in his papery blue gown. How diminished.

I cover my mouth and go to him, grasping the side of the bed and taking in his pale face, the dark circles under his eyes so much worse than my own.

"What happened?" I glance at Hilroy.

"He got shanked in the shower."

My mouth falls open. "Shanked? My *father* got *shanked*? At *Wakeman?*" Every single part of that sentence sounds like it's wrong, a line from a cheesy TV script.

"It's rare, but it happens." Hilroy's cheeks are pink, telling me this is the party line, not his own level of indifference. He's shaken, too.

I see the tears fall before I feel them, watch them soak into the edge of the off-white sheet. I cover my father's hand with my own, squeezing his fingers gently, feeling his bones, his skin, his frailty. I feel hopeless and guilty. And angry.

His eyes flutter open and take a second to focus, flitting from me to Hilroy, then the door. He tries to smile but it doesn't really work. "Hi," he says, his voice raspy.

"Hi, dad. I'm…" I don't know how to finish the sentence. I'm here? I'm sorry? I'm going to fix this?

I feel the slightest pressure on my fingers, either a reassurance or a warning. The look in his eye tells me it's the latter. I'd seen the same look when I visited him at the precinct following his arrest. Whatever's happened to his body, his mind is unchanged. Always whirling, always plotting.

I glance at Hilroy. "Can you give us a minute?"

He hesitates, then nods and leaves. I hear him confer with the guards, then it's quiet.

"You got shanked? Dad… Why… How…"

He shudders. "It's bad, Reese."

"Obviously!"

"I thought they'd be happy with what they had, but they're not. They want the rest." I don't ask who "they" are. I'm pretty sure we've met.

"How much?" I ask. "I have some savings. If somebody's threatening you, I can—"

"No, Reese. That's not going to cut it."

I think about Angela's estimate. A million dollars would wipe out everything in my bank account, all my dreams and escape plans. Never mind her exorbitant interest rate.

I picture Hilroy and the guards. I picture a bug under the bed, in the lamp on the nightstand, behind the heart monitor. I picture everybody listening to every word, just as they always have, the same question on their mind: *Where's the money, Reese?*

I want my dad to be different. But he's not.

"I told you to get it," he rasps. "I told you where it was."

"I went," I tell him, wiping at the tears dripping off my chin. "I told you I went to get it and it was gone."

"Reese."

"You shouldn't have asked me. I didn't want to know."

"I couldn't ask Alex. You were the only one."

"It was too late. I went where you told me. I searched everywhere, and it was gone."

"That can't be true, Reese. Only I knew where it was. And I only told one person. You."

"Anyone could have found it!" I snap. "It doesn't—"

"I need it," he interrupts, eyes flashing desperately. "Look at me! They fucking shanked me!"

My fingers curl into my palms, digging into the torn flesh, making it burn. "Did it never occur to you to warn me that there was someone out there who might *want* to shank you? Who might want to shank *me?*"

Some of the fight goes out of him, and he finally sees past the clumsy makeup. "What did they do to you?"

"You did it," I bite out. "You sent Chris after me. You're the only one who knows where I work. Where I live. When I visit.

You told him where to find me. Here. The Food Bank. You gave him *my address*. You started this mess and you dragged me into it. You ruined your life trying to help Alex, and then you ruined mine."

"Pieces, no—"

The heart monitor starts to beep a little louder.

"You care about that money more than you care about me."

"I need it, sweetie. We can—"

"You never *needed* anything. You had enough!" I snap, my voice breaking. "You had everything. We had everything. And it wasn't enough for you. It was never enough."

"Whatever you did with it—" he begins, eyes widening as I shake my head. There's something in his stare now, something desperate, something removed from the father I know. Something that says the money is what he really loves, that three years in prison hasn't taught him anything.

Well, it's taught me lots.

The media says I'm like my father. That I'm selfish and I'm mean.

If they only knew.

I lean in close, my lips next to his ear, the words only for him. "It's gone," I whisper.

"Reese, honey—"

"I burned it."

"No, you—"

"I took it out to the forest, I dug a hole, and I watched it burn."

"I don't—"

"You made this mess," I tell him, backing away. "*You* clean it up."

The heart monitor starts a frantic, high-pitched squeal, and I back away slowly, my father's eyes widening as he reaches for me. Hilroy and the guards burst in, and I cover my face and burst into tears. "Help him!" I cry. "Help him, I don't know what's happening!"

Two nurses and a doctor rush in, and Hilroy guides me to the side, awkwardly patting my arm as I look on in faux concern. We always joked that I got my father's talent for money and Alex got our mother's gift for performing, but it turns out we got an even split, right down the middle.

20

I linger in the hospital waiting area until a group of nurses leaves for lunch, then slip into the crowd alongside them. I take the bus three stops past my apartment, then get off and walk back. I don't see anyone following me, but I also don't care. If this is my last time strolling these streets, I want to take them in. Holden is the only home I've ever known, and I want to remember the way the sun glints off the buildings, the way the sea of business people swallows you whole, the way it's so easy to blend into the insufferable swarm if you just try.

I buy a bottle of cheap wine and duck into a random parking garage, stripping off my nurse's scrub top and throwing it under a car so I'm in a plain black T-shirt. In the next garage, I lose the pants. Now I'm in black leggings.

I say goodbye to the wig in the third garage and arrive in my own parkade dressed only as myself. I take the elevator all the way to the roof and sit on the ledge, my feet dangling. I twist the top off the bottle and toss the tin cap over the edge, watching it disappear. I'm going to hell for a lot more than littering.

I close my eyes and feel the sun on my face as I drink. I think about the Food Bank and Rodney and Lyla and Hilroy and Mr. Pedersen. I think about how when I lost my old life, I never got to say goodbye. I tried, but no one would speak to me. There'll be no goodbyes this time, either, but at least it's on my terms.

I gaze north toward the cemetery, the grassy block obscured by gleaming office towers, the Carone logo glinting gold in the light. I think about my mother and brother, their graves unearthed by thieves, their unmarked plots unknown even to me and my father. I think how it's possible to think you've lost everything, and lose still more.

⸫⸫⸫ ⸫⸫⸫

Chris is pacing frantically when I walk through the door. "What the fuck?" he exclaims, skidding to a halt. It'd be funny if not for the very sincere panic on his face. "You were supposed to be back hours ago! I was going—" He breaks off and frowns at my appearance. "What happened to your hair?"

I touch the tangled black mess. "It got a little windblown."

"Windblown? What were you doing?"

"Hanging out on the roof. Thinking."

"Think—" He comes close and pauses, sniffing. "Were you drinking?"

I shrug. I'd had less than a quarter of the bottle, but enough for him to believe I had more. "It's been a rough day."

"Reese."

I watch him, but I don't think he was eavesdropping on my conversation with my father. I don't think he knows I broke his heart, the way I broke everybody else's. I don't think he knows what was true and what was not.

"I don't know if my dad will be okay," I admit, staring at my feet. "He's so—" I don't have to fake the tears, not when this part of the lie is real. "When he got arrested, he told me he'd hidden money in the basement of the theater. He told me where to find it and I went to get it for him. But it was gone." I sniffle miserably. "Because, on the way over, I got scared and I stopped. I sat in a parking lot and tried to process everything, tried to decide if I could do this. I waited and someone got there first. All these years I felt like I let him down, let down Alex. Like maybe if I'd found it and turned it in, they wouldn't have sentenced him for so long. Maybe Alex would be alive. Maybe every—" My face crumples and Chris catches me when my knees give way.

"Shh," he says, stroking my hair. "Come on."

"They were right." I sob into his shoulder. "All those people. Those things they said. I'm responsible. I killed Alex. If I hadn't stopped, then I could have gotten there first—"

"Okay," Chris murmurs. "It's okay."

They checked my car's GPS from that day, but I hadn't moved it from the parking garage. They checked the traffic cameras and security cameras from the nearby buildings, but there was no blond hair. No pink Maserati, no high heels, no one looking for attention. That was my first time venturing out incognito, and today will be my last.

Chris continues to hug me and smooth my tangled hair, but I'm the one who makes the first move. I kiss him goodbye like I never got to do on our failed date, the goodbyes I can't exchange with anyone else. The one person who saw me for who I was and chose not to hate me for it, even though he should have. He hesitates, his hands tensing on my hips, waiting for me to change my mind again.

I intend to change my mind. I intend to stop. Except it's so nice the way he feels and smells. It's nice the way he holds me and sees me and ignores all the jagged edges. It's nice that he believes in me, even if I know it can't last.

I pull my shirt over my head, and he reaches for me, then hesitates. "Are you sure?" he asks. I nod and pull off his T-shirt, and soon enough our pants are gone and it's just tangled limbs and gasping breaths. We're too beaten up to go at it on the floor, so we fumble our way down the hall, much like that night at his place, only we're at my apartment, my real one, and this time the light is on and nothing is hidden. The scars are out in the open. Today he knows my name. He says it often.

Everything I've been feeling and trying not to feel is bursting at the seams. I bite my lip to keep it in, to not say something I'll regret. Chris covers me with his body, and I sink into the mattress, enjoying the weight, the anchor, the fleeting idea that someone might want me to stay, might want to keep me. It's too late, but it's a pleasant thought.

I kiss him like there's a chance everything will be okay, like it's possible. He doesn't know this kiss is a goodbye and an apology. He doesn't know that with every second I'm promising myself I'll stop, even when my panties are gone and he's pushing inside and I'm so ready for him.

"Reese," he mutters, the words slipping through my hair, warm against my scalp. He threads his fingers through mine and rocks his hips, making me shudder. The pressure of him is wonderful, but it's my name on his lips that does it for me, that feels better than anything else ever could. He tells me to keep my eyes open and this time I do. When he looks back on this moment, I want him to know it was as real as I could allow it to be.

It feels like time slows down and we're here forever. It's misleading but it's right, like the calm before a storm. Those final moments before the phone rings and you mute the TV because you think that in a few minutes you'll turn the volume back up and everything will continue on the way it was. But it won't, and it never will.

I come with a cry that Chris catches in his mouth, smothering his own muttered words of satisfaction. My short nails dig into his back, too short to leave much of a mark, but maybe a small impression. A reminder. A memory.

He collapses on top of me, his heart galloping against my breast bone, and it's the most alive I've felt in a long time. The castle bridge is down, but instead of waiting for the enemy to come in, I'm going out. The decision has been made. There can be no siege if there's no princess.

"I need a drink," I whisper, biting his ear.

He grunts and lifts up enough so I can edge out. I pull on my panties and gather my bra as I walk to the kitchen. I dress quickly then return to the bedroom where Chris lies prone on his stomach, arms over his head, as always. He doesn't open an eye as I approach, doesn't see me lock the handcuff to the headboard, doesn't fully awaken until I secure the other around his wrist. I jump back before he can grab me, his post-sex reflexes surprisingly sharp when he's been betrayed.

"Sorry," I say, rolling a bottle of water up against the foot of the nightstand. "You'll be okay."

"What the fuck are you doing?" He sits up, outraged, and catches the briefs I toss at him. I give him sweatpants, too, so it's less embarrassing when he's found later.

"I'll call the police in a few hours," I tell him. "You can scream the place down in the meantime, but there's no telling who'll come."

"Reese—"

"I can't do this anymore." I grab my purse, the one with my real ID, my passport, and my keys. That's all I need.

"Reese." He yanks furiously at his hand. "They want their money. If you go, they'll kill your father. If you go, they'll kill me. They'll never stop looking for you."

"They'll stop," I assure him. "Don't worry about it."

"Where are you going?"

"Everywhere. You saw the maps."

He holds my gaze for a long moment. "Yap is cheap," he says.

I roll my eyes. "Don't kid yourself."

WHERE

21

Three years ago

"Sleepless in Seattle Seahawks," I mutter, blowing on my fingernails. The *Jeopardy!* contestant rings in a second later with the same response, earning herself four hundred dollars.

I scrutinize my new polish color. They say it has actual diamond flecks in it, and, for the price, it should. I apply another coat and listen to the next answer. "Pulitzer prize fighter," I say.

"What is Pulitzer prize fighter?" the contestant guesses for six hundred dollars.

My cell phone rings and I sigh at the unknown number. Despite changing my number three times in the past year, I still get a lot of calls from random losers. Bitter people like to post my details online for petty revenge, which means I have to deal with weeks of heavy breathing and "You're a whore!" calls varied only by the occasional marriage proposal and dick pic.

I know I shouldn't, but I mute the television and answer anyway. If it's a pervert I'll just hang up. Again.

"Hello?"

"Is this Reese Carlisle?"

I steel myself for the insult. "Who's this?"

"Officer Lee Jacobs with the Holden City Police Department. Am I speaking with Ms. Carlisle?"

I sit up a bit straighter. Yes, I got in a fight with Jill Waters at the Bolster Club last night, but those hair extensions were coming out anyway—who cares if I gave them a helping hand? Everybody knows she's the one who sold that crotch shot to the highest bidder. It's the least she deserved.

"You are." I use my most polite voice as I prepare to defend myself. If I get in trouble again this month, my dad is going to cut me off.

"I'm calling about your father," he says.

The world stops spinning. I've seen the commercials warning against the perils of drunk driving. A nice lady opening her front door to two pitying police officers, mouths moving as the bad news is buried under the screech of sirens, the woman collapsing in a devastated heap to reveal two small kids huddled behind her.

"He's been arrested," Jacobs continues.

My mouth opens and closes uselessly as I try to figure out what to say. This is probably a prank. Some paparazzo trying to get me to show up at the police station so he can get a shot of me going inside and sell the world a story about how I've turned myself in for one stupid reason or another.

"What for?" I pick up the polish. I need a third coat. Honestly, this manicure would have been cheaper at a salon. I press play on the remote but keep the volume muted as I read the questions. *Personal space invaders*, I mouth. One thousand dollars.

Jacobs starts listing some pretty serious charges, and it sounds like he's planning to ramble on for a while. I have to do my hair, choose my dress, and figure out if I should start my night at Josie's married boyfriend's new restaurant or just head straight to the club. The last time Josie had a chef boyfriend, we all got food poisoning. I lost six pounds in two days, but it wasn't worth it.

"Why aren't you calling his lawyer?" I interrupt. "Where did you get this number?"

Jacobs pauses. "Your father gave it to me," he says. "He wanted to call you first."

"Uh-huh."

"Ma'am. You need to come to the station."

"I'll bet."

"And you should come now, before word gets out."

I lie and say I'll come, if only because the police station is on the way to the restaurant, so I can drive past and look for "Officer Jacobs" lurking in the trees with his telephoto lens.

I hang up, then nurse a glass of champagne as I try on outfits, discarding shoes and jewelry and hairstyles for an hour until I settle on something short and silver to match my nails. Black leather stiletto booties give the outfit some edge, and I leave my blond hair loose and tousled, hanging halfway down my back.

I text Josie and tell her I'm on my way. There'd better be an open bar at this thing; I'm not traveling to the opposite side of town for a bottle of water. She texts back with assurances, and I buzz the doorman to ask him to get me a cab. He calls back a few moments later to say the taxi's waiting, and soon enough we're en route to the restaurant.

Normally the Holden City Police Department is a quiet, understated building that takes some effort to identify. Tonight, however, the glare of spotlights and headlights illuminate the block, and traffic has slowed to a crawl.

"Something big going on," the driver remarks.

I abandon my text conversation with Josie and crane my neck to see. The parking lot is full of news vans, reporters staring solemnly into cameras, while a few pedestrians look on. The entrance is crammed with paparazzi, far more than I normally warrant, and that's when I start to take Jacobs a little more seriously.

"Circle the block," I tell the driver, slouching low in my seat.

"The restaurant's straight ahead," he says.

"I know. Just circle."

He shrugs and flips on his blinker. I turn on the light on my phone and shine it out the window like I'm filming, but really I'm preventing anyone's camera from getting a clear shot of my face as I take in the scene. This is a city of stockbrokers and investment bankers, where money and politics are king. Life is rich but boring, and the Carlisles are the closest thing we have to a celebrity family. If this is where the action is tonight, it's because my father's inside.

My dad's lawyer is also my godfather, so I call him up in my contacts and press dial. It goes straight to voicemail. "Lincoln," I say, covering my mouth in case the driver is listening. He knows who I am; whether or not he cares is a different story.

"It's Reese," I continue. "Have you heard from my dad tonight? I think he needs your help. Come to the police station."

We inch around the block, the streets crowded with

haphazardly parked cars, the sidewalks filling with nosy locals hoping for cheap entertainment.

"Stop here," I say, when we pass the entrance to the parking lot. "This is close enough."

"You sure?" the driver asks. "I'll take you the rest of the way."

"Here's fine. Thank you." I pass him cash and climb out. For a few seconds, nobody even notices me, but I'm dressed to turn heads and soon enough there are cameras and shouted questions and I'm being swarmed.

"Did you help your father, Reese?"

"Are you here to turn yourself in, Reese?"

"Where's your brother, Reese?"

I feel the hot burn of a hundred flashbulbs, the bump of a padded microphone on my cheek, too many gusts of breath and pinching fingers to count.

The officers guarding the doors quickly figure out what's going on, and after a few suffocating moments I'm being escorted into the station, half-blind, ears ringing. My skin is clammy, my palms slick with sweat. I tell myself it's the warm weather, not terror.

The doors close behind us, muting the worst of the cries, but it takes a second for my eyes to adjust to the fluorescent lighting and the overwhelming quiet of the station. The officers wait patiently while I collect myself, tugging down the hem of my dress. I wish I had a jacket, but it's eighty degrees out, and I really didn't think I was coming here.

"Is my dad, um… Is Kimball Carlisle here?" I ask. "I got a phone call."

The officers exchange a look. "Mm hmm," they say. "Hang

on just a second. Would you like some water? A soda?"

I shake my head, wishing I had something stronger. They leave, and I check my phone. Lincoln hasn't called back. I send another text. *At police station. Dad is here. Come now.*

A minute later a tall, thin man in a cheap suit comes out, his smile razor sharp. He looks more like a shady accountant than a detective. "Reese Carlisle," he says, extending his hand. "I'm Kyle Trapper."

I shake his hand limply. "Uh-huh."

"Your father has asked to speak with you."

"Uh-huh."

"It's unusual for us to allow a suspect to meet with a friend or family member, but given your father's status in the community, tonight we're going to make an exception."

I'm used to being given free things. Prime tables, designer clothing, bottles of alcohol. But it's never really free, and even though Trapper continues to stare at me like he's being kind, and even though I can feel my entire world tilting on its axis, I'm never so off-kilter that I buy it.

"Thank you." I bite my lip and gaze at him with wide eyes, my best impression of a lost puppy. "Thank you so much."

His smile stretches. "Of course, Reese. Right this way."

I follow him through a low swinging gate and down a linoleum-covered hallway that threatens to crack under my heels with every step.

"Is he…okay?" I ask when we pause in front of a heavy gray door in a hall of similar gray doors. The walls are chipped cement. The whole thing is depressing.

"He's not injured," Trapper assures me, pulling out a key and unlocking the door. "We'll give you a few minutes."

"Thanks." I hope I sound grateful.

I peer into the room before I enter, just in case it's some kind of terrible trap. It resembles every interrogation room in every TV show. Plain walls, a small table tucked in the corner with cheap plastic chairs on either side. There are two cameras in the corners, red lights blinking, and I feel unseen eyes tracking my progress.

My father, who was supposed to be at a business dinner tonight, sits in his rumpled suit, tie undone, nursing a Styrofoam cup of water. I cross the room, ignoring the click of the door behind me, and he stands to wrap me in a hug.

"It's in the theater," he mutters into my hair. "Basement crawl space. Get it. Hide it. Don't tell Alex."

I pull back in confusion, remembering the cameras and screwing my face into a mask of dismayed outrage. "What are you doing in here?" I exclaim. "What have they done to you? Look at you! Your clothes are ruined. Your hair's a mess." I swipe at his hair as though I can fix anything. I don't know what he's talking about at the theater. No one even goes into the basement. People barely ever go into the actual fucking theater.

"It's a misunderstanding, sweetie." My dad gestures for me to sit and pats my hand as he takes the seat across from me. Even though he's a little roughed up and dented, the glint in his eye is unmistakable. He's the smartest man I've ever known. And he's in trouble.

"What are they saying? Is this some trumped up speeding thing? There's so much press outside. They probably—"

"They're saying I stole money," he interrupts. "From my clients."

My jaw drops, the shock real. "What? How could they—" My father doesn't need to steal. He earns every one of the millions of dollars he makes each year because he's good at his job. His clients are his friends. They adore him. They trust him.

So do I.

"Two hundred and twenty million," he adds.

If possible, my mouth opens even more. "What?"

"They said they followed the money and found two hundred million dollars in off-shore accounts. But there's twenty million still missing." His stare is unflinching. "They don't know where it is."

It feels like the cameras are zooming in, reading every spike of my pulse. "Do you know where it is?"

"Of course not," he says.

I bury my face in my hands, trying to compose myself. "Of course not," I repeat. "This is a misunderstanding."

"Absolutely. They don't understand. But you do, Reese."

I'm scouring my brain, trying to work through the ramifications of what he's saying. If he knows where the twenty million is—if it's in the fucking theater basement, of all places— then my father is a thief. And he wants my help. If you read the papers, you know I'm a lot of things—whore, ditz, socialite— but I'm not a thief and I'm not a liar.

A knock on the door makes me jump, and we turn to see an irritated Trapper shuffling back to allow my dad's lawyer, Lincoln Anders, to enter.

"Linc." My dad looks surprised as he stands. And so, so guilty.

"Kimball," Lincoln replies, glowering at Trapper. "Not another word, you understand?"

"Yessir," he answers.

"Daddy," I say.

He gives me a tiny nod. "I love you, Pieces. Take care." But *take care of it,* is what he means.

Trapper jerks his chin to indicate it's time for me to go. They didn't get what they wanted, so the Good Cop has taken his leave. He skims over my outfit with a contemptuous sneer. "Party's over," he drawls.

I was twelve the first time I tried a pair of high heels. My dad's then-girlfriend taught me how to walk. I remember my ankles twisting and my knees banging together as I limped up and down the hall, determined to master the skill. Now I head outside on the shakiest heels I've ever worn, swallowed up by the screaming swarm of press and onlookers. I don't have words for them. I don't have words for anything right now.

There's a free taxi in the center lane, and I slip through stalled traffic to get in the backseat. The photographers pound on the windows so hard the car shakes, a million stars exploding as they take my picture, each one a flashing dollar sign.

I tell the driver I want to go home.

≫ ≫

Half an hour later, I stumble off the elevator and into the dark penthouse. "Alex!" I shout, kicking off my shoes and striding into my dad's office, *tequila* my only desperate thought. We have a bar in the living room, but this is where he keeps the good stuff. "Alex! You'd better be here, you fuckwit! Something's up with Dad, and I need your help!"

No answer. I'd called him a dozen times on the interminable

drive home, but each call had gone directly to voicemail. I can't even remember which performance they're putting on at the theater tonight, but it had better be truly fucking phenomenal if I'm dealing with this crap by myself.

My dad's office smells like cigar smoke and cedar. Paper and ink. Time and money. The walls are lined with heavy wooden bookcases, every square inch filled. The desk is made of the same wood, designed to be imposing but functional. Before I worked at the firm, I used to come in here and sit in one of the upholstered seats opposite his big leather chair and wonder what it was like to be the richest person on the eastern seaboard. I wanted to know what it was like to have that money at your fingertips, to know you'd earned it and everyone knew.

Now I slouch into that same leather seat and fumble beneath the drawer for the key I know waits there, stuck to a tiny magnet. Alex and I found it when I was ten, playing a game of hide and seek, though we'd always been forbidden from playing in the office. I was thirteen the first time I tried the tequila; sixteen before I developed a taste for it. My dad must have known, but he never moved the key.

He keeps shot glasses in the same drawer, so I pull out the bottle and fill two glasses to the brim. Part of me is desperately praying Alex will come home and help sort this out. That my father will walk through the door, laughing with Linc, and say it was all a misunderstanding, those stupid cops don't know what they're talking about, Reese, get out of the office I told you not to play in there.

But that wasn't what he said when he hugged me.

I drink.

The alcohol burns on the way down and doesn't stop my hands from shaking. I'm sweating behind my knees and my hair feels too heavy for my head. I've never had a panic attack and I'm determined not to start, even though I'm pretty sure the choice isn't mine anymore. There's only one choice tonight and I cannot make it. I don't care what they say in the press. I'm not just a dumb blonde. I'm not the product of nepotism. I'm not an accomplice.

My phone rings, and I snatch it up, stopping just before I accept the call. It's not Alex or Linc. It's Josie. *Where the fuck are you?* she texts when I don't pick up. *The party's awesome and you're missing everything!!!*

I don't reply. I don't know what to say. I don't know anything.

I down the second shot, but it doesn't make me feel any better. I stash the bottle back in the drawer and return the key to the magnet, then stare at the desk, three gleaming computer monitors, neat stacks of paper, a hefty paperweight made from a piece of meteorite recovered from Siberia. I turn slowly in the chair, absorbing the bookshelves, the locked drawers, the panel under the Persian rug that no one knows holds the real family jewels, the DaVinci sketch on the wall that everyone knows hides a safe.

But he didn't tell me to empty the safe.

Or the floor panel.

Because that's too obvious.

Those are the first places anyone would look. The penthouse, our primary residence. Then the beach house, the brownstone, the yacht, the plane. My mother's apartment. The theater.

I take the shot glasses to the kitchen and peer out the window at the street below, now just a giant, swarming mass of lights and bodies. It's like the view from a concert stage, except I'm not a performer and no one asked if I wanted a part in the play. They just thrust a script into my hands and told me to read.

Frustrated tears fill my eyes when I call Alex again and get no response. I stopped leaving voice messages after the first four, worried I might say something that makes everything worse. "Did you know dad was stealing from everyone?" I imagine myself saying. "Hey, can you quickly check the crawl space in the basement of the theater to see if there's any cash stashed down there? I don't want to do it myself because of the rats."

My phone beeps with another text, and I sigh when I see the message is from a blocked number. *Hey, whore. Heard your money's as dirty as your cunt.*

If I were at the restaurant with Josie, we'd read this out loud and laugh hysterically before deleting it. Because it's different when you know in your heart it's not true.

Now I'm not so sure.

Another text. *You lying bitch. You're going to prison.*

Another one. *Rot in hell with your mother, thief.*

The screen lights up with message after message, so many I can't keep up. The words swim together, a sea of hate, so heavy and seething I turn off the phone completely, something I haven't done in years. I stumble down the hall to my bedroom, where I catch a glimpse of myself in the sparkly dress and yank it off. A strap tears, but I don't care, sobbing as I pull on a black T-shirt and a pair of dark jeans. I find sneakers I haven't worn in eons and a black baseball cap. Alex has random costumes in his closet so I root around until I find a shoulder-length brunette wig.

Normally I love walking out into a crowd, hearing them shout my name, cameras flashing as they take my picture. I love my unmistakable pink Maserati, the way it's guaranteed to get noticed.

Alex hates the attention at home as much as he loves it at the theater. Since opening a few years earlier, he's spent every waking moment there, desperate to prove to my father that he can be a success even if he doesn't care about money the way we do. He's got a dark gray Lexus that blends easily into the throng of luxury cars that fill the streets of downtown Holden, but there's no way anyone's leaving this building tonight without picking up some sort of tail. That's the kind of thing you get used to when you cultivate a following the way I have; it's the kind of thing you need to avoid when your dad has stolen two hundred and twenty million dollars.

Fortunately, Alex has a system in place for this. I used to tease him and say there's no reason to have a system, since he never goes anywhere interesting, but a UTI and a frantic early-morning visit to the doctor in utter obscurity was enough to show me the value of flying under the radar on occasion.

I grab my purse and a garbage bag, then take the elevator to the second level of the parking garage. I pluck my sticky T-shirt away from my chest and try to walk quickly but casually through the parkade. It's dark and humid down here, the air thick and gross with the smell of gasoline. I see no one as I make my way to Alex's crappy second car, parked on the fourth level of a garage two blocks over.

To further the idea that it's a car not worth stealing, Alex doesn't even lock the doors and keeps a key stashed under the driver's seat. When I reach the car, I keep going, just in case there's a reporter hiding nearby, waiting to see which vehicle I get in. I circle the lot, using my own car keys as both a ploy and a possible weapon, doing my best to look like I've forgotten where I parked.

When two laps of the garage turn up no unwanted guests, I return to Alex's car, snag the key, and stick the garbage bag in the glove box. It smells like pot and old leather in here, and I roll down the driver's side window a crack, expecting a hand to reach in and grab me at any second. I'm sweating profusely when I leave the safety of the garage, the darkness interrupted by the brightly lit mob scene two blocks away. I turn in the opposite direction, disappearing into the night as I picture our wealthy neighbors cursing the Carlisle family for turning them into hostages in their own homes.

≫≫ ≫≫

The theater is dark, the parking lot empty. I stare at the garish tiger wing doors as I cruise past, the only light coming from the tiny gas lamps hanging on either side. There are no cars out front, and none in the back where the staff parks.

I check my watch. A little after eleven. Alex said he had a show tonight, but if there was a show, there would be people here, cleaning up, going home. Maybe I got the day wrong. He always accuses me of being self-absorbed and not paying enough attention to him.

I reach for my phone, fingers fumbling on the cheap leather

seat before I remember I left it at home. It's probably for the best. I've watched enough television to know the police check cell phone records, and the last thing I want is to lead them here. I feel bereft without my phone, but that's the least of my twenty million worries.

I park the car, lock the doors, and wait as long as my nerves will hold out. Five minutes, maybe ten. I don't know what I'm waiting for. Alex? My dad? The police? No one comes. There aren't a lot of good reasons to hang out in this area after dark, and plenty of reasons not to. Maybe it's better if no one shows up.

I take a steadying breath, grab my purse and the garbage bag, and get out of the car. No one jumps me. My footsteps are the only sound as I cover the short distance to the back of the theater and unlock the fire door. Alex gave me my own key so I could come and go anonymously, saying it was so I wouldn't be hassled at the front, but we both know it's so I don't steal the spotlight on opening nights. That was always a bit of a joke, as are opening nights. He's doing his best to make this place a success, but it's usually empty, and as a result there are no security cameras. Alex insisted they weren't necessary, that anyone who stole something would realize its worthlessness and abandon it in the parking lot, anyway. It's weird, but I trust him.

The fire door clicks shut behind me and I check to make sure it's locked. I'm in a long service corridor lined with tiny orange emergency lights, the walls cast in eerie shadows. Framed pictures from old movies and theatre productions hang crookedly, painted faces leering at me.

It takes a second for my eyes to adjust, my nose twitching at the smell of must and old wood. I follow the hall straight through to the lobby, passing four closed doors on my way. I know there's a basement, but the doors aren't marked, so I try each one and they all open easily. There's a small staff bathroom, a space for the bookkeeper, and Alex's office, identifiable by his sticker-covered laptop and a few family photos. Opposite his office is the door to the basement. I know they store props down there, so it can't be quite the rat-infested, blood-spattered dungeon I'm imagining, but I'd really rather not go in, no matter what secrets are hidden down there. But I have to.

My hands are clammy and my fingers tremble as I feel for the switch on the inside wall. The bare overhead bulb flickers on and I halt, expecting a swarm of armed men to swoop in and arrest me, but apart from a moth waking up and slamming repeatedly into the bulb, nothing happens. I try to convince myself to descend the narrow stairs, but I can't. The air is thick with dust and paint fumes and I think of Alex's set designs, remember watching him sit at the dining table with his papers and pencils spread out, creating these new, fake worlds to sell to unsuspecting crowds. There'll be some down there now, painted trees and rainbows and blue skies. A forbidden castle, a jungle, the entrance to a gold mine. All preferable alternatives to this new reality.

You always want to believe you'll be the hero of your own story. That in a moment of terror you'll exhibit grace under pressure, remain calm and clear-headed, do the right thing. I do none of that. Tears I didn't even know were falling drip off my chin, and my palms are so damp they slip right off the handrails I cling to on my shaky way down. If I were on death row, I imagine my final walk would be just like this. A sniveling, terrified mess. A confused wreck of a stupid girl, wondering just how she came to be in this position.

I reach the bottom of the stairs and squint through the sickly glow of three more bare bulbs. Every square inch is jammed. Furniture and lamps and blank-eyed mannequins, trunks and racks overflowing with garish costumes. The painted backdrops are there, promising worlds far, far away. I trip over a plastic flamingo and nearly have a heart attack.

The walls are concrete, cool to the touch, and there are no windows. I don't know where the fucking crawl space is. I check under the stairs, but there's no door. I do my best to edge my way around the perimeter of the room, encountering an alarming number of taxidermy animals, their beady eyes watching my progress with disdain.

Then, finally, on the far wall, I find the crawl space. It's not so small I actually have to crawl, but it's low enough I have to bend in half to fit. It extends about ten feet back, and it's full, too. Every inch of this basement has been used to hide something, some of which will serve a new purpose in a new story, most of which will not.

I edge my way inside, past a large porcelain dog and a cracked sink with a pair of false teeth sitting in the basin. Progress is slow, and I think about the money. Running the calculations in my head, if it's hundred dollar bills weighing a gram apiece, that's five hundred kilograms' worth of money. Twelve hundred pounds. I saw a million dollars once, arranged in a single stack nearly as tall as me. What the hell does twenty million look like? And what am I supposed to do when I find it? The garbage bag

I brought to help carry the load crinkles in my hand like it's cackling at my stupidity.

The crawl space is deep, and I feel like I've been in here an hour when I finally reach the far wall. Next to a set of dust-covered bedside tables and a lamp that's missing its shade, are four large suitcases. They're identical, tall and gray, the type destined to incur extra handling fees at the airport if you dare fill them to capacity. They're too nice to be props.

I nudge one with my foot, and it doesn't budge. It's full. The light from the main room barely filters all the way back here, and when I fumble for a zipper, my fingers wrap around a small travel lock. I grab the handle of the closest suitcase and back my way out of the crawl space, banging my head on the low ceiling and losing the wig. The bag is incredibly heavy and it's all I can do to keep it upright, my spine wailing at the effort. I curse and sneeze as I retreat, my previous fears temporarily shelved.

The lock is small but high quality, and I can't wedge the zippers apart enough to stick in a finger to feel for the money. The sheen of sweat on my arms gleams in the meager light as I run up to Alex's office for a pair of scissors, then hurry back down. The suitcase is expensive and well-designed, and I feel blisters developing as I saw through the thick fabric until I have a hole big enough to see a neatly banded stack of bills in one hundred dollar denominations.

I drop the scissors and slump, sweat burning my eyes as I brace myself on a prop canoe. The money is real. And now here I am, a sitting, idiot duck, with millions of dollars not even a team of trained investigators could find.

Yet.

They probably think what any rational person would think—no one would have this much money in cash. It has to be hidden in an account somewhere, the millions arranged in a neat series of zeroes and commas, not four dingy suitcases. Who would even want this much cash? It's literally too much to carry. We're already rich—why would he do this? What could he have been using it for?

I peer at my watch. Just after midnight. Fuck. As a non-criminal, I really have no idea how long criminal transactions take. I've been in here a long time. I've left fingerprints and footprints and tears and sweat and hair everywhere. I have to make a decision. Help my father and implicate myself, or direct the police to the money and hope the gesture of goodwill results in a more lenient sentence. I think of Trapper, his disdainful sneer. I think of Alex, his sweet, hopeful face. If they want a scapegoat, I'm the obvious choice. The same million people who downloaded my crotch shot would love to see my mug shot.

I need to think. I have to get this money out of here, to a place no one can find, and no one will ever think to look. My dad won't be further implicated, Alex will never know, and I'll deny deny deny until everybody forgets about it and a bigger scandal hits the front page.

It takes forever, but eventually I've got the four suitcases lugged out of the basement and lined up in the hallway next to the back door. I'm sweating buckets and my muscles ache from the effort. There's a vending machine in the lobby so I go out front and dig coins from my purse to buy an orange soda. I drink deeply, wondering if this will be the last drink I have as a free woman. I close my eyes and enjoy it, trying to think of where the hell I'm supposed to hide twenty million dollars. I run through the obvious options, ruling out each one for that all too obvious reason. I think about attics and treasure chests and safe deposit boxes. I picture loading the suitcases onto the yacht and sailing into international waters, living out my days on the upper deck, eating sushi and developing a tan as I fan myself with fistfuls of cash.

I think about going to the private hangar at the airport and boarding a plane for Brunei or Comoros or Montenegro, countries that don't have an extradition treaty with the United States. My dad brought up the topic at dinner one night about a year ago. I had no idea what he was talking about. Or why.

But if I'm thinking about the plane, then Trapper is thinking about the plane. And anything I can think of he's likely to have thought of, too. The investigation must have taken months, if not years. I'm smart, but not so smart that I think I can outwit a team of professionals without any time to plan.

I pace around the lobby, jittery with nerves and sugar. I look at the framed playbills on the wall, the schedule of performances, the small art gallery. All these created worlds, fragments of imagination. Real until they're not. Near the doors hangs a full-color map of Holden County with pins noting other galleries and places of interest for those hoping to take advantage of our lean cultural offerings.

I start to walk away from the map, then pause. Very slowly, I turn back. It's a stupid idea, but it's all I've got. I find a pen near the cash register, uncap it, and stand back about six feet from the wall. Then, using the pen like a dart, I aim it at the map and let fly.

It bounces against the paper, then falls to the floor. I scoop it up and squint at the map. In the dim light it's hard to find at first, but then I see it. On the outskirts of Holden, about sixty miles away, there's a tiny dent in the paper and a miniscule spot of ink, like a period. The end of a sentence. The end of the story. If I didn't think of it, Trapper won't.

I hurry back to Alex's office, then reconsider and use the computer in the book keeper's office instead. I call up a map of Holden County and zoom in on the spot I'd marked on the map. I don't click on any of the tiny farm towns clustered in that area but make a mental note of the names. For good measure I do a search for the airport hangar address, the rules for arrests made in international waters, and how to buy a fake passport. I return to the basement to cover my tracks as best I can, dragging in props to fill the empty spaces left by the suitcases, swiping an old cape over the floor to redistribute the dirt.

I collect the wig and hunt through the props until I find a shovel and a change of clothes, then I go back upstairs and load the money into Alex's car. It's almost one o'clock in the morning, but I'm no longer tired. With the window rolled down, the night air rushes in, cooling the sweat at my temples. The roads are clear on the hour-long drive to Newtonville, a small farm town at the very outskirts of Holden County. I never come out here, and as I drive I pass stretches of farmland, broken up by forest and interspersed with feed stores and agricultural supply companies.

There's a gas station with an all-night diner, its lot full of semi-trucks. My stomach rumbles, but I know I can't stop. I think about sneaking up and adding a suitcase to each truck, imagining them driving to the four corners of the globe, letting someone else find the money and determine what to do with it.

I keep going until I find more forest, then pull in on a logging road until I'm convinced no one can see me. I get out, grab the shovel, and begin to dig the first hole I've ever dug in my life. It's incredibly hard. There are tree roots everywhere, and the shovel hits rocks and rings in my hands, rattling all the way up to my shoulders. Despite the cooler weather, I start to sweat again. It drips into my eyes, stinging, and soon my hands are burning, then tearing, the torn skin catching on the wooden handle and ripping more. I return to the car to look for gloves, but of course there are none. I brought a garbage bag, like that might hold twenty million dollars, but nothing of any real use.

I blow on my stinging hands, feeling loose pieces of flesh sway. My stomach lurches, bile burning the back of my throat. To add insult to injury, my half hour of digging has resulted in little more than a trench barely big enough to bury the shovel. I'm spiteful, so I do just that, kicking dirt over the top and spitting for good measure, then I get back in the car and slowly reverse down the logging road until I can see the moon again.

I don't know where to go. I've got a half-tank of gas, and I'm not going to waste it by driving in circles. I have to decide. To the east of the flat plains of farmland there's a smattering of lights from an industrial park, so I make my way over, craning my neck for some place to store twenty million dollars in stolen money.

And then I see it. *Newtonville Storage*, reads the glowing orange sign. *24 hours*. I pull into the deserted lot and ease past the front door. Inside I see a bearded guy reading a comic book, his feet propped on the small desk. If he notices me he doesn't react, and I circle through the narrow lanes that divide the storage sheds, each corrugated door locked and identical.

It's so perfectly *obvious*. I can't keep the money in the trunk. I can't dig a hole. I can't go home with it. I should *store* it.

I park out of sight and flip on the overhead light, then dig out tissues from my purse and wipe smears of dirt from my face. I tie back my sweaty hair and hide it under the wig and add a baseball cap for good measure, then a pair of sunglasses. With the light and a clearer head, I see that the costume I stole was, for some reason, a pink shirt with black piping and a pleated apron you might find in a fifties diner. Beggars can't be choosers, so I strip out of my dirty T-shirt and put on the costume. I've always wondered what it would be like to be a waitress.

I keep the jeans and sneakers, then get out of the car and go around to the trunk. I find the suitcase I'd cut open and wedge in my fingers until I've pulled out four thousand dollars. The sign says it costs fifty dollars a month to rent a locker, so this should buy me more than enough time to figure out what to do.

I steel myself and go inside. I think of Alex describing his techniques for inhabiting a character and wish I'd done more than roll my eyes and pretend to listen. My heart has resumed its steady pounding, and I'm newly sweaty. I'm conscious of keeping my tattered palms hidden when the attendant stands to greet me. His nametag says Roy.

"Hi there," he says.

I nod and wipe sweat out of my eyes. "I'd like to rent a locker."

He hesitates and I keep my head down, doing my best impression of a criminal waitress. "All right," he says eventually, sliding over a clipboard with a rental form and pen waiting on top. "Just fill in the boxes. What size unit are you looking for?"

"The smallest one you have."

"That'd be five by five."

"That's fine."

The sunglasses slip down my nose, and I push them up with one hand, the other trembling as I reach for the pen. My palm touches the paper and leaves a pink tinge.

Roy notices all of this.

"I'm sorry," I mumble, dropping the pen, then quickly picking it back up. I'll have to steal it. The police can use it to find my fingerprints. My DNA. It's on the paper, too, so I try to peel off the top page, but my skin hurts and my fingers are greasy and oh my god I'm going to prison.

"Hey," Roy says, his voice surprisingly gentle. "Don't worry about it. You just want to get out of town, make sure he can't find you. I understand."

I freeze as the words sink in. The sunglasses. The diner clothes. The injured hands. He thinks I'm a battered woman.

I'm going to hell.

Or prison.

"I can't let him find me," I hear myself whisper.

"He won't," Roy says. "I'll fill in this paperwork for you. You got any money?"

I nod weakly. "Yes. A little. I don't know when I'll be back."

"Never," Roy says adamantly. "Right?"

I lift the hem of my shirt and retrieve the four thousand dollars from the waistband of my jeans. "How much will this get me?"

Roy's mouth falls open. "Um…a lot. A long time."

"I might need a long time," I say. "And I need to make sure no one ever knows I was here."

"Absolutely. Absolutely." His eyes are locked on the cash.

"I have to go," I say. "Is there a key or something?"

Roy remembers himself. "Of course. Of course. You want an indoor or outdoor unit? Outdoors is a little cheaper, because it ain't air conditioned. Inside it's cooler. Depends what you're storing."

"Outdoors is fine. Out of sight of the road, if possible."

"Of course it's possible," he assures me. "Anything's possible."

Five minutes later, I have an indefinite rental term on a tiny unit at the back of the lot. There are no other vehicles in sight as I pull up to my locker, the dark blue garage door rattling as I unlock it and heave it over my head. The unit smells like dust and concrete, but it's clean and anonymous. I unload the suitcases, then use my T-shirt to wipe them down as best I can. I'm pretty sure any junior forensic expert would easily be able to find my DNA everywhere on the bags, but going through the motions makes me feel better. Like a criminal with promise.

I lower the door and twist the lock, the odd-shaped key cool in my throbbing palm. It's short and cylindrical, smaller than a regular key. A cheap tin tag with a paper center dangles from the end, C-76 written in marker in Roy's neat script. I unclip the tag and roll it between my sore fingers as I drive back to Holden, repeating *C-76* until there's no way I could ever forget it, though it'd probably be better if I did.

When I cross the Holden River, I roll down the window and toss the tag off the bridge. In the city center I cruise past my street, but it's crowded with news vans and bystanders, too many people to risk. I turn east, toward my mother's apartment. It's been sitting empty for the past year, but stale air won't be the worst thing I encounter tonight.

A couple of people stroll down the street, smoking and laughing, and they pay no attention to the car as I cruise past. This area is cheaper and more artsy than the financial district I live in, and Alex's car blends well. I circle the block, but see no cameramen, no reporters waiting to pounce with questions and accusations. They think I'm at home.

I park around the corner, then hurry into the building, taking the elevator to the third floor and letting myself in. The apartment is dark and warm, and the moonlight eking through the windows offers enough guidance that I don't bother with lights as I shuffle into the bedroom. I strip out of my dirty clothes and stuff them in the garbage bag, mostly to convince myself it has a purpose.

I take a lukewarm shower to rinse away the grime, my hands burning the whole time. There's no food in the fridge or the cupboards, so I mollify my rumbling stomach with mouthfuls of water gulped straight from the tap, then return to the bedroom and toss the duvet onto the floor, crawling in naked beneath the thin fitted sheet. It's 3:07 a.m.

I lie awake until nearly six, unable to slow the whirring wheels in my brain. I wonder if I slept, if this has all been a dream. If I went to the restaurant opening and had a little too much to drink and ended up in this strange apartment and everything is fucked up but as it should be.

But I know this apartment. I see the bag with my dirt-smeared jeans, the pink apron, the wig. I reach for my phone and remember I don't have it. I'm alone. No one knows where I am. I picture the swarming mob, the hisses, the texts, the insults, the accusations. It's one thing when you know what they're saying is untrue, quite another when it's not.

My bladder is nagging me but I don't move. I don't usually like being alone, but right now—just for now—it's kind of nice.

>>> >>>

Thanks to my father's sentimental streak, I was able to raid the closets holding my mother's clothing for something not filthy and incriminating to wear home this morning. Now I'm in a black flapper-style dress, a gaudy costume jewelry necklace, and a pair of shoes one size too small as I return Alex's car to its secret spot then make my way out of the garage to street-level. I'd fixed up my face a bit with the compact and lipstick I had in my purse, and tied my blond hair up in a sloppy morning-after bun. My sunglasses mask the fact that my eyes aren't puffy and swollen from my usual hangover, just lack of sleep and an excess of criminal activity. I totter carelessly up the street, wincing at the bright sun. It's nine o'clock in the morning and the press is out in full force. I hear them before I see them, like a swarm of bees.

The first cameraman recognizes me when I'm a block away. Everyone else has their focus trained on the front doors, stupidly convinced I'm hunkered down inside. A shout goes up and they turn as one to mob me, the cries and questions deafening. Cameras and microphones bump my face, and I feel grasping hands and fingers on my arms, my legs, the hem of my skirt. I'm wearing yesterday's panties, so we can rule out a new crotch shot.

"Reese!" they scream in unison. "Is it true your father has

been arrested? Is it true he's been stealing from clients? Were you helping him, Reese? There's rumors of missing money! Do you know where it is, Reese?"

I force a vapid smile and clutch my purse to my chest as I shoulder my way toward the front door. Over the heads of the reporters I see Trapper's stern face as he stalks through the crowd, flanked by two men in dark glasses.

"It's just a misunderstanding!" I say dismissively. "Everything will be fine."

"Where were you last night?" someone asks.

"Who were you with?"

I grasp the bag even tighter, keeping my palms hidden.

"She looks like she's been drinking," someone adds.

"What's new?"

"Who designed your dress, Reese?"

This is hardly my first walk of shame, but it's the first time I've actually felt ashamed of what I did the night before.

A hand grips my arm, and I know it's Trapper even before I hear his voice ordering the crowd to give me some space. The men in shades have earpieces, dark wires coiling into the necklines of their navy jackets. The same jacket Trapper's wearing, *FBI* stenciled across the breast in yellow.

The letters barely have time to sink in before he's ushering me into the lobby, my toes squealing in the tight shoes. I stumble, and he mutters something under his breath. The only word I catch is "stupid."

This morning when I left my mother's apartment I threw the sheets and each item of clothing from last night into a different dumpster. I poured bleach down the shower drain and ran the hot water for ten minutes. I found a pen and sketched a tiny diamond on my wrist, then tried to wash it off, leaving a faint blue stain.

"Where have you been?" Trapper asks, waving away the alarmed concierge and poking the button for the elevator.

"I don't know," I mumble. "Out."

"Out where?"

I turn over my wrist to show the blue smudge. "Here, maybe. I don't remember."

His sigh is pure exasperation. "You changed your dress."

"Yeah."

"Why?"

I finger the dark material. "Black suited my mood."

We reach my floor, and I take out my keys, but before I unlock the door it's wrenched open, Alex standing on the other side, mouth slack.

"Pieces!" he cries, hugging me tightly. His big blue eyes are wet with tears, his tousled brown hair even messier than normal. No matter how old we get, he'll always look young to me, always be my little brother. "Where the hell have you been? Oh my God, did you hear? What's happening? What's going on?"

In response, Trapper reaches into his jacket and pulls out a folded sheaf of papers. "Search warrant," he replies.

Alex releases me. "A search warrant? For what?"

"Twenty million dollars, among other things."

Alex pales. "What?"

"They're saying dad stole money," I tell him. "Maybe it's sitting in his office in an envelope somewhere."

"Start there," Trapper says to the closest agent, who nods and pushes past me. Two more elevators open, and a flood of men and women in matching jackets and hats spill out.

"You can't do this," Alex says, though it seems pretty obvious that they can. They're swift and efficient, filling boxes with books and computers and file folders. I see them take my phone, still sitting on the counter.

Trapper watches me, missing nothing.

Missing everything.

"You're wrong," I tell him.

"I'm not."

"There's a safe."

"Reese!" Alex exclaims.

Trapper nods. "I know."

"About the floor safe?"

Alex gawks at me. "Reese! Stop!"

"There's nothing to hide, Alex. Everything they take can be replaced. I have you, and you have me, and dad will be back in no time."

"Your dad will be back in twenty-five to thirty," Trapper replies. "Where's the floor safe?"

"Under the rug by the desk," I say, nodding toward the office. "Any others?"

"Just the two in here. There's one in the beach house, in the back of the closet in the blue guest room."

Trapper's nostrils flare, then he pulls out his phone and types out a message. That's when I realize how big this is. They're not just here. They're everywhere. The beach house. The yacht. The airplane. The office.

Someone walks past with my laptop, its glittery pink casing winking goodbye.

"That's my—"

"We know," Trapper says.

He never looks at Alex, only me.

"Two years probation," he says. "If you testify."

"To what?"

"To knowing your father was embezzling."

I hear Alex gasp.

I curl my broken nails into my palms, the pain bringing tears to my eyes. "He would never do that."

"You've got until noon to take the deal."

A woman passes with Alex's tablet, identifiable by the Andy Warhol collage that covers the surface.

"You can't—" Alex protests.

"We can," Trapper says.

Alex turns to me. "We have to get out of here," he says. "We'll go... We'll go to—"

"Your assets are frozen," Trapper interrupts. "The beach house will be repossessed. The yacht, the airplane. Everything you think you own, you don't. Everything you thought was yours...isn't."

I finger the long necklace that hangs around my neck. A cheap chain, a piece of costume jewelry my father saved along with the dress. The tasseled brass pendant dangles between my breasts, now amended with something small and cylindrical. Trapper takes note of the jewelry, then zeroes in on my mangled nails.

"What happened to your hands?"

I turn them over, like I can't quite believe what I'm seeing. "I must have fallen," I say.

"That's quite the fall." He smirks at his own joke. You don't grow up in the penthouse suite of the most exclusive building in town without someone wanting to see you brought down a peg. Or twenty million.

A stream of agents filters past with boxes full of everything. Things they can't possibly need. Things they're taking because they don't want us to have them. The living room is almost empty. I can see the bare shelves of the office from here. But I'm the only one who knows where to find what they're looking for.

"Reese," Alex whispers, clutching my wrist and pulling me across the room, away from Trapper's smug stare. "Do you know what they're talking about? Money? Hidden... here?" He looks sick and betrayed, one fat tear rolling down his baby-smooth cheek. Worried about our father, our future. When he was three, he cried for a month straight when he realized he didn't have a mom. I used to sleep curled up next to him, stroking his back and promising everything would be okay. I would help. I remember my dad carrying me to my own bed, whispering what a good sister I was as he tucked me in.

22

Present

I leave Chris cuffed to the bed and drive to Newtonville Storage in a blond wig, a baseball cap, sunglasses, and my black tights and T-shirt. I stick to the speed limit and use my blinker appropriately. I'm going to do what I should have done three years ago, and I'm going to do it right.

There are a handful of vehicles in the lot, but the only people outside are a middle-aged couple unloading their car in the next aisle. I'm alone when I park in front of C-76, the blue door lowered and locked, innocuous and identical to all the rest. I clench the key in my hand, making my torn palms ache. This morning I'd made a little label out of tape and written *C-76 Newtonville* in block letters.

I haven't been here since that night, and I don't know what I'll find when I lift the door. Maybe something. Maybe nothing. Maybe I imagined the whole thing. Maybe I'm just as crazy as I've always feared but have been too afraid to confirm. For three years, this money has been an anchor, weighing me down, keeping me here.

Today it ends.

I place my hands on top of the steering wheel and glance around covertly for security cameras, spotting one on the garage behind me and one a few doors down. Eventually Trapper will watch this footage, and it needs to be convincing. I grab my bag and climb out of the car, then squint at the key in my palm and check it against the number on the door, confirming I'm at the right place. For posterity's sake I reach for the car like I'm having second thoughts, then bravely stiffen my spine and approach the locker, crouching down to test the key.

It slides in easily.

I fall back onto my butt, a clumsy blonde fool, then look around, embarrassed, before twisting the key and giving the door a tentative push. It glides up three feet, like it's happy to be open, to have its secrets revealed. I crane my neck and peer inside, then straighten and push the door another two feet so I can duck under. When I release it I give it a quick tug so it slides back down, hiding my actions from view of the camera. I switch on the light. It flickers, then hums to life.

Four identical gray suitcases stand upright against the back wall of the small unit. One has a gash at the top, just enough room to pluck out four thousand dollars. It's exactly as I left it.

I don't have a lot of time, and if the cameras can't see me in here there's no need to play the hesitant twit. I reach into my satchel and pull out the bolt cutters I bought on my way out of town, then snip the lock on the damaged bag and unzip it fully. It's as expected. Rows of banded hundred dollar bills, pristine and waiting. Pandora's box, beckoning. But I'm not tempted. I have money and I have plans that don't involve jail time.

The currency strap tells me each bundle is worth ten thousand. One thousand tidy hundred dollar bills, not so tidily earned. I count out a hundred packs and remove the top bill from each, giving me ten thousand dollars in non-sequential hundreds. From my satchel I remove the five black garbage bags I'd brought as filler and toss them into the corner, then slide the loose bills into the pre-paid Priority envelope I bought on the way over. I take the remaining nine hundred and ninety-thousand and stuff it in my bag, then study the lumpy satchel. It looks the same as it did with the garbage bags, if considerably heavier.

I leave the opened suitcase as is and ignore the others, then pause and listen carefully. It's quiet outside. I want the camera to witness my exit, not actual humans. Fingers crossed that my luck holds out, I turn and run to the door, shoving it open and scrambling out as though I'd found a body. I slam and lock the door, then hurry to the car. Looking around helplessly, I brace myself dramatically against the hood, a stunned daughter composing herself in the face of an unbelievable discovery. Shakily I climb into the driver's seat, shocked but determined to do the right thing.

The closest courier office is on the outskirts of Holden, connected to one of their depots. I make the short drive over and wait in line until it's my turn. I'm wearing the ball cap, but I've ditched the sunglasses. I want Trapper to be able to identify me. The attendant is polite but bored, not interested in my stammering, shocked performance. I ask to borrow a piece of paper and scribble a quick note.

I found this key inside a picture frame. I went to the locker and looked inside. There were four suitcases. I opened one. It's full of money. I don't know how much. I don't know who put it there, but I hope you can return it. Now fuck off.

I sign it with my own name, then fold the paper in half, add it to the envelope with the key, and address the package to the Holden branch of the FBI. I pay for next day delivery, then get back in my car to make my final stop in Holden.

≫≫ ≫≫

I still bear the scars of my last visit to the Chopin Lounge, but it feels like something that happened a long time ago to a different person. This time I'm the one who ignores the hostess and strolls to the back, my cash-filled satchel over my shoulder. I'd dropped the Priority envelope in a mailbox down the block, so the only thing left in this bag is nine hundred and ninety thousand dollars and a lock. I enter the kitchen, and the chefs look at me in surprise, but no one says a word. They know what the secret room is for and they know how to see nothing.

I step into the back hallway just as Angela strides through the guarded double doors, having gotten word of my arrival. "May I help you?" Her eyes glitter with contempt, ringed with heavy slashes of black eyeliner, the dark braid coiled over her shoulder. Today's dress is embroidered blue silk, her silver heels picking up the gleaming threads.

"Call them," I say.

"Who?"

"Who do you think?"

She stares at me for a second, then pulls out her phone. "It's me," she says. I hear a man's voice on the other end. It could be

Chris. It could be the police. It could be Johan or Davor. "She's here."

The voice raises.

"Tell them I'm leaving," I say, "and I have a going away present." I don't bother negotiating for my father's safety or for Chris's. I know well enough that when people care about money, they'll do anything to get it and anything to keep it. There's no sense inviting more drama once they've been paid.

"Prove it," Angela says.

I unzip the bag and show her the cash. She reaches for it but I slick the bag closed and fasten the tabs together with the lock. When she opens her mouth to argue, I take the phone from her hand. "It's a million dollars and there's a combination lock," I say into the receiver. I don't know if it's Johan or Davor, and I don't care. "If the bag is damaged when you get here, Angela stole from you."

Angela's indignation is replaced with pure rage when I hang up, text the combination to the number she'd just called, then toss the phone on the floor and stomp on it, shattering the screen with my heel.

"Good luck," I tell her.

"Wait. You—"

I waited three years for my father's appeal. Three years to convince myself it was all some sort of misunderstanding. Yes, he had twenty million dollars in sequential bills stashed in suitcases, but maybe he had a good reason.

He didn't.

So my father is paying the price for what he did, and if Trapper checks his mail, he's likely to continue to pay for another twenty-two years.

Alex will pay forever.

But I'm done.

This is not my mess.

Not my secret.

Not my choice.

Not anymore.

≫≫ ≫≫

Because Holden is small but rich, the Holden City Airport is also small and rich. I park my Mercedes in the extended-stay lot, another overpriced automobile in a matching sea. I stroll inside and buy a one-way ticket to the first place that comes to mind. I pay with my credit card and show the agent my passport. I sign my name, *Reese Carlisle*. He tells me to have a safe trip.

Before passing through the security checkpoint, I meander through the concourse and stop at one of the shops to purchase a new set of clothes. A floral-print skirt. A peasant blouse. A pair of flip-flops that would be ten dollars elsewhere but cost sixty here. I don't care. It's my money. I earned it.

I stop in a bathroom and change. I throw away the blond wig and wash my face. An older lady dries her hands and spots me, then looks away. When she looks again, I realize my escape injuries are on display. The scuffed knees and elbows, bruises up and down my arms. But these aren't scars. They're badges.

I study myself in the mirror. I'm not the Reese Carlisle from before the scandal, not the Reese Carlisle after. Not Ella or Francine or Giselle. Not anybody's business.

On my way to security I take out my phone and call the police. I tell them there's a man handcuffed to a headboard who needs their help. I give them my address and hang up, turning off the phone and dropping it in the trash.

I place my duffel bag in the plastic bin and wait my turn to pass through the security gate. I know this routine, and the alarms stay silent as I step through. No threat here. The agent calls me forward and scans me with her wand, subtly tallying my injuries. She looks at my lonely bag when it rolls up, then back at me.

"Where you headed?"

"Yap," I tell her.

She nods.

"It's a fresh start," I add.

"Okay."

"I broke up with my boyfriend," I throw in.

She eyes my bruises. "Good," she says.

I take my bag and walk to the departure lounge. There are no disguises in this bag, just a few basic toiletries, a bathing suit, a couple changes of clothes. Everything else I can buy in Yap. Or Estonia. Or Argentina. No more make believe borders, no castles, no moats. I'm no longer willing to be a prisoner of my own making, paying the price for a crime I did not commit.

I figure Dumb and Dumber will take their lightly discounted money and leave Chris and my father alone. My dad will wile away his days in white collar prison, swapping ramen and working on his tan. Maybe Angela will continue to write to him, but probably not.

Trapper will find the suitcases, count them out, and get over the fact that there's a bit missing. The twenty million dollar mystery will be ninety-five percent solved, and he can move on with his life. There's no need to look for me. None of that money has ever been in my bank account, nor will it be.

If Rodney opens the envelope, it's his decision what to do with the ten grand. He can become a chef or a video game designer or take up canning—it's his life. He can live it.

I accept a glass of complimentary champagne and stare out the windows at the planes taxiing down the runway. I don't think about where they're going or where they'll end up. I just watch them lift off, rising into the clouds until they're gone, out of sight.

23

I have a tan. I've put on six pounds. I'm not sure how, since all there is to do is read and swim and eat fish and coconut. And I walk. I slather on sun block, and I walk. A lot. I walk without ducking into parking garages or putting on disguises or keeping my head down. I say hello to my neighbors, most Yap natives, but a few expats, friendly people from England and Australia and a chatty couple from Brazil. In the month that I've been here we've had dinner five times, and each time I've introduced myself with my own name, sat down to a meal as myself.

It's not as easy as it sounds. I've resolved to tell only the truth, but that doesn't mean I'm going to tell the *whole* truth. This leaves gaping holes in my story, in my past, in the fabric of this friend they're making. I can see the hesitation in their smiles, and sometimes on my walks I see them together, sharing drinks or chatting without me. It's hard to accept just part of a person, to know they're keeping pieces of themselves hidden. It's hard to build a relationship with so many gaps in the foundation.

But it's fine. I spent three years as a hermit. Too much companionship is like too much of anything. It makes me sick.

I'll have to build up my tolerance.

I bought an e-reader at the airport, and I've been reading lots. Some fiction, some travel. Getting ideas on what to do with the rest of my life. If I thought time stretched out endlessly while I hid in the apartment, I was mistaken. Here it goes on forever, extending as far as the sea, melting into the horizon, no promises, no lies. Just time.

Two weeks into my stay I visited one of the resorts and paid to use their internet, checking the news from home. Trapper found the money, and they've decided to close the case. My father's appeal was heard; the conviction was not overturned. He's still alive, so I assume Johan and Davor got their money and have moved on to other victims.

Now, as I do most days, I'm sitting in one of the wooden beach chairs planted in pairs in the sand at random intervals by the nearby resort. There's just one other person twenty yards away, preoccupied with her own life and ignoring me.

I sip my orange soda and stare out at the interminable sea, the water smooth and unbroken. The sun is high, reflecting off the surface, reminding me how many hours are left in this day, this life. I curl my toes in the sand and press until I can feel the cooler grit beneath, rubbing my heels over it, creating an indent. When I lift my foot, white sand floods back in, erasing my work. I sigh and shift in the chair, the slats pressing into my thighs, and glance at the other guest, now reading a magazine and holding down a floppy hat with one hand. She's busy, the kind of busy you are when this is your vacation, not your life. Not the rest of your life.

When I was fourteen and Alex was eleven, my dad took us to

Barbados. I'd been more preoccupied with my tan and my highlights than family bonding, so they'd left me at the pool and gone on excursions together, a jungle trek, jet skiing, lessons on cracking coconuts. One day, we went to the beach. They splashed in the water while I stayed on my towel, watching my skin gleam and darken. Beads of sweat trickled between my breasts and behind my ears, and I grew more and more tense as I baked and they played. Finally I got up and walked to the water's edge.

"Come on in, Pieces!" my dad shouted, at least a hundred yards out. Alex bobbed beside him, beckoning me, like they owned the ocean.

I waded in up to my knees, the water so clear I could see my pink pedicure, my feet glowing a pale white. I dove under and swam toward them, and when I resurfaced it was too deep to touch the bottom. I swam farther and came up for air. My father and Alex were watching, waiting. I submerged myself again, deeper this time, using my arms to press me lower and lower, until my toes found slippery sand. Then, instead of continuing to swim forward, I swam sideways. I slid through the water like a shark, my eyes slits, fingers carving a path to nowhere.

I kicked until my lungs threatened to cave, then I let myself glide upward, seeing the sun come into sharper focus, then it was too bright. I broke the surface, spitting salt water and wiping my stinging eyes, and behind me I could hear shouts and commotion. I spun around to see my father and Alex frantically splashing in the water closer to shore, where I'd gone under. They'd recruited other swimmers in their quest, and now they dug through the water like maybe I'd been buried.

For a second I didn't move, just watched the show, my heart swelling with satisfaction. I knew I could have done it differently, joined them on the hike or participated more in the dinner conversation, been a better sister, daughter, person, but I liked this. I liked being looked for. And sometimes, I guess, I liked being found.

Eventually someone spotted me swimming toward the fuss, and I pretended I'd simply gotten turned around under water, my mistake, sorry for worrying them. The other swimmers disappeared back to their vacations, and my dad hugged me and asked if I wanted to go shopping instead.

I sip my soda and smile at the memory, the selfishness, the past.

I see the shadow a split second before it slides into the seat next to me. The bottle slips from my fingers, bounces off the arm of the chair, and spills into the sand, turning it chemical orange. I stare at the spreading stain and feel him watching me, the way I'd felt him so many times before. I hear the chair squeak slightly as he settles in, like he's come to stay.

He doesn't speak.

Eventually I turn my head, just enough to see from the corner of my eye.

I see his knees first, the hair flecked on his legs. Light shorts, a green T-shirt, sunglasses, mussed hair. A paperback in his lap. No incriminating bookmark this time.

My mouth feels as sticky as the sand, my emotions the same. Fearful and flattered, panicked and pleased. I'd chosen Yap for a reason, after all. Hoping maybe someone would come for me, would look in the right place for once.

"Hey," he says finally. "I'm Chris." He extends a hand to shake, but doesn't touch me, not even close. He's waiting.

I turn my hands over in my lap, staring at my palms, the skin no longer scraped and torn. With time, it stitched itself back together, cells forming, joining, renewing. The skin is smooth and even, maybe a bit thicker than before, but there are no scars, no sign of the past.

I use a finger to flick away a grain of sand, then shake his hand.

THANK YOU

If you've read my previous romance novels, thank you so much for giving this one a try! I've been interested in writing in a new genre for a while, and this is the hard won result. If you're new to my work, thank you for choosing my book! My favorite thing to write about is difficult people, and Reese certainly fit the bill. Challenging characters give you the freedom to write unapologetically, which means no matter what crazy situations they find themselves in, I'm always having fun. I hope that joy translated to the page and your experience reading it!

If you enjoyed the story, I'd be very grateful if you would leave a review on Goodreads or wherever you bought the book. Positive or negative, reviews help other readers find my work and I appreciate them all.

If you would like to know when my next book is available, you can sign up for my newsletter at www.juliannakeyes.com/newsletter.html. I'm too lazy to send newsletters often, so you'll only get them when I have a new book coming out or something incredibly exciting to share.

You can also find or follow me on the following pages:

www.juliannakeyes.com

http://facebook.com/juliannakeyesauthor

https://twitter.com/JuliannaKeyes

Email: info@juliannakeyes.com

ACKNOWLEDGMENTS

I know I sound like a broken record at this point, but of course I'm thankful to Natalie Perret for her enthusiasm and willingness to read. I'd set this story aside for over a year before picking it up again, and I only found one typo. Natalie found a dozen. More than anything, I'm grateful for the peace of mind that comes with knowing I didn't put "rise crisp" into the world.

Thank you as ever to Khoi Le for his help with the cover, and for reviewing many images of scantily clad couples and telling me which one would look best in silhouette. Fun fact: Totally by chance, the picture he chose is the same couple that appear on the cover of *Undeclared.* It was meant to be, obviously.

I also have to thank my agent, Jill Marr, for loving this story enough to sign me as a client, and continuing to champion my writing. This can be a lonely world and a tough business, and her positivity and encouragement make staring down a blank page just a little bit easier.

BOOKS BY JULIANNA KEYES

NEW ADULT

My Roommate's Girl

BURNHAM COLLEGE SERIES

Undecided

Undeclared

CONTEMPORARY ROMANCE

Just Once

Going the Distance

TIME SERVED SERIES

Time Served

In Her Defense

The Good Fight

CHARLESTON THRASHERS SERIES

Team Player

Bench Player

NOVELLA

Bad Princess

www.ingramcontent.com/pod-product-compliance
Lightning Source LLC
Chambersburg PA
CBHW062007170626
46813CB00001B/67